T0095193

Life was just an accident

Life was just an accident

Philip Donaghy

LIFE WAS JUST AN ACCIDENT

Author Photographs by Brian McKenna Photography, Maghera, Northern Ireland

iUniverse books may be ordered through booksellers or by contacting:

iUniverse
1663 Liberty Drive
Bloomington, IN 47403
www.iuniverse.com
844-349-9409

ISBN: 978-1-4502-0157-5 (sc)
ISBN: 978-1-4502-0158-2 (e)

Print information available on the last page.

iUniverse rev. date: 02/28/2024

Dedicated to the memory of Caoimhe Kerr

Preface

In writing this book, I have had the chance to look back at my life and contact many people from my past. It has been a painful experience at times, for them as well as for me. Even the good times are sad because of what has happened to me. But I would say to people, don't feel any pity for me. I have achieved more in my life so far than a lot of people with ten times my opportunities. I had a rough upbringing and an insecure life. I am insecure to this day. I was reared in a children's home and then fostered out before ending my childhood in another children's home. From the age of 11, I have been looking for my father, a man I never knew. Then, just when I was beginning to face my future as an adult, I had a car accident that left me paralysed. I have learned the hard way the value of life and this book describes what I have achieved, against the odds. I want my life to be an inspirational story for people who think they have been abandoned by their families and by life itself at times. I never had money in my life to help me achieve things. All I had was willpower and I have plenty of that. Willpower is like love; the more I use it, the more I have. It doesn't matter if I am paralysed. Willpower, like love, makes no distinction.

I have always said, "You can't choose your family, but you can choose your friends" and I am proud of the friends who have stood by me. I am proud to call them my friends. To protect the innocent, I have changed the names of most of the people I met before my accident in 1998.

Sr. Paula, who reared me in St Joseph's Babies Home in Belfast until I was six years old, has been like a mother to me all my life. Any sense of justice and honesty that I have comes from Sr. Paula and the care she took of me as a child and again as a young adult. I thank Sr. Paula for her support all my life.

The Byrne family in Cookstown took me in when I had nothing and nobody. They have continued to support me with advice and friendship. I always feel welcome in their home. If I could choose a family of my own, I would choose the Byrne family. I couldn't hope for a better one.

The Magill family in Cookstown sheltered me when I was a frightened child. They tried to protect me and they believed me when no one else would. I will never forget them for doing that.

Feargal Logan, of Logan and Corry Solicitors in Omagh, has been a loyal friend in the years before and since my accident. I still rely on Feargal for his good advice and support. People say to me he's only doing his job, but Feargal has gone out of his way for me on many occasions. I am grateful to Feargal, his wife Eileen and their young family.

I would like to thank my accountants McAleer, Mullan and Jackson in Omagh for their good business advice. I always say they charge me enough for it! But in the long run, they help me to manage my finances and make the right decisions. Quinn Direct has also offered me excellent support over the years. Without a family to rely on to help me make important decisions in life, I am grateful to these companies for their continued professional guidance and personal support. Thanks are also due to Collie McGurk, the architect who helped me to design my first home and Rodney Stewart, who maintains my computer systems. Rodney's electronic gadgets help me to live independently in my own home.

Beaumont Hospital in Dublin, the National Rehabilitation Centre in Dun Laoghaire, the Musgrave Park Hospital in Belfast, and St John's Hospital in Sligo, worked hard to restore my health and gave me back the will to live. I am grateful for their care and attention. I am especially grateful to Dr John McCann at the Musgrave Park Hospital who taught me that being paralysed doesn't mean that life has ended.

I met literally hundreds of carers and residents at the nursing homes where I stayed as I completed my medical rehabilitation. There are too many to mention here, but they know who they are. Some stand out. The night staff at the nursing home I stayed at in Magherafelt was fantastic. Michelle Brown and her partner Paul have continued to stay in touch with me long after I moved into my own home. Karen Mitchell took leave from her nursing home job to come with me to Lourdes. I befriended the late Mrs. Bertha McCready while she was a nursing home resident. Her son, Gilbert McCready, and his wife, Mae, continue to visit me at home. Helen Dawson looked after me at weekends for several years and I have a lot of appreciation for her. Paula O'Neill has also become a good friend to me. Helen and Paula are two women who didn't know me before my accident, but who made the effort to get to know me. A lot of women in Ireland don't know what to say to a man in a wheelchair. Helen and Paula are not among them and they are good friends to me. I am grateful to the carers and residents of the nursing homes who looked after me and cheered me up as I completed my medical rehabilitation.

There is a team of carers who look after me in my own home. They are loyal and dedicated and they are always there when I need them. Special thanks are due to Bernie Boyle, Pat Jordan, Linda Little and Clare Monaghan, who visit me every day. They have to put up with a lot of cheeky chat from me. I might not always show it, but I am truly grateful to them for their care of me. Clare introduced me to her friend Cora McLaughlin and I would sometimes go for a coffee with Cora. She has been a good friend to me for a couple of years now.

I play Westlife songs for Clare and Cora: "Unbreakable" for Clare and "Obvious" for Cora.

Thanks are due to all of the newsprint and television media who took an interest in my story. They only know about the car accident and how I cope with that. This book goes a lot deeper.

I am proud of my association with the Roadsafe Roadshow and the Youth Justice Agency. I am proud to have been able to give something back and I thank all the people I have worked with on road safety down the years, especially those who are suffering as victims of road carnage.

Tom and Ann McGucken are regular visitors to my home and I have a good friendship with them since my accident. My former neighbours in Mullabeg have been very helpful to me in remembering aspects of my childhood when I lived among them. My current neighbours, particularly the Kellys and the Beatties, have been supportive and welcoming.

My uncle Joseph and his wife and family have hosted my mother for Christmas every year. I thank them for that. Joseph is the only member of my mother's family who I see regularly and he has been supportive of me and my mother recently as we have tried to resolve the issue of my paternity. That was a very big thing for Joseph and my mother. I am truly grateful to both of them for seeing it through.

Katarzyna, or Kate as I knew her, was the first live in carer I employed to look after me at home. Kate gave me the hope that I could have a more normal life. It was a pleasure to know Kate and to meet her sister Agnes when she came to stay for a holiday. I am grateful to Bogdana for caring for me and for introducing me to Eva, who is a very special friend to me. Eva has kept the dream alive of one day having a family of my own to love and support and I thank her for that. Eva has also helped me to become a bit more independent and she trusted me to share in her life for more than a year when she lived with me in my home. Eva, it was the best year I have spent in my time on a wheelchair.

I would like to thank Martin McKenna who brings my medication from the chemist in Kilrea. Mary and Seana McKenna have been good friends and always have time to spend with me. Shauna McTeague from Purely Hair comes and does my hair for me at home and I would like to thank her for keeping me looking so good.

Brian McGovern knew me as a party animal in Sligo and he didn't forget me when my party days looked like they were over for good. I thank Brian for his continued friendship. When I was walking, I worked with Pat Hagan and Colin Darcy in Sligo, carrying coal. We had good times together and I thank Pat and Colin for their support.

I dedicate this book to all my friends, past, present and future.

Is this some kind of a joke?

One evening in late October 1998, I was involved in a two-car crash near the town of Castlebar in Co. Mayo that left me paralysed. I was in my early twenties at the time. I can hear you thinking, "*Same old story. Boy racer heading out on a Saturday night in his souped-up Subaru, music blasting out, driving like a maniac, no respect for the road, showing off for his friends.*" But it was not like that at all. In fact, I have never driven a car in my life. I never will now.

It was months before I found out what happened that night. After the crash, I remember nothing. I don't remember being taken to hospital in Castlebar. I don't remember the phone call my friends made to Sr. Paula, the nun who brought me up. They told her that I might not make it. I don't remember being transferred to Beaumont Hospital in Dublin, where I had surgery and was in a coma for about six weeks. I don't remember the visitors who came to see me in Dublin, believing they had come to say goodbye. There were times in Dublin when my eyes opened and my arm stretched out as if to greet people, but those were reflexes. I don't remember any visitors at all. It is cold comfort to the families, but if my experience is anything to go by, crash victims who die at the scene feel no pain. I felt no pain.

A few years ago, the parents of Michelle McDaid, a young girl who was killed in a car accident, came to see me. They had watched me on a TV show talking about road safety. They wanted to hear it for themselves that Michelle would have felt nothing. They have tortured themselves with thoughts of their young daughter dying in agony. More recently, the parents and sister of young Caoimhe Kerr came to see me. Their daughter and sister died in a crash. She was their angel and they can't bear the thought of losing her in such a tragic way. I told both families that I felt nothing; I have no memories of the accident; I have no memories of pain. I was a young lad heading home from my work with hardly a care. I hope that my experience gives those families peace of mind.

Since I can't remember the six weeks after the accident, I have relied on friends and family to fill in the blanks during that period of my life that was barely life at all. Not everyone could be trusted to do that for me. Some family members in particular had their own reasons for keeping me in the dark. It was the habit of a lifetime for them and they couldn't break it, even in the most extreme of circumstances.

The first thing I remember is wakening in a hospital bed. I couldn't move and I was thinking to myself "*Where am I at?*" My eyes blinked and I tried to see where I was. There were Christmas cards and some decorations by my bed. "*How could it be Christmas?*" I said to myself, for I was sure it wasn't even Halloween. I was aware of other people nearby in hospital beds. I was aware of the lighting, the smell, and the sounds of an institution, which unfortunately I knew far too well. I said to myself, "*Somebody is playing a prank on me. Is this some kind of a joke?*" I felt like I had a massive hangover more than anything else. It was as if I had a feed of drink in me and someone had tied me down in the bed. I felt like saying, "*Very funny, lads, now get me out of here*", but I couldn't get my thoughts and my words to work together. I was lying in an awkward position and I couldn't seem to right myself; I was stiff and my throat was dry. I had a choking sensation as I tried to catch my breath. I couldn't move my head to look around me and that was what started to scare me. "*Where am I at?*" I tried to say the words, but I couldn't speak them. It sounded like I was whistling. Something was blocking my voice. It was like in a nightmare, when you try to scream for help but no sound comes out of your gaping mouth and nobody hears you. I could feel a rising sense of terror and panic. There was nobody at my bedside to comfort me. There was nobody there to say, "Thank God. Philip, you're alive and awake. Thank God!" That was nothing new in my life; I have always had to face my fears and terrors alone. Luckily for me, this time there was a nurse nearby who was able to talk to me and calm me down a bit.

I got the shock of my life when I was told I was in a rehabilitation centre in Dun Laoghaire, south of Dublin. I didn't even know what a rehabilitation centre was at that time. But I learned I had broken my neck in a car accident. I think I was told at that point about the extent of my injuries, and the likely outcome, but I just didn't hear the words. Like someone who was told they had a terminal illness, I couldn't take the information in. I was in shock. I heard nothing after the first sentence. My body and my brain rebelled against what the doctors were telling me. A broken neck? That would heal, wouldn't it? I wasn't dead, so I would get better, right? I was hooked up to a ventilator, which was why I couldn't get my words out. The ventilator was breathing for me and making my voice sound like a whistle. In the back of my mind, I was still expecting one of my friends to jump out and tell me it was all a joke and I'd fallen for it, like a big eejit. But it was no joke. I really had no idea at that time just how ill I had been, how lucky I was to be alive and what a miracle my life was. My life is a miracle to this day.

Once I regained consciousness, I had a lot to learn. I discovered I had been in a coma. I learned that of six people in the two crashed cars, everyone except me had walked away uninjured. One of those things nobody can explain, like a bullet with your name on it. I was told about all the people who had kept watch at my bedside while my life was held in the balance. These included family members I had not seen in years, and had no wish to see. I would love to have been a fly on the wall watching my friends from Sligo and Castlebar meeting my relations from Cookstown for the first time. You see, when I made a fresh start in life in Sligo in the mid-1990s, I told people I had no family. I told them Sr. Paula had reared me in a children's home. It is true; Sr. Paula reared me in St Joseph's children's home in Belfast until I was fostered at six years old. It was Sr. Paula I turned to when my life was falling apart at the age of 20. Sr. Paula hoped and prayed my accident would help me to reconcile with my family. Her prayers are unanswered to this day. Plenty of times I asked myself, "*What use is it to me to even know my relations?*" Maybe some day I will have an answer to that question, but at the minute, I wouldn't even call them my family.

Dublin and Dun Laoghaire were very far away from home and it was a big strain on my friends and relations to spend time with me, especially when I couldn't communicate with them at all for those first six weeks. Sr. Paula told me that my eyes opened now and again. She recalled me staring at my cousin Cathal as if I were searching for something familiar to hold on to while I made the journey from death's door back to life. Everyone thought I would die. Some said their goodbyes and went home to wait for the bad news they were sure would come. One of my best friends, Maurice Byrne, couldn't speak when he saw me. He saw the tubes connecting me to all sorts of machines, the metal braces that held me rigid in the bed, and the scar on my face that was prominent because I was so deathly pale. Maurice had known me since I was 11 years old and we have had some laughs together. Up until my accident, we were both strangers to sickness of any kind. We were two young men in the prime of our lives. Maurice felt he couldn't face me again in this life, as sick as I was. He went home expecting the worst. "Don't go," he said to my friend Tom

Magill, "Don't go down and see Philly. He's that bad looking and I don't think he's going to make it. Don't put yourself through it." Maurice thought he would never get my image out of his head, and if I died, he would only remember me as a man in a coma strapped into a bed and hooked up to a life support machine. It was not the image of me he wanted to remember.

But I have been a fighter all my life and I fought my way back. I sometimes wonder why I fought so hard. The life I returned to is very different from the one I had made for myself in the few happy months before the crash. I was taken off my feet just when I felt I had landed on my feet, with a good job and a good life in Castlebar.

In the rehabilitation centre in Dun Laoghaire, slowly, I realised how serious my injuries were and how helpless I had become. I was brought up the rough way and I have never been a man to feel pity for myself. Pity is no use to me. Through all the setbacks in my life, I have always managed to find a way to pick myself up and get on with it. But this was different. By the time I regained consciousness, I weighed just seven and a half stone. I needed help with feeding and I had to take a funny kind of drink that was disgusting but was supposed to build up my strength. I needed the ventilator to breathe for me. I needed nursing staff to turn me in bed, to clean and shave me, to dress me, to fetch and carry for me. It was a lot to get used to and it was very hard. It still is. In my body, I felt like a baby again, but in my mind, I was still an independent young man. I am sorry to say that I fought the nurses at times. It was hard for them to strike the right balance. I wanted to be treated as a normal person, but I was paralysed and I could do literally nothing for myself. If I got the feeling that the nurses were treating me like an invalid, I made life difficult for them by refusing to cooperate. Most of the time I did my best, but sometimes I just got skundered with all the adjustments and changes I had to cope with. I lashed out at whoever was there, and usually it was the nurses.

Maurice Byrne's parents and his sister, Clare, came down from Cookstown to visit me in Dun Laoghaire. They were directed to a ward full of patients recovering from all types of terrible injury. They described the atmosphere in Dun Laoghaire as morbid and they were embarrassed to stare at the patients as they scanned all the beds looking for me. They thought they had come to the wrong place. They went to leave the ward and Clare turned round for one last look. That was when she saw me. A couple of nurses moved away from my bed and Clare saw a failed looking, skinny chap lifting his arm up in greeting. I had a bed close to the door of the ward and I liked to see all the comings and goings. "There he is, there's Philip," Clare said to her parents. "It couldn't be," they said. I was nothing like the tall, cheeky young man, full of life they had known before. They got a terrible shock at the sight of me. They had heard I was conscious and making a recovery. Nothing could have prepared them for this. They said that my eyes were dead, as if a light had been switched off inside my head. They wondered at first if I might have been brain damaged in the accident. That was the rumour going round back home. But once they sat down with me and we started to talk, they realised it was the same old Philip, keen to hear all their news and to share a joke. The Byrnes went home asking themselves the question I had not got round to asking myself: "*What kind of a recovery is Philip going to make?*" They were not hopeful. In those early days, the Byrnes found it hard to imagine how I would cope with the life I was facing. The Philip they knew would rather be dead than live like that.

The Byrnes might have been shocked at the sight of me, but it was nothing compared to the shocks I was getting on a daily basis. I started to become more aware of all the things that had to be done for me and what my future life would be like. I had a quick look under the bedclothes and nearly fainted when

I saw a tube coming out of my penis, taking out urine and putting it into a bag hanging down the side of my bed. These days, I have a supra-pubic catheter, which drains urine directly from my bladder through a tube inserted in my abdomen. It has given me back some of my dignity. But in the early days, I did not have that relief. I had worked as a volunteer in nursing homes for the elderly and in hospitals in my past life. I knew what was going on, but I couldn't understand why I needed a catheter. I had not fully understood the extent of my paralysis. Whenever I saw a nurse coming towards me with a bucket, I said to myself, "*I don't like the look of this*". It usually meant the nurse was coming to clear out my bowels. Every time, I tried to push the nurse and the bucket away but I had no power to do that. All I could do was put up with it and cry my eyes out. I felt so degraded, so exposed and uncomfortable. Not for the first time in my life, I felt like dirt. To this day, even though I know everything there is to know about catheters and enemas, the removal of waste from my body is still the most degrading aspect of my disability. I will never get used to it. I will never be able to accept the fact that someone has to empty my catheter and clean my backside. I am embarrassed by myself all the time. Maybe if I was 90 years of age, I might expect to rely on other people for my personal care, but not as a young man in the prime of my life. What can I do about it? Nothing. Not a damn thing. I just set my jaw and let my carers get on with it.

It wasn't all doom and gloom in Dun Laoghaire though. I will always remember Christmas Eve, 1998. I wasn't long out of the coma when I had a visit from two beautiful girls, Orla and Diane. They were relatives of the Byrnes in Cookstown, and they were living in Dublin. I remember I had a notion of one of them, but I won't say which one! They brought me my favourite beer, Budweiser. I was as delighted as a child waiting for Santa. Orla called one of the nurses over.

"We have brought Philip a present", she said, "Would it be okay if we gave it to him?"

"Of course it would," said the nurse, "What is it?"

"It's beer. Budweiser. It's Philip's favourite," the girls said.

"Well, alright," said the nurse. "But not too much now Philip. We don't want you flying. You know you're on a lot of medication."

"You're the boss," I said, "Cheers and a happy Christmas to you."

As a teenager, I tattooed the word "Bud" on my arm. That was how much I liked Budweiser. Let me tell you, it was the best beer of all time and it was the only festive thing about Christmas 1998 for me. Those two girls treated me like a normal person. It was the first time that had happened since my accident, and I appreciated it. What was every other 21-year-old in Ireland doing on Christmas Eve? Having a beer with friends, just like me. From that moment, even though I had very little idea of what lay ahead, I thought to myself, "*I want a normal life, where I am treated as Philip and not some disabled statistic.*" A good part of my life since the accident has been taken up with building that normal life for myself. It is a lifelong project and the biggest test of my determination.

One of my most constant visitors through the months of illness and rehabilitation was my girlfriend, Rachel Desmond. She travelled regularly from Castlebar and Sligo to be with me, staying in a bed and breakfast near whichever hospital I was at. Her mother came with her too sometimes, and so did friends from McDonalds where I worked, and from Sligo. Rachel was a beautiful girl and I remember meeting her for the first time in Sligo and being too shy to ask her out. I spent weeks acting the goat with her before I plucked up the courage. I am glad I did. Rachel was full of life and I enjoyed being with her. I felt comfortable with her and we had a great time when we were together. I often wonder if we would be married now, if things had been different. We both made the move from

Sligo to Castlebar in the early summer of 1998 to work in a new McDonalds restaurant, where I was Customer Service Manager. We had lots of friends, and although we were falling in love, we still spent time doing our own thing. For me, that was playing football, beers with the lads, clubbing at the weekends, or heading up to Dublin for a concert, normal stuff I would give anything to be able to do again.

I was also looking out for good business ideas. The day after the accident, I was due to take over a car wash business in Castlebar. I had already printed up the leaflets and distributed them around the town. I was going to operate the car wash during the day and work in McDonalds in the evenings. I even sent a leaflet to Sr. Paula, although I knew she had no car, just to let her know that wee Philip from the children's home was making a life for himself and settling down. I have never been afraid of hard work, or dirty work. Maurice Byrne's father, Danny Byrne, always said to me, "There's money in dirt," and I was keen to prove that saying right. I had worked for Danny Byrne in his petrol station back in Cookstown. Washing cars was one of my many specialities, as Danny could tell you! If things had been different, what would I be doing now? Running a successful business, providing for my wife and children, giving them the love and support I never had growing up. That is what I would have hoped for. It is still my dream today.

Lying in a hospital bed in Dun Laoghaire, the car wash business was the last thing on my mind. I realised I had escaped death but I was facing a life sentence. People looked at me a bit funny when I said I would walk again. The doctors said I was paralysed for life, but I thought I could prove them wrong. I have always struggled against people who told me what I could and could not achieve in life. In my experience, they were just putting barriers in my way to give themselves a quiet life. I saw it as my job to knock those barriers over and achieve what I wanted to achieve. But maybe this time the doctors were right. I just couldn't accept it at first.

For a long time, the details of the accident were kept from me. The funny thing was, I never asked what exactly happened on the road that night. Maybe somewhere in the back of my mind, I knew. In any case, my friends decided it would be better for my recovery if they waited until I had built up my strength before telling me about the accident. When I was eventually told, I understood why they had waited. It was my solicitor, Feargal Logan, who explained to me what happened. Feargal has always been a good friend to me and I trusted him. There were not too many men I would have trusted, but I knew that Feargal would never do anything wrong by me. I had no doubt that what he said was true. I had very mixed feelings when I learned that Rachel, my girlfriend, was driving the car at the time of the accident. She had picked me and a colleague up from work at McDonalds in Castlebar, and was driving us home. I was in the back of the car, because my colleague was getting dropped off first. There were no rear seat belts fitted. Rachel made a right turn into the path of an oncoming car. On impact, I was thrown 40 feet through the windscreen.

Rachel was devastated about what had happened. She carried the guilt of what she had done all the times she came to visit me and stay with me in hospital. She agreed with my friends not to talk to me about the accident itself, and that was a terrible burden for her. I often think to myself, what a strain it must have been on Rachel. At first, when I was told, I just accepted it as one of those things. I told myself it was not Rachel's fault, she certainly didn't mean to cripple me. It was an accident. But at the end of the day, it was her fault. She was driving, she did something careless, and I was the one who suffered for it. She walked away from that car to phone an ambulance and I would never walk again. It seemed so unfair. Over the months of my rehabilitation, I struggled with love for Rachel and the thought that if it wasn't for her, I wouldn't be in this terrible mess. I was grateful she spent so much time with me in hospital, but I admit I started to resent her. I was sometimes very short with her when she came to visit me. I remembered the life we had before the accident and the hopes I had for a future life together. In that dream life, I was a man, a husband, a father, a provider. I would work hard for my family. I would sit down in the evenings and talk things over with my wife. We would make plans together. We would support each other. We would get a babysitter and go out dancing now and again. We would celebrate birthdays and anniversaries together. We would take holidays. Maybe, in time, we would take a trip North to visit my relations. That was the kind of life I imagined for myself. There was no place in it for a man taken off his feet or a woman devoting her life to his care. That was no part of my plan. The gap between my dream life and my reality was too wide. I looked at myself at that time, helpless in a hospital bed, and I had no respect for myself. I thought of myself as a useless, dirty bastard. With those feelings taking over my mind, how could anyone stand to be with me? I couldn't imagine a beautiful young girl like Rachel having to do everything for me. I genuinely didn't want Rachel to waste her life on me. I was so full of disgust with myself, I couldn't see that she might choose to be with me. I thought no one in their right mind would want to make their life with me.

My own feelings on the matter were not helped by family members who implied that Rachel was only with me because she expected me to come into insurance money. That's what type of family I have. They told me that during the time I was in a coma, Rachel was wearing an engagement ring when she visited me. They said she wouldn't let them near my bedside. Other people have told me it was my uncle Francis who wouldn't let anyone near me, including Rachel. Uncle Francis fostered me when I was 6 years old. I never had a happy day in his home. He is the last person I would have wanted to keep a vigil at my bedside. I don't know what really happened during the time I was in a coma. I was not engaged to Rachel, I know that much, although I like to think we would have got engaged one day if I had not had the accident. If Rachel was protective of me, I am not surprised. She was one of the people who believed I had no family. She was one of the people who knew Sr. Paula as my family. After all, it was Rachel who contacted Sr. Paula from the hospital in Castlebar to tell her about the accident. Sr. Paula contacted my family.

In the end, about a year and a half after the accident, I broke off our relationship; I had to let Rachel go. We both had to move on. The life I would have liked to have with Rachel was no longer possible. But I didn't want her to miss out because of me. Rachel had to have the chance to make a new life, meet somebody else, get married and raise a family. I realised we both had to get on with our lives. Our relationship was not going to be healthy if she felt guilty and I felt resentful. It has taken a long time, but I forgive Rachel and I forgive myself. It was, after all, just an accident. It changed the course of both our lives, but nobody died. Life was not over for either of us. I revisited the scene of the accident that changed everything for us. I had to see for myself that stretch of road where I lay dying. It was a very strange feeling to see cars speeding over the spot where my broken body was flung. It was like watching a ghost. I sat in my wheelchair at the side of the road and cried. I thought of the happy times I had spent with Rachel in Castlebar and Sligo. Those happy times ended with a crash. I wouldn't like to be in Rachel's position but I wish her every happiness in the world. Rachel got married a few years ago and she had a baby. I sincerely wish her young family all the best in life. I have no regrets about meeting that beautiful girl and spending time with her. If I have to live with the consequences of the accident, then so does Rachel in her own way.

By the time Rachel and I split up, I was getting stronger in myself and making plans for my future. I had regained some of my confidence and self-respect. But back in the National Rehabilitation Centre in Dun Laoghaire, five months after the accident, I still wasn't sure if I had a future or what way it would be. It was time to come off the ventilator. It was time to learn how to breathe again on my own. It was time to get to know my body again. I was hoisted out of my bed into a manual wheelchair and taken for physiotherapy. I hated that manual wheelchair. I hated having to rely on a nurse to push it. There was one nurse in particular who pushed the wheelchair too fast. I don't know if it was a flashback from the accident, but the feeling of being out of control scared the wits out of me. That nurse was an ignorant fucker and if I could have decked him, I would have. But that was the old Philip. The new Philip didn't have the strength to swat a fly. In physiotherapy, they taught me how to breathe again and speak again. My left vocal cord is paralysed. Sometimes I sound like a boy whose voice is breaking and then my real voice kicks in. I suffer from frequent chest and lung infections, and I had to learn how to cough again and how to manage the build-up of mucus. If you think about it, a good cough starts in the pit of your stomach. You take a deep breath and feel your ribs and diaphragm moving; you cough and you can feel it right through your body. You can. I can only remember that feeling. In Dun Laoghaire, when I couldn't manage to cough myself, I often had to have suction tubes inserted to remove fluid. It was not a pleasant experience. It was not anywhere near as satisfying as a good cough. I had to learn how to exercise my body, both the parts I can move, and the parts I can't. I had to learn how to examine my skin for any signs of a pressure sore developing. For paralysed people pressure sores, or bedsores, are dangerous. They can become infected if they are not recognised and treated early. Spots, burns, friction, bruises, cuts, even a touch of sunburn are all part of everyday life for most people, but for me they are danger signs. For a start, I can't feel them so I have to look for them. One time, when I was living in a nursing home, I had a sore at the base of my spine that ate away my flesh into the bone. That took a long time to heal. I had to lie on my front in hospital for six weeks waiting for my skin to heal. Learning and re-learning basic skills was like being a child again in many ways. The main difference is that when I was a child everything was new. But now that I am paralysed, everything is a reminder of how much I have lost.

When I got my first automatic wheelchair in Dun Laoghaire, I felt like I was the cool kid on the ward; it was deadly. Most of all, I liked being in control of where I went around the hospital. I didn't have to call for a nurse and then wait until someone was free to take me for a spin. I am not a holy man, and I would not describe myself as a good Catholic, but I spent a lot of time alone in the chapel in Dun Laoghaire. I was wondering what to do next in a life that had already had lots of turning points, lots of crossroads, lots of bad decisions, most of them taken on my behalf. I was determined to do things my way, and if I made mistakes, so be it. Danny Byrne has always said to me "Philip, you will learn from your mistakes," and he was right. The quiet of the chapel gave me time and space to think. It was good to get away from the wards and away from the nurses and the visitors. Everyone had the best of intentions, but I was getting fed up with people telling me what to do and how to live. I knew it was time to start making some decisions for myself.

As soon as I was fit enough, I asked to be transferred from Dun Laoghaire to the North of Ireland. I had a feeling that I wanted to go "home", although in fact I had no home to go to there. In any case, in the state I was in, I would have to spend a lot more time in rehabilitation and nursing homes. Dun Laoghaire was so over-crowded that I think the staff were delighted I was moving on. Having made the decision to go home, I was becoming more aware of how little I could do for myself and how alone I was in the world. Now that it was clear I would live, the people who had visited me in hospital had to get back to their normal lives. I started to get depressed about the future, and to wonder if I had any kind of a future. It was very hard to pass the time on a wheelchair. It was impossible to be glad I was alive all of the time. I got bored and frustrated and depressed. I have always seen life as a journey, and I took it one step at a time. But when I was taken off my feet, it felt like a journey cut short. At the start, there were times when I honestly thought I would walk again. I still thought I could prove the doctors wrong. My legs were moving and I took it as a sign that life was returning to them. What I didn't realise was that the movements in my legs were involuntary spasms. The cut off nerve endings were trying to send messages back to my brain. I think amputees go through something similar, and chickens whose necks have been wrung. It would be many months before I understood I would never walk again. It would take even longer for me to accept it. To this day I take medication to control the spasms in my legs and body.

By the time I was transferred to the Musgrave Park Hospital in Belfast, I was probably at my lowest. I was very uncooperative and bad-tempered. I was in Belfast to complete my medical rehabilitation and I just didn't want to know. I was with Sr. Paula, the nun who brought me up for the first six years of my life. I still consider Sr. Paula to be like a mother to me. She remembers that I was depressed in Belfast, and refused point blank to cooperate with the nurses. I always hated being told what to do, and the fact that I was virtually helpless in a Belfast hospital just made me even more stubborn. Sr. Paula came to visit me one day and found me lying in bed, unwashed and unshaved.

"Philip, are you not well?" she asked me, her voice full of concern. I grunted back at her. A nurse came by.

"Are you ready to get up now Philip? You could go with Sister to the cafeteria for a coffee," she said.

"No!" I shouted at her, "I'm not getting up. Stop asking me." Then the tea trolley came round.

"Tea or coffee Philip? And yourself, Sister? If yous are quick, you'll get the chocolate biscuits today." The nurses and care assistants at Musgrave Park were always so cheerful, but I was having none of it. I turned my face to the wall. Sr. Paula got me a coffee but it stood on the table, untouched.

"Philip, what is it?" Sr. Paula asked me. But I wouldn't answer her. I felt like I was on strike. I felt like all the other patients in Musgrave were doing what the nurses and doctors told them, but they were not getting any better. They were just becoming institutionalised. I definitely did not want that to happen to me. I suppose I thought that if I refused to do what I was told, then I wouldn't turn into a vegetable. I meant no disrespect to the other patients, but that is how I felt at the time. I wouldn't let the nurses get me up. I refused to eat or drink. I wouldn't get shaved. I wouldn't discuss what I was feeling. Nothing. I just shut down. Sr. Paula was trying to encourage me, but she knew I could just as easily send her away with a flea in her ear. She really wanted to help me and to be there for me, as she has always been. For Sr. Paula, the fact that I was alive was a blessing from God. For me, well, I was beginning to wonder about that.

Then Dr. John McCann, who was treating me at Musgrave Park, came to see me. He spoke very bluntly to me. He told me I was paralysed from the chest down, I would never walk again, and that I would need 24-hour nursing care for the rest of my life. He said to me, "Philip, you can decide either to lie there in that bed and do nothing, or you can decide to cooperate with the people who are trying to help you make the best of what you have got. It is your choice. It is up to you." Dr. McCann left me then and Sr. Paula started to cry. I think for the first time she realised the kind of life I was facing. The doctor's words and the nun's tears got to me.

"That's it," I said, "I am not happy with this. What a completely ignorant man that doctor is."

"Now Philip, really, he is trying to help ..." Sr. Paula always sees the good in every situation. It must be part of a nun's job description. I interrupted her.

"Imagine leaving you in tears like that. How could he do something like that to a nun?" I was ashamed of my behaviour and it was good for me to disguise my shame with concern for Sr. Paula.

We called the nurse, and I got myself ready to be hoisted up out of the bed to start the final phase of rehabilitation in Belfast. It wasn't easy for Dr. McCann to speak to me so bluntly, but I was grateful he did. At that stage, the last thing I needed was a softy-voiced doctor filling me with false hope. Dr. McCann told me the bare truth in a way that got through to me. He also told me that how I managed my disability was mostly down to me and to my attitude. In every hospital and nursing home I have stayed at, I have seen people who are so much worse off than me in every way. I get down in the dumps at times, but I hope I am never guilty of too much self-pity. I hope I will always remember to be grateful for what I have. One thing I never forget is my gratitude I was not brain damaged in the accident. During the time I was in a coma in Dublin, that was on everyone's mind. Thank God it didn't happen. There was one poor girl I met in Dun Laoghaire. She had been in an accident but she was walking and didn't appear to have any disability. When she spoke, I realised she was brain damaged. No two words that came out of her mouth made sense. They were all scrambled up. She couldn't put her thoughts into words at all. She couldn't communicate with anybody. At least that didn't happen to me. I still had my brain, thank God.

At the Musgrave Park Hospital, I finally came to terms with my paralysis. As I got stronger and healthier in myself, I was better able to accept the bad news about my medical condition. I didn't just break my neck in the accident, my spinal cord was severed. The spinal cord is like a tube running from the back of your head to the base of your back. It is like a motorway for communication between the brain and the body, with directions at every junction. The spinal cord is very fragile and it is protected by the bones in the neck and spine. The outcome for someone with a spinal cord injury depends on exactly where the injury is. As soon as the doctors know where the cord is damaged, they know what level of disability the patient will have. Each section of the spinal cord is responsible for the different actions and movements the body makes. My injury is a C6/C7 injury. That means my spinal cord is severed between the sixth and seventh cervical vertebrae. These are the small bones in the neck and there are eight pairs of them in total. The bit of the spinal cord that is protected by the first five pairs of cervical vertebrae is okay for me. That is why I am able to breathe on my own. But below the site of my injury, no signals can pass between my spinal cord and my brain. They can't jump across the severed cord. All of the functions of my body that are controlled by sections of the spinal cord below the sixth and seventh cervical vertebrae are gone. So, the messages that should pass between my brain and my bladder letting me know that I need to use the bathroom, can't get through. The signals that would make me get up and walk to the bathroom, can't get through. All of these signals travel through the unbroken spinal cord and a normal, healthy 20-year-old wouldn't even give them a second thought. In my case, communication is broken. There is always hope that there will be a breakthrough in the treatment of spinal cord injuries. For the moment medical equipment, such as wheelchairs, hoists and catheters, is the only way for me to manage the broken relationship between my brain and my body.

But believe me when I say I am one of the lucky ones. First, I am alive. Second, I did not suffer brain damage. Third, there is lots of stuff I can do on my own. I can breathe; I can move my head and facial muscles; I can still have a laugh and joke about. I have movement in my neck and shoulders; I can move my arms and I have limited movement of my hands and some of my fingers. I can operate my electric wheelchair, which is fitted with a control like a joystick. I can make phone calls and send text messages. I can change channels on the TV. I can't write, but I can record my thoughts and ideas on a voice recorder and have them typed up. I can't make my own tea, but I can hold and drink from a lidded, two-handled cup, like a child's beaker. I have just learned how to put toothpaste on my toothbrush, and I can use a toothbrush to clean my teeth. I can't put shampoo on my hair, but I can wash my hair if somebody puts shampoo on it for me. These might seem like small achievements, and I couldn't do any of them when I was hospitalised. But they are massive achievements to me. They help to make me more independent and in control of my life. They make me feel normal.

I look after myself too, probably better than most men my age. I have a healthy diet and a stable weight. A lot of people in my situation put on weight. They eat to relieve the boredom of sitting in a wheelchair. I have never had a big appetite and I am glad about that now. Carrying extra weight adds to the health problems that paralysed people face. I don't overdo it on caffeine or dairy products, which can cause blockage problems in my supra-pubic catheter. I exercise to build up the strength in my upper body and to keep my leg muscles toned. I don't smoke any more, although I am addicted to nicotine gum. I hardly have any opportunity to drink, but the few times I do get out to the pub, I make sure I enjoy myself! I am tuned into my general health and immunity. A common cold could mean hospital for me, so I am careful about getting close to infection. I ask visitors to stay away if they think they have a bug.

Even though I consider myself to be one of the lucky ones, I have lost count of the number of people who say to me, "Philip, you've got over your accident." I say to them, "Yes, I have got over my accident, but I am still learning to live with it." By the time I left Musgrave Park Hospital in

Belfast, I had got over the medical aspects of my accident. My broken ribs had healed as much as they could. My broken neck had stabilised. The cut on my face has left a scar, but it is not disfiguring. My nickname, when I was walking, was SPFP, which stands for Sexy Pretty Face Philip. No scar can change that; I still have my good looks! But learning to live with the accident will take the rest of my life.

Even though my medical condition was stable, I was still in bad shape after I left the Musgrave Park Hospital. I had less mobility than I have now, and I wouldn't have been capable at that time of leading any kind of an independent life. The next part of my rehabilitation was to go and live in a nursing home, where I would get the 24-hour nursing care I needed. Ireland is a small country with a small population. Despite the troubles, frequent road crashes, industrial injuries, and genetic disorders, there are not enough people with my level of disability to justify the cost of a specialist unit for young disabled people. That is what the politicians tell us. But how many disabled people do you need in order to provide a decent service? The lack of service for disabled people in this country is a disgrace. The only option for me was to live in nursing homes specialising in the care of the elderly.

Now, I did voluntary work in nursing homes in the past, and I have a good relationship with elderly people. I have a lot of respect for them and the hardships they faced in their lives. I have always made the effort to be friendly with elderly people. But, as a young man getting used to life in a wheelchair, I couldn't recommend living in a nursing home for elderly people. The fact is, no matter how disabled you are, the needs of a young person are different from those of a 90 year old. I have lived in children's homes and I know how hard it is to provide the right kind of care. I know how it feels when you are not sure if the care you are getting is what you need. I knew this as a child and I was discovering it again as a young, disabled adult. If I hadn't taken matters into my own hands, I could have been spending the rest of my life in a nursing home for the elderly. I hate to think how I would have turned out if that had happened. I am sure I would not be here today.

I lived in nursing homes for nearly five years, both North and South of the Irish border. That is a hell of a long time. It is a wonder I am not institutionalised, but I moved around a lot so maybe that kept me from going under. At the start, I needed the 24-hour nursing care the homes provided. I was still getting used to life as a paralysed victim of a road traffic accident. At the same time, I was working with Logan and Corry Solicitors on my insurance claim. While that was in progress, I had no choice but to live in a nursing home. I had no home of my own to go to and no family members I would have been comfortable to live with, even if they would have had me. At that time, I was homeless, penniless and paralysed. But hey, I didn't let that stop me!

I made a lot of friends among the staff and the residents of the nursing homes. I met people I would never have met in my life when I was walking. In one of the nursing homes, in Newtownards, I met members of the police force who had been paralysed in shooting incidents and bombs during the troubles in Northern Ireland. When I was walking, the only time I ever spoke to the police was when I was in trouble. Unfortunately, I was often in trouble growing up. So, it was a new experience for me to meet the police as "equals" in the nursing home. One of them said to me,

"I suppose Philip you would never have talked to me if we both were walking?"

"You're right there," I replied, "Although I might have told you to fuck off." We laughed about it. It is funny how life can turn you and your prejudices upside down, and how paralysis takes away your differences.

Despite the friendships, and some really excellent staff members, I was always very critical of the care I received in nursing homes. Most of these homes were operated in the private sector and I sometimes wondered if they were properly inspected by the health service. There should be spot checks with no notice on all residential nursing homes. The private sector is making a great deal of money out of the health service and they should be kept on their toes. I was charged plenty when I lived in the nursing homes. They said I needed more care than the average resident. That was rubbish in my opinion. I was hospitalised with a pressure sore while I was living in a nursing home. That should never have happened, and if it happened to me with all the so-called "extra" care I was paying for, how many old people end up with pressure sores? I am much better at looking after my skin now, but in the early days I relied on the carers to check my skin for me. They didn't do a good enough job and they couldn't control the sore once it took hold. That was why I ended up in hospital, with all the additional costs to the health service. I feel very strongly that people who have paid their taxes all their lives deserve the best of care and a good quality of life if they eventually have to live in nursing homes. To me, it doesn't matter what age you are, you do not want to sit in a chair staring at four walls all day long. You do not want to have to share shower facilities and toilet facilities. You want to be able to attract the attention of a nurse when you need one, not when one happens to be passing by. These nursing homes spend a lot of time filling in forms and making notes on everything you do. But most of the time, what the residents need is just some human contact. There was one day in a nursing home in the North when I came across a very old lady in some distress. In my condition, I couldn't help her but she was calling for a nurse. No-one came.

"Shout out the name 'Gerry Adams'," I told her, "Shout it out at the top of your voice."

"Gerry Adams!" she cried, and I don't think the poor lady had a clue whose name she was calling. "Gerry Adams! Gerry Adams! Gerry Adams!" Within seconds, all the staff on duty were at her side, looking for Gerry Adams.

One thing I did have plenty of in the nursing homes was time. Time to think. Time to get depressed. Time to consider ending my life, which I thought about a lot. Time to ask the million dollar question: "Why me?" I have to admit I have been asking myself that question for most of my life. I have had an insecure life and I never had anyone there to explain "Why?" to me. I had to provide my own answers and most of the time I didn't have the experience to give myself the kind of solid advice I needed. It was very hard to pass the time sitting on a wheelchair. It would have been dead easy to become institutionalised and just live my life to the beat of the nursing home routines. I tuned in to shift changes, getting up time, shower time, meal times, visiting times, bed time. It never changed. Even when I had a good laugh with staff or residents, there was no variation to the routine. With so little to occupy my time, I was forced to think hard about my future and to examine my life in more detail than I had ever done before. "*Why am I here?* I asked myself. I believe I am on this earth for a reason. I just needed to work it out.

I moved North to be closer to my idea of home. I didn't have a family I could rely on, so home for me was about friends. Living with a disability in a nursing home taught me who my friends were. I was able to see clearly who the people were who would stand by me through this latest ordeal in my life. I didn't blame people for not wanting to face me, for wanting to remember the "old" Philip. It is more of an effort to be my friend now, I know that. I can't just meet someone in the street and go for a coffee with them or a pint. It all has to be planned in advance; it takes time. People have other things to do, different priorities. I understand that. It makes me grateful for the friends I still have who accept me as Philip. They say to me, "You're the same Philly, just in a wheelchair." It is easier now that I live in my own home. I can invite people to come and see me. But back in the nursing homes, there was a routine and both me and my visitors had to follow it.

By moving North, I also faced the Donaghy clan for the first time in years. Having been reared in children's homes and fostered by my uncle Francis and his family, I have opinions on family life that maybe not a lot of people share. But then, no-one has been in my situation. Children's homes and foster homes are not an experience I would wish on anybody. But they were my experience and they have an influence on me to this day, both good and bad. They play a big part in how I see myself and how I feel about myself.

Being paralysed in a car wreck was not my only accident. From the little I know about my mother's life and the circumstances of my birth, I'd say I was an accident from the very start. I didn't ask to be paralysed in a car wreck. It was something that happened to me through no fault of mine and because someone else was careless. I didn't ask to be born. It too was something that happened to me through no fault of mine and because someone else was careless. I have been trying to find out exactly how I came to be on this earth for more than 20 years. I think there were a lot of people back then, when I was a baby, who couldn't have cared less about me. There were a lot of people who thought it best to forget about me. I would like them to know what their carelessness has cost. I would like them to know the kind of life I have had as a forgotten child. I would like them to understand all the things I have lost out on because nobody gave a damn about me. People say, "Poor Philip. He has lost out on so much because of his accident." That's true, but I would also say that I have lost out because I was never loved as a child.

In writing this book, I have started to lift the corner of the carpet and to see all the crap that has been swept under it for more years than I have been on this earth. It is about time I aired that old carpet and swept away the dirt.

Setting the bunny rabbits free

I was born a few weeks early by Caesarean section at the Daisy Hill Hospital in Newry. I weighed 6lb 11oz. Two weeks after my birth, I was still referred to as "Baby Donaghy" in the hospital reports, even though my mother gave me the name "Philip". I don't know who gave me my middle name, "Kevin". I don't know for sure, but I think it was about seven or eight years before my mother saw me again. I believe I was taken from her shortly after I was born and transferred to Craigavon Hospital where I was treated for breathing problems. My mother got to hold me for a few minutes, but she never got to care for me in the first days of my life. That early disconnection between mother and son has continued between us to the present day. There are many reasons for it and they have made our relationship difficult at the best of times, and impossible at the worst. It is hard for us to have a connection with each other when the most basic of relationships between a mother and her child was not allowed to develop. People say, "Oh, but back in that time things were different. Your mother couldn't have looked after you; she wasn't fit to do it." They talk about my birth as if it was 100 years ago and not 30. What I say to those people is, "Was my mother even given the chance to care for me? Did anyone consult her in the matter? Did anyone offer to support her? Did anyone explain to her what would happen to me?" Nobody has answered those questions, and my mother gets very distressed when I ask her about it. I think she was made to feel ashamed of herself and her pregnancy, and I am probably a reminder of that shame. I look around the town now and I see lots of single mothers. They have the support of their families in many cases and the support of social services. Their position in life may not be perfect but at least they are given the chance to rear their own children. My mother did not have that chance.

Grace Donaghy, my mother, doesn't want to be involved in the writing of this book and I respect her decision. But one thing I have noticed, she talks about herself at the time when I was born as if she were talking about someone she hardly knows. She'll say something like "I don't know anything about Philip's mother," or "How would I know if his mother sent him to a home?" So much time has passed that Grace hardly recognises the woman she was. I wouldn't be surprised if she has tried to block the memories altogether. I think it is sad for both of us that we don't really count for much in each other's lives. We have lost out on so much and we don't see our mother and son relationship as one of the most important relationships there is.

By the time I was given a clean bill of health as an infant, my mother was gone. She went home first and then back to the psychiatric hospital in Co. Tyrone where she has been an in-patient for most of her adult life. I was taken by a social worker to St Joseph's Babies Home in Belfast. I lived there for the first six years of my life. At that time, St Joseph's Babies Home was a Down and Connor diocesan home run by the Nazareth nuns. It was where unwanted babies were sent and cared for before they were adopted out by Catholic families. There is a long history of unwanted babies in Ireland. In the old days, they came to St Joseph's from all over the country. It used to be the policy to send babies far away from their birth place. This made it harder for a child to trace the natural family, and easier to cover up any scandals. There was a lot of shame to deal with at that time. Families didn't want to know about the babies born to unmarried mothers. The mothers were expected to give their babies up and to forget they ever had them. Some mothers managed to do that. They went on to marry and have legitimate children. Their unwanted babies were never spoken of. There were some families too who wanted to forget about the orphaned children of their brothers and sisters. They gave them over to children's homes. Some were adopted and others were not. In most cases, family groups were split up and sometimes the family connection was never re-established. Now and again, a baby would come to St Joseph's and it would not get adopted. Babies over the age of three had very little chance of making it into a new family at that time. They were taken out of St Joseph's and placed in the Nazareth Lodge children's home. If the children had problems growing up, they were sent to training schools. Training schools were harsh places, usually in the middle of nowhere. There are not too many success stories coming out of the training schools of Ireland. Over time, attitudes have changed. There is a lot more tolerance for single mothers now and support for abandoned and neglected children. There are fewer children available for adoption now. But when I was born, I think my family was still stuck in the old days of shame. It is hard to imagine that Ireland was so backward in the late twentieth century, but I am living proof of it.

Most babies who came to St Joseph's when I was there stayed for a very short time while the paperwork from their natural mother and the adoptive parents was sorted out. St Joseph's was like a holding centre. A neutral place where babies were cared for but mothers were excluded from. At that time, they didn't worry as much about checking the background of the adoptive families as they do now. Usually local doctors and local clergy worked with the nuns and the families to process the babies through the Catholic Family Welfare Society. Social services were not often directly involved. I don't think it would happen like that today. I arrived at St Joseph's with another baby boy. The other baby left with his new parents shortly afterwards. Very few adopted babies made contact with the nuns in later life. They were at St Joseph's for such a short time, there was no special bond or relationship with anyone there. The nuns knew from the start that I would not be leaving them any time soon. I was the responsibility of social services. There was no doctor and no priest paving the way to a new family for me. When I arrived, I had nothing, not even my own nappies. The social worker who placed me in the care of the nuns wrote:

"The relatives have been prevailed upon to provide a dozen new nappies. I will be up in Belfast on Tuesday and will leave these nappies in with you at St. Josephs. I am sorry I cannot get them to you sooner.

"The baby's birth has been registered, and I will forward the birth certificate to you as soon as I get it. There is some doubt as to where the original certificate is, and I may well have to obtain a copy certificate from Newry."

I don't know about the nappies, but my original birth certificate never turned up. Paperwork gets lost all the time, but I do not believe that my birth certificate was lost. I believe it was deliberately withheld by members of my family. My missing birth certificate has affected the direction my life has taken ever since I discovered, at the age of 11, that my father was "Unknown". It is often said you come into this world with nothing. In my case, it seems I had less than nothing. No nappies, no mother to care for me when I was born, and no father.

I have always wondered why I was never adopted as a child. Not knowing my real parents, I have always wished I had parents who were strangers, and who would love me because I am Philip and because they chose me from all the babies at St Joseph's. Even if they changed my family name, they would love me because I am Philip, and because I am in this world. It is only recently I have discovered I was never going to be adopted. I managed to get my records from the years I spent at St Joseph's and it nearly broke my heart to read them. I was so alone in the world from the day I was born. There were three reasons why adoption was not for me. First, my mother either could not, or would not, give her consent for me to be adopted. For all I know, she was never even asked. Social services were responsible for me from the moment I was born and I do not believe my mother had any say in the matter. Second, my mother was a long-term patient in a psychiatric hospital. Her illness has followed me all my life, like a bad smell. The funny thing is, nobody can tell me what it is she suffers from. I am fed up hearing that Grace "loses the head". What does that mean? Don't we all lose the head from time to time? Even so, whatever Grace's illness is, it has tainted me. Third, since no-one had admitted to knowing who my father was, he was assumed to be another psychiatric patient. The way people thought at that time, there was no way the child of two mad people was going to be put up for adoption. The child was bound to be mad himself. No-one challenged this opinion, not once. In the children's home, it worked in my favour in a way because my development was regularly checked and plans were made to give me any extra help I needed to catch up with other children my age. But once I left the children's home and all the time I was growing up, I can remember people in my family saying, "It's only Philip, sure Philip's like his mother, mad in the head." It is a terrible thing to carry around with you all your life. Pretty soon, you start to believe it yourself.

Next to a real family, St Joseph's Babies Home was a great place to be reared in. It was a big red brick building in the grounds of the Nazareth House on the Ravenhill Road in Belfast. It is closed down now and scheduled for demolition, but the Nazareth Village is still there caring for elderly people. I don't have too many memories of St Joseph's, but the ones I have are all happy and I was well looked after. I revisited St Joseph's when I was about 15, when I was trying to find out more about my natural parents. But the visit didn't add anything to my memories. I am told I was a favourite with the nuns, because, unlike the other babies, they had time to get to know me. They got very attached to me. Long after I had left, there were still framed photographs of me in St Joseph's and the nuns still talked about me and laughed at the things I got up to. In fact, I met a social worker much later in my life who had done a placement at St Joseph's after I left. She remembered the photographs and the way the nuns talked about me. She felt she already knew me when she met me for the first time. Some might say I was spoiled at St Joseph's, but I don't think children ever remember being spoiled. I certainly don't.

As time went on, there were fewer unwanted babies for St Joseph's to care for. There were more older children and family groups from troubled homes, and I joined these children in the Nazareth Lodge children's home on the same site as St Joseph's. The other children were my friends and I had plenty of company. I didn't worry about who everybody was. It didn't matter to me if these children were my brothers and sisters, or my cousins, or strangers. They were all my friends, and the ladies in veils and blue skirts were all our mothers. Nobody that I can remember made us feel unwanted or like wee bastards. We were all just accepted and cared for as children and there was no difference made among us. The Nazareth nuns did a fantastic job. There are so many stories now of abuse in the homes run by the Catholic clergy. The notorious Fr. Brendan Smyth was a visitor at Nazareth Lodge children's home. I never experienced any abuse. Far from it. I felt I had the run of the place and could always be found playing and messing about with the other children; or running wildly down the wide corridors, shouting and laughing at the top of my voice. I was a bit of a show-off. I had a big personality as a young child and no inhibitions. I enjoyed life and I was as noisy and carefree as any child could be. Maybe the nuns would have preferred a quieter child, but they never said so. In my personal opinion, I don't think the innocent nuns and priests get enough recognition for the fantastic work they do with abandoned children and the elderly, the unwanted people in our society. All the attention is on the abusers, and in my experience, they are a minority. They might do a lot of damage, but they shouldn't take away from the good work the rest of the nuns and priests do. If I have any sense of right and wrong in this world, if I have any sense of justice, if I am ever generous or kind, I learned those things at St Joseph's Babies Home and I learned them from the nuns, especially Sr. Paula.

Come to think of it, as a child, I had no idea what nuns were – all these women running round in their navy blue skirts and veils, saying "Sister this" and "Sister that". I thought they were all my funny looking sisters and mothers. Sr. Paula was like a mother to me. I asked her if I called her "Mummy", but she told me no, I called her "Sister", like everyone else. Sr. Paula got me up and dressed in the mornings; she took me to nursery school; she listened to all my jokes and stories; she scolded me when I was bold and she comforted me when I was sick or sad. I remember going to the chapel with Sr. Paula and she nudged me to put my pennies in the collection basket when it went round. I didn't want to let my money go, and I can imagine that I fought Sr. Paula over the pennies. Some would say I am still the same way about my money!

The nuns, and Sr. Paula in particular, were the constant figures in my early life. Unlike a real mother, I never saw Sr. Paula in her bathrobe, or dressed up to go out for the evening. She was always dressed the same in her nun's habit. I have no other image of her in my mind. She is a tiny lady and to me her appearance has not changed. A few years ago, I was at a road safety event in Dublin called "Slow Down Boys" and Sr. Paula came with me. We stayed in a hotel and during the night, I rang for a glass of water. Sr. Paula brought it to me, and I didn't recognise her. It was the first time I had ever seen her without her nun's veil and I got the shock of my life. "Holy hell Sr. Paula," I said to her "Jesus, your hair's all white!" Sr. Paula gave me a drink and told me to mind my language. She would still try to tell me what to do at times, and I would still resist her. Sr. Paula has stood by me through all the trials of my life. She has always been there for me when I am troubled in myself, even though she would be the first to admit that at times she had no idea what to do with me! Sr. Paula knows me as a mother would. She knows me better than my real mother does. I owe Sr. Paula a great deal and I have a lot of respect for her. When I was told, clearly and bluntly, I would never walk again, Sr. Paula was there. She has always been there. Just like a real mother. I hope in my own way I can give back to Sr. Paula some of the care and attention she has given me throughout my life. If she were ever to need anything, all she has to do is ask.

Like any family, the nuns in St Joseph's would work out what was best for the children they cared for. They discussed our education and our progress. They worked on our behaviour and discipline problems. They gave all the children a good Catholic basis in life.

I had a weakness for toothpaste at St Joseph's and was regularly told off for taking great squirts of the stuff at all times of the day and night. I suppose if there had been packets of biscuits lying about, I would have taken them instead, but there weren't. There was only toothpaste. The nuns would tell me all the time that toothpaste was not for eating, but I didn't listen to them. I remember too there were a couple of rabbit hutches full of bunnies for us to play with and look after. I loved those bunnies. I used to open the doors of the hutches and let the rabbits run free. The nuns would be running after them down the corridors, skirts and veils flying, screaming for the rabbits to get back in their hutches, and telling me I was a holy terror. I would laugh, secretly hoping the rabbits would never get caught. Sr. Paula still teases me about this.

At that time, although social services were responsible for me, they had very little involvement in my day-to-day care. I did not have a relationship with anyone in social services, and there was nobody like Sr. Paula there. Occasionally, social services called for a review of my progress but apart from that, they had very little to do with me. The nuns celebrated our birthdays with us, and our Christmases, and they made it all as happy as they could. At Christmas time, when I was two years old, social services wrote to the nuns.

"I now enclose a cheque for £6, being Philip's Christmas allowance. I am sorry that it is not possible for one of our Social Workers to take Philip to buy a Christmas present, but unfortunately with our present level of staffing and the numbers of children in residential care scattered over the province, this is just an impossible task."

Sr. Paula was "Santa" that year. She would never criticise anybody. She would always try to see the other person's point of view. But I wonder what she thought when she got the £6 to go and buy me a present. She must have felt some anger and sadness at the thought of a small boy so alone in the world that he had to rely on strangers and public money to give him a happy Christmas. She must have wondered about the boy's family, leaving him alone year after year, every Christmas and every birthday.

St Joseph's was not a real family, but I felt happy and secure there. It was probably the only time in my life that I did feel secure. There were big rooms to play in, endless wide corridors. You could make noise there. I was always a bit boisterous, a bit of a showman and a comedian. I haven't changed much. The nuns might scold you, but I quickly learned how to turn on the charm and they were never cross with me for very long, no matter what I got up to. I am still the same. I enjoy a bit of cheeky chat with my home helps. I like to put a smile on their faces. It helps me to cope with the indignity of 24-hour nursing care. It releases the tension and it helps me to cover up my real feelings. At St Joseph's, I had no feelings to cover up. I was just myself, charming my way round the nuns and enjoying my young life.

A photograph of me from my time at St Joseph's shows a small boy with huge eyes, wee short legs and a pudding bowl haircut. I don't much like the look of the clothes I'm wearing in the photograph, but I don't suppose the nuns kept up with fashions. Even if they had, there probably wasn't the money for more than the basic clothes. I have that photograph framed on my sitting room wall now. When people ask me who it is, I say, "That's the wee bastard in the children's home". They take another, longer look. "Are you serious, Philip?" they say, "Who is it? Is it you?" I am not smiling in the photograph, but I look like I am about to burst out laughing.

Because of my mother's mental health problems, there was a question mark over my development from the earliest days of my life. I was seen regularly by a paediatrician and an educational psychologist while I was at St Joseph's home. In my very early years, my development was below average. I didn't hit the milestones as quickly as other children my age. I was slow to walk and to talk, although Sr. Paula remembers that once I got started, I couldn't stop! I wonder now if my mother's medication and treatment, both before and during her pregnancy, might have affected my early development. I have no way of knowing. When Grace got pregnant, she was sent away, even though there was a general hospital about a mile from the Willow Hill psychiatric hospital where she lived. My mother spent around six months of her pregnancy at The Good Shepherd Convent in Newry, where she worked in the laundries and waited for me to be born. As I have already said, I was a little bit premature and Grace never had the chance to care for me. She held me for a few minutes when I was born and then I was taken off her. It must have felt like she was never even pregnant. Maybe it would be better for her to think that. It was not the best start for any baby, or any mother. No wonder my development was slow. It has also been said that as I was one of many children at Nazareth Lodge, there was not enough love to go around and make me thrive. I don't know about that. I know what it feels like to be unloved, and I believe the nuns did their best for me and I believe I was loved when I was there. When you think about it, no children's home can replace a loving family, no matter how good it is.

When the time came for me to go to primary school, I was assessed by the educational psychologist. She recommended a special school, and added:

"It is really too early to make an accurate forecast especially in this case where development was so delayed in the early stages. I would like to keep Philip's progress under review as with directive treatment it might be possible to return him to the normal school at a later date."

My first primary school was Harberton School in Belfast; a small special needs primary school where Sr. Paula thought I would do well.

At around this time, when I was about four, there was talk of fostering me out. Adoption continued to be out of the question for me. Social services became a bit more interested in me at that point. Maybe there was a change of policy on children's homes or something. Maybe I needed a change of scene. St Joseph's was in the heart of Belfast and in the early 1980s, although I knew no different, it was not the best environment to grow up in. In any case, the search began for a family who would take on a child who was considered to be mildly mentally handicapped. It was hoped a foster family would keep me at Harberton School as planned, at least until I caught up with other children my age. My friends and business contacts today would be surprised to learn that I was considered mentally handicapped. It was a total shock to me when I found out that was what people thought of me back then.

Several families came forward to foster me, but for one reason or another, they were not selected. Then, an advertisement with a photograph of a laughing child in dungarees was sent to the newspapers and the parish newsletters of the Catholic Church. When I read this advertisement now, it makes me feel like a child for sale or an abandoned dog. But I have to admit, it succeeded in bringing potential foster parents forward, who might not have thought about someone like me. Here is the advertisement in full.

"We are looking for long term foster parents for Philip who is a 4 ½ year old Catholic boy. Philip has lived all of his life in a children's home as his mother is ill and cannot look after him. He is medium sized for his age with unruly brown hair, a lively nature and a ready smile. Philip is just a little bit slower than average and it is planned that he will go to a special primary school in Belfast where he will get a little extra help, though it is hoped that he may be able to return to a normal school in the future.

"For this reason we would like to find foster parents for Philip either within the South Belfast area or within travelling distance of that part of Belfast. Philip has a slight speech difficulty in that although he can speak quite clearly, his vocabulary is fairly limited and he will need to learn lots of new words and expressions.

"Philip mixes well with the other children in the home and is generous with his belongings. Although he can be high-spirited at times, he poses no particular problems to the staff. He is very secure within the children's home and, naturally, it will take a considerable time to introduce him to a foster family, and for him to get used to a normal family routine. He is a very pleasant and affectionate child. He will amply repay the affection and attention of foster parents."

I cried my eyes out when I first read that advertisement just a year ago. I didn't have a clue that I was advertised in the papers. My friends have said to me that they don't know how I cope with reading that very short story of my early life. Considering what happened to me after that advertisement was published, I don't know how I cope either, but I do.

I spent nearly six years at St Joseph's and up until the time I was fostered, I had one visitor from my natural family on my mother's side. I don't remember the occasion at all. I am told I was two years of age. My maternal grandmother came to see me. She was in a wheelchair at the time and her daughter-in-law brought her, my uncle Joseph's wife. As well as my mother, I have an aunt and four uncles. Some of them were working away in England and North America, but they all came back. They all had children of their own. None of them ever came to see me the whole time I was in St Joseph's. I don't know my father's side of the family, not yet. I have often wondered if my father would have come to see me, if he knew where I was at. I wonder if he ever tried to find me.

It was a surprise to everyone when one of my mother's brothers, Francis, presented himself, his wife, and his large family as a potential foster family. Did he see my face in the parish newsletter and feel a stab of guilt? If so, guilt for what? Abandoning me? Abandoning my mother? Or did he not want any other family in the parish to have me? Maybe he thought that at six years of age I was half reared, so there would be little work for him to do. I don't know what his motivation was and he didn't discuss it with his brothers or sisters. Some of them were told of his decision and some, including my own mother, were not. Nobody in the family was consulted. A child's natural family is usually seen as the best option for fostering. The child is supposed to get more of a feeling of who he is and where he is from. I can see the reason for that opinion. But in my case, I don't agree with it at all. My foster family never helped me to find out who I am.

When the child is unwanted by the family from day one, and lies abandoned and forgotten in a children's home with only one visitor in six years, how can it be a good idea for that family to take over his care? When the child's mother had to spend her pregnancy in a convent far from home, how can it be a good idea for her family to take on the care of the child they hid away and didn't want to know? When the child's family had to be "prevailed upon" to provide a dozen nappies for him when he was born, how could that family be trusted to love and care for the child? I will never understand it. I will never understand why my uncle wanted to foster me in the first place. I will never understand why social services allowed it to happen. Was it too expensive to keep me in a children's home? My foster parents had a big family of their own and not much money at that time. There were other families in a far better position to take me in and love me, families who could have given me the support social services knew I needed. There was no love in my foster home that I could see. How could there have been any to spare for me? How could it have worked?

Of all the families who were interested in fostering me, one in particular was quite a way through the process. Then my uncle Francis appeared on the scene. I wish to God he had been turned away at the door and the other family had taken me. I recently met a lovely young woman in a shopping centre. She came up to me and said "Philip, you could have been my brother." It turns out this girl was fostered by the family who were pushed aside when my uncle came along. She is doing well in life and she was very happy in her foster home. I am glad for that family who were able to give a child a solid start in life and a loving home. I am glad they continued to be foster parents to somebody even though they didn't get me.

When I first met my uncle Francis, aunt Bernadette and cousins, they came to see me at St Joseph's. I don't remember meeting them but I have seen the bit of paper in my files that my uncle submitted for petrol expenses to cover the trips they made to visit me. On the first visit, they didn't even phone to make an arrangement to see me, they just turned up. I was not told at first they were part of my family, just in case we didn't get on and it would be difficult for me to accept. But I am told I was delighted with these new people. Remember, I had almost no experience of visitors, so anybody coming to see me was a big change in my routine. The Donaghys made several trips to see me and the files say that the more I got to know them, the better I liked them. I was excited by the visits, and I spent them showing off to my cousins, big time. My favourite TV programme back then was "*The Incredible Hulk*" and I identified my uncle with the Hulk. He was a big man then, a farmer, with thick black hair and glasses. He had a loud and booming voice. I was sort of afraid of him, but in that excited way, like at Halloween when children want to be terrified. I had practically no experience of men at that time. My uncle was as different as you could get from the wee, soft-voiced nuns of Nazareth Lodge. I was running round him and ducking out of his reach shouting "Hey Speccy, you're the Incredible Hulk! You're the Incredible Hulk!" My cousins were quieter than I was, much less excitable, and they didn't join in the game. That made me even more anxious to entertain them by showing off. One of my cousins thought I was overstepping the mark with my uncle and that he wouldn't like the way I was behaving. Sr. Paula recalled meeting me not long after my foster placement started and I was as quiet and subdued as my cousins by then. Where did all that life go? Where was the special boy who was the nuns' favourite? He was long gone by then.

The family visited me a few times at St Joseph's and then I visited them with my new social worker and Sr. Paula at their home on a farm in Mullabeg, outside Cookstown. Although I was not quite six years old, I was a real city boy, with a Belfast accent. I loved the farm, the fields and animals, the freedom. Everything was different and new to me, and I thought it was brilliant. I had been told by then I might be coming to live with this family and I had been told they were my relations. I had no idea what the words "family" and "relations" meant, but it didn't matter to me then. It was an exciting adventure for me. Before returning to Belfast, I wanted to know where I would be sleeping when I came to live in Mullabeg. Everyone agreed that this was a good sign.

In early May 1981, I spent a long weekend by myself at Mullabeg with the Donaghys. This was the next step in introducing me to my new family. As the fostering advertisement said, "*[Philip] is very secure within the children's home and, naturally, it will take a considerable time to introduce him to a foster family, and for him to get used to a normal family routine.*" After the weekend visit, I was supposed to go back to St Joseph's and the fostering process would continue for another three months or so, until I was ready to move to Mullabeg permanently. If everyone had stuck to the plan, and if I showed good signs of settling into my new life, I would have been starting primary school in Mullabeg in September 1981. But things weren't moving fast enough for my uncle Francis. It must have been a right pain for him to drive up and down to Belfast to pick me up and leave me back. He probably didn't want to spend the summer driving up and down the road. He was a farmer, he would have been busy. Plus, there would have been a lot of security checkpoints at that time and the journey would have been slow, even though it is only about 40 miles each way. I did not return to St Joseph's as planned in May. My uncle said I was unhappy on the journey back, so he turned the van round and came home. He sent me to the local primary school the next day, and the day after that, he phoned social services and told them what he had done. Because my uncle took the fostering process into his own hands, social services confirmed my placement sooner than was planned. I would say this was the first, and maybe the biggest, mistake social services made in the 18 years they were responsible for my care. Think about it. If that happened today, it would cause a scandal. My uncle Francis broke the agreement he had with my legal guardians by not sending me back to them at the end of the weekend. It doesn't matter that he was blood related to me. He was a stranger in my life and he had no right to break the timetable for my fostering. He was not reprimanded in any way. Far from it. I was signed over into his care immediately.

With hindsight, the process should not have been speeded up. The checks social services made on the suitability of foster families back then were not as strict as they are now. Plus, since my foster family was part of my natural family, there seemed to be even less reason for concern. Social services wanted this placement to work. They seem to have only wanted to see good things in my uncle and his family. Not only that, there was a change of staff at the local office and I have the feeling that the outgoing social worker wanted to leave a tidy caseload behind. I fell between two social workers. Nobody had a complete overview of the fostering case. There was a lack of communication with my carers at St Joseph's and I would say that social services couldn't care less about the work the nuns had done with me. There was also less family support at that time to prepare foster parents and children for what lay ahead. In my case, there was not enough groundwork done. I didn't understand the existing blood relationship I had with my foster parents. I didn't know anything about my mother. I didn't understand what my position would be in the family of my uncle. I wonder if my foster family knew what they were taking on when they decided to foster me? Did my aunt know that the burden of my day-to-day care would fall to her? Did my cousins know who I was and what I had been through already in my life? Was my uncle prepared to open his heart to me as well as his door? Maybe if my foster family had taken more time to think about what they were doing, and why they were doing it, they might have acted differently and left me in the children's home. There was a good family interested in fostering me, and they were elbowed out of the way when my uncle came forward. The plans that were carefully made for my education fell by the wayside. Not enough time was spent getting to know each other and understand each other. If I was too boisterous, or too slow, or too mad, or too bold, or too difficult, all of these things could have been discovered in time for my uncle to change his mind about fostering me. Or to get help. But he wouldn't take the time and he is not a man to ask for help. I paid the price for his haste and his stubbornness for nine years. In many ways, I am still paying the price.

From my personal experience, I would say I disagree with family members fostering the unwanted children of their unwanted sisters. I was abandoned by my family. Despite what they may say, I was never loved and I was never wanted by them. A child knows when he is loved. I was an embarrassment to my family from day one and I felt my foster parents were ashamed of me. I still am an embarrassment to them. When I appeared on TV, they would rather I just stayed at home and shut up. Maybe they blamed me for what happened to my mother, I don't know. But I felt like a bastard in that house before I even knew what a bastard was. I was the living proof of a sister who was hidden away from the world. And when she got pregnant, she was hidden even further away, in a convent. It was many years before people in Mullabeg found out that Grace was my mother. It was all a big secret and a great shame on the family. In my opinion, the foster placement was doomed from the start. It has done more to harm my sense of identity than living among strangers could ever have done. Strangers might have taught me to respect my mother in spite of her illness and not to fear her for it. Strangers might have introduced me to their friends and families instead of putting me out of the room when visitors called. Strangers might have helped me to make contact with my real parents instead of brushing my identity under the carpet. I don't believe that strangers would have made me feel like a mad bastard all my days the way my foster family did.

After that long weekend in May, I never returned to St Joseph's to live. Most of my things were still there, and I felt very alone in a strange house. My cousins were very quiet and I missed the noise of the children at the home. The novelty of my foster family quickly wore off and I started to fret. I wondered when the holiday would be over, and when I would be going home to Sr. Paula. When I realised that my foster home was my home, I would lie in bed at night wondering why I was there and why I couldn't go back to the children's home. *Why me?* I used to suck my fingers for comfort in bed at night. Sr. Paula visited a couple of times, I remember, and then she didn't come back. She was transferred to another Nazareth House. This was always likely to happen, and it was why she was so glad to see me settled with a family before she left. I didn't understand this at the time. To me it was like being abandoned. Again. My foster parents kept in touch with Sr. Paula, to let her know how I was getting on and to send family snapshots. Sr. Paula believed I was happy because that is what she was told. Happy was a word I no longer understood. Smiling in a family snapshot is not the same thing as being happy.

All the joy had gone out of life for me. I was six years old. All the times I had gone running down the corridors of the children's home, laughing my head off, were like faraway memories. We didn't do much joking about in my foster home. There were very few noisy games. There wasn't the loving interaction between parents and children I see in the families of my friends. I was part of a family in one way, but I never felt sheltered or protected by that family. I was never at ease. I don't remember ever being kissed or cuddled after I left St Joseph's. I don't remember being spoiled by my other uncles and aunts. I don't remember playing with their sons and daughters. I was kept away from the extended family. If they came visiting on a Sunday afternoon, I was brought into the room to meet them and then put out again. I wasn't encouraged to play with my other cousins, or even to talk to them. One cousin remembers me staring at him as if I was dying to talk to him and play with him, but I wouldn't open my mouth. I left the room when my uncle or aunt told me to, and that was it. Over time, my cousins passed no remark about me. They knew I was there, but that was all they knew. Through no fault of theirs, they got used to ignoring me. They probably were told I was mad like my mother. They never had the chance to get to know me.

It wasn't long before I started to forget St Joseph's. It is good in a way that your memories fade because you can't live in the past. You have to move on and adapt to the life you are living now. As a child, I found that hard to do. The past was a fading memory. The present was anxious and difficult. I didn't understand who I was in my uncle's house. I felt I had nowhere to go and no-one to turn to when I had problems or worries. I felt I didn't belong anywhere and I think that is where my restlessness and insecurity come from. I had to rely on myself too much and too early. I was confused. People who remember me from the time I was fostered say I looked like a lost boy. That is a good description. I was lost. Most young children have at least one adult who is at the centre of their lives and who can guide them through and make growing up a little bit easier. I had insecurity at the centre of my life. I had to learn from my own experience. It was a hard life and I wouldn't recommend it, but in some ways it has made me the strong person I am today. It has made me better able to cope with the life I have now. But back in Mullabeg, I didn't feel like I was coping. I was watching my step and my back all the time.

My so-called family

My foster home was the home my mother was reared in until she was first hospitalised at the age of 19. It is a farm in a place called Mullabeg in the heart of the Mid-Ulster countryside. Slieve Gallion in the Sperrin Mountains rises up behind the farm. I used to love going up the mountain, not for the scenery or the fresh air, but because I could look down at the house and see how small it was from up there. Just four whitewashed walls, and a few outbuildings, that was all. There were dozens of lanes connecting the small communities of isolated farms round about Mullabeg. The roads were narrow and twisting, and they were almost free of traffic at that time. The earth in the fields was red; the hedges were high with grassy verges. There were lakes and a quarry in the distance. As I got to know the area, I quickly learned about the importance of the land and the rights of way through it. I also found plenty of hiding places and boltholes, places I could escape to when I needed to. Every inch of that ground is of value to somebody and I got to know where the safe places were.

My cousins were older than me, except for the youngest daughter, and they were all living at home when I came to stay. I shared a room with my cousin Cathal who was five or six years older than me. I was quite close to him growing up, but I never felt that we were as close as brothers. I never felt that closeness with any of my relations. Cathal was sent to work in England at probably the most vulnerable time in my life. It was a vulnerable time for him too, but I was so wrapped up in my own problems that I didn't understand what he was going through. I saw plenty, but I thought Cathal was coping with it, being a son of the family. I have never had much to do with the two oldest sons. They were close to their father and very like him. When I arrived at Mullabeg, I played with the younger children. I remember a donkey in the field that I used to like. One of the daughters looked after it. I remember a red tricycle we played on and a dog called Dot. I broke my heart when Dot was shot for worrying sheep. I was told off by my foster mother for putting on a babyish voice when I played with my young cousins. She made fun of me for wanting to play with girls in the first place. I was expected to act like a man from the age of six.

There had been a lot of discussion in Belfast about my education. I was to go to a special needs primary school that would help me to catch up with other children my age. Social services were concerned that the local primary school in Mullabeg would not be able to cope with me. I was not aware of any of this at the time, but I have since learned from my files that my cousins and their parents had all attended the local school. According to the head teacher, none of them had been anything more than average, so I was not likely to stand out in the household as being particularly slow or stupid. I think my foster parents would be surprised to learn their "retarded" nephew was no slower than they were at the same age. They ought to be ashamed of themselves for putting a child down before he even had the chance to prove himself.

Social services came to see me regularly for the next 12 years of my life, until I turned 18 and was free of the care order that had tagged me from birth. In all that time, I never felt close to anyone from the social services. I am sure they were busy and had lots of other people to see, but I think they knew me no better at the end of 12 years than at the beginning. You would think 12 years was enough time to build a trust with somebody. But I never trusted social services, not as far as I could throw them. Towards the end of my time in care, I was very demanding and I gave the social workers a mouthful of abuse whenever I felt they let me down, which was most of the time. I was completely fed up with them by then. I had tried to cooperate, but at the end of the day, they were not interested in me. They were more interested in doing what their bosses told them. I went through more than one social worker for the last few months of the care order, stressing them out one by one. But back when I was fostered as a 6-year-old, I was no trouble at all. I was just a small boy trying to find his way in a new family as best he could. Right or wrong, I have always believed social services were working for my foster parents and not for me. I never saw it as a three-way relationship. Maybe I was too withdrawn and quiet for the social workers. Maybe dealing with the needs of foster children was not their speciality. My uncle and aunt became the main source of information about Philip Donaghy. The boy himself was a nobody. But I am grateful to social services for one thing. They kept very detailed reports and I have relied on their reports to help me with this book. Under the Freedom of Information Act, I have been able to request the files that were kept on me since birth. I don't remember things the same way as the social workers. They wrote in their reports hings like, "When I arrived, Philip was in the kitchen enjoying a cup of tea." What I remember was my uncle or aunt saying "Get yourself in here and be quiet, the social worker is here." I will leave it to the readers of this book to make up their own minds about where reality sits. I was no saint and I did some stupid things in my time in care. Without strong leadership in my life, I made some bad decisions and acted on them. But I was not a bad person. The nuns in the children's home taught me right from wrong, and they taught me well. Looking back, it wouldn't have taken much in the early days to unpick my bad behaviour to see what was behind it. A wee bit of loving care and attention might just have turned my life in a different direction.

Having been reared in a children's home, I don't think my foster family or social services realised I would miss it when I left. To them it was probably the worst kind of institution to be reared in. But the children's home was all I knew and after a few days in Mullabeg, I wondered when I would be going home. Although it was explained to me that Mullabeg was my home now, I didn't really understand what that meant. I fretted in my bed at night, remembering all the people in St Joseph's, my friends, my toys I had left behind. I was already starting to forget things. For comfort, I would lie in the dark remembering, and I would suck on my fingers until I dropped off to sleep. This was a habit I had from a young age, and until I was fostered, it had not seemed to bother anyone. It vexed my uncle Francis and it was probably the first sign of trouble between us. He said sucking my fingers was pushing my teeth out. He was probably right about that, but I wasn't thinking about my teeth when I sucked my fingers. It was just a habit. The more unhappy and insecure I felt in my foster home, the more I sucked on my fingers at night for comfort, and the angrier my uncle Francis became about it. It was the first of many vicious circles in our relationship. If he had been helped to understand why I was sucking my fingers, the habit might have been broken more easily. Probably the first time I was ever called a liar was over sucking my fingers.

One morning, I came downstairs. Uncle Francis was sitting at the kitchen table having his breakfast. He looked hard at me as I came creeping quietly into the kitchen.

"Were you sucking on them fingers?" he asked me.

"No," I said, too quickly, because I knew it vexed him. Uncle Francis got up from the table and took my chin in his large, calloused hand.

"What's this then, you wee liar?" What I didn't realise was that I had a telltale rash at one side of my mouth where drool had gathered as I sucked on my fingers. It was a small lie I told to keep out of trouble, but it was a lie. Later, my uncle took me into the town. He bought me a toy gun and a pair of plastic handcuffs from Wellworths. I thought they were a present. It was the one and only time he took me shopping for toys. That evening at home, he produced a wooden box he had made, about the size of a shoebox. It had a lid and a lock, and there were two holes cut out of the side of it. He told me to put my hands into the holes. Then he put the toy handcuffs on me. He closed and locked the lid of the box, and told me to go to bed. I had to go up the stairs lugging that wooden box with my two hands trapped inside.

"That'll learn you to suck your fingers," my uncle said, and he laughed. I had to sleep with that box on top of me. I don't remember how long I had to wear the box at night. It felt like ages, but it probably was not that long. Sometimes, in the morning, my uncle was gone out to the farm before I wakened and I had to wait until he got back before the box was opened and my hands were freed. I was not able to go to the toilet, have my breakfast, or get dressed until that box was taken off my hands. It didn't work anyway. The first night I was sent to bed without the box on my hands, I went back to sucking my fingers. Uncle Francis had several other tricks up his sleeve to cure me of my habit. I had manure smeared socks put on my hands, but what finally cured me was being thrown into a cupboard for the night. It was a dark old hot press in the kitchen with a lock on it. I was thrown in there with a quilt and locked in all night. It only happened the once, and I never sucked my fingers after it, but it has left me with a fear of the dark. When I think of being alone in the dark, I remember anxious moments sucking my fingers as a child. Even now, I hate to wake suddenly in the night and feel the darkness all about me as I lie there. It reminds me of that locked cupboard with the child trapped inside.

Life in my uncle's home was very different to the life I was used to in the children's home. Sr. Paula has remarked that I was so desperate for a father in my life, that I would have done anything to please my uncle. She was probably right about that. I had no male influence in my life for the first six years, no man who could be a role model for me. Instinctively, I turned to my uncle. Even at the age of six, I wanted to admire and love him. Most of all, I wanted him to love me back. Whatever he asked me to do, I did it to the best of my ability. But it was never good enough. My uncle was not a man who was easily pleased, neither by me, nor by his own sons and daughters. Or anyone else for that matter. Love didn't come into it. He was not liked, and in a small, rural community where people have to rely on each other, whether they like it or not, it is important to keep good relations with neighbours. You never know when you might need them or when they might need you to do them a good turn. My uncle didn't give a damn about his neighbours. He laughed at their misfortunes and encouraged his children and me to do the same. I did what I was told, but I was never comfortable with that. I liked my neighbours. I was at school with their children.

From the earliest days, I was expected to pull my weight around the house and the farm. This is not a criticism, because I was a very willing worker, although not a very skilled one. All of my neighbours back then remembered me as a hard worker and a boy who would go out of his way to help them if he could. They remembered me in my white Wellington boots taking sheep over the lanes and up the mountain, or standing by a hedge watching the men at work in the fields, too shy to speak to them. In the country, children were expected to help out on the family's farm, but some of my neighbours thought I was too young for the amount of work I was expected to do. At six years of age, I had no experience of any kind of work. Not only was I a city boy, but I was used to having everything done for me by the nuns. Compared to my cousins, I was spoiled. But the nuns only did for me what they did for every child they cared for. It was not my fault if I didn't know my way around the household chores the way my cousins did. But I was desperate to please, and this marked me out as a skivvy on the farm and in the house. I wasn't able to do any of the important jobs, so I was given a lot of the donkeywork to do. My first chore was to gather sticks for setting the fire in the morning. I also kept the fire supplied with coal and turf. It pleased me whenever I didn't have to be asked to get the turf. I kept a close eye on that fire. I was a skivvy the entire time I lived at my uncle's; a whipping boy. I have heard of boys from orphanages in Ireland being hired out to farmers, home boys as they were called, who were treated no better than a dog. That was how I was reared in my foster home, long after the traditional orphanages were closed down. I had a roof over my head and I worked for it. That was all.

The social workers noted in almost every report that when they called at the house to see me, I was out in the yard or on the farm working. I was kept busy. It could be getting fuel for the fire, dipping sheep, feeding calves, or washing my work clothes at the cold tap in the yard. The reports from that time painted a picture of a young boy in his element on the farm. My foster parents told my social workers I liked farm work. In a way I did because it got me out of the house. But it was never my ambition in life to be a farmer. If my social workers could have dressed me up in a powder blue costume and put a crook in my hand, I think they would have. But, in reality, while I was out of the way working, my social workers talked to whichever of my foster parents was in the house. When the time was up, they would be off to write their report. I am not saying that social services never saw me, or never talked to me on my own. But the time available to build a relationship was taken up mainly by discussions with my foster parents and not with me. That made me feel uncomfortable and so I was withdrawn whenever a social worker spoke to me. In a typical conversation I would have given "yes" or "no" answers to any question I was asked. If I ever gave any more than that, social services took it as a sign of progress and happiness and they wrote about it in their reports. I was also warned by my uncle not to tell the social workers anything about the family. My uncle is very secretive, even about his most ordinary, day-to-day business. Social services saw me through the eyes of my foster parents, and when I read their reports, I didn't like what they were seeing. No wonder I felt I couldn't trust them. My foster parents had them wrapped around their wee fingers. It was my foster parents who controlled the relationship and the information about me that was passed on to the authorities. In report after report, my foster parents complained about me like I was some kind of faulty machine and they wanted their money back. "Philip tells lies." "Philip fights with his cousins." "Philip is immature". They never said that Philip was a breath of fresh air about the place, or Philip was a great wee worker. They never reported one good or positive thing about having me in their lives.

Another aspect of life that was new and strange for me at that time was physical punishment. I had been told off by the nuns plenty of times at the children's home. I might have had the odd slap, but if I did, I don't remember it. I know for certain I had never been hit a slap in violence or in anger. I had never in my life been cursed at. I had never had a man's voice or hand raised against me until I went to my foster home. My aunt said at the time I appeared to be afraid of men and more fond of women. The only man I knew was my uncle Francis. And she was right, I was afraid of him. I still am in some ways. I don't employ men to care for me now, even though they would be physically more able than women to do the heavy lifting that is involved. I couldn't bear the thought of being that vulnerable and exposed in front of a man again. It is a fear that I have my uncle Francis to thank for, through years of rough treatment.

Probably, back in that time, most children I knew would have got the odd slap off their parents. They would have expected it, if they had been caught doing something wrong. At school too, you would have expected a slap by the teachers for acting the goat or fighting in class. Things are different now. Teachers are banned from hitting pupils and my friends don't hit their kids. They love and support them and rear them as best they can, no matter what they do. If the children need to be punished for something, they know at the end of it there will be no hard feelings and no grudges. Although I have no memory of ever being slapped by the nuns, I think I would have expected a slap for bad behaviour. It was just accepted at the time.

It was a big shock to me to hear my uncle Francis shouting and cursing at his children in the crudest kind of language. He had us down on our knees every night saying the Rosary, but at all other times he was very free with his shouting and cursing around the house and farm. I can tell you, I learned what a hypocrite was very early on in life. People said you could hear the shouting from our house for miles around Mullabeg. The neighbours all heard it, and kept half an ear on it, but what could they do about it? That was how uncle Francis ran his home. It was his business at the end of the day.

Uncle Francis was a big man then, well built and strong. His voice was always loud in my ears, even when he wasn't angry. Even now, although he is getting older and more frail in his health, that voice remains powerful. Sometimes, from a distance, you couldn't tell his mood from the sound of his voice, and you had fear in your throat; you hoped he was in good humour as you quickly went through in your mind something you might have done, or failed to do, that would vex him. I was shocked when he turned his anger towards me. I was scared out of my wits and that just made things worse. I was constantly looking for ways to keep out of trouble, and my uncle was constantly catching me out in stupid excuses.

Lies, as he called them. It must have made him feel like the big man to get the better of a child of seven or eight years of age. A visitor to the house said to me that I had a way of carrying myself at that time, as if I were a dog expecting to be walloped.

"Did you check on the sheep up the field?" Uncle Francis said to me.

"Yes." I knew I had forgotten to check them, but I thought I could sneak out and do it and uncle Francis would be none the wiser. But when I went out into the yard, he was waiting for me.

"Where are you off to?" he would say, with a smirk on his face, knowing fine well that he had caught me out.

"Nowhere, just out," I stammered back at him.

"Get back inside," he said and I sat all evening fretting about the sheep, hoping they were alright. Sometimes they were, but not always. I was sure to get the blame if they got out of the field or if one of them died. As I say, I would have expected to be punished for doing something wrong. The problem was, half the time I never knew what I was being punished for. I was always trying to guess what way my uncle was thinking and what he wanted from me. He took pleasure in catching me out. When I got hit for something, I would cry. And then I would get hit again for crying and told to stop crying like a baby. If I told a lie to avoid getting into trouble, I would get hit a good few slaps until I told the truth. Then I would get hit again for telling lies. If I was telling the truth, I would get hit for telling lies. So then I would tell a lie to avoid getting hit, and I would get hit again for lying. It was a vicious cycle, I couldn't get out of it and I could never win. In a very short time, my foster parents were complaining to the social workers that I told lies. The reason for telling lies, to escape punishment, or "chastisement" as it was called in the reports, was never looked into. The form "chastisement" took, slaps that turned into beatings over time, was never looked into. I soon realised whatever way I behaved, it was wrong. No matter what I did, it was not good enough. I used to end up getting told off by the social workers as well as "chastised" by my foster parents for the same thing. And I had no-one to turn to. That is what I remember most about my foster home, the feeling I had no-one to turn to if I was upset or unhappy. I didn't blame my cousins for turning a blind eye to what was happening to me. They were probably in fear of their father too, and plenty of times I saw them getting the brunt of his anger. They know I did. The only ones I never saw being punished were the two oldest sons. But blood is thicker than water at the end of the day. I think my cousins knew that I was more harshly treated than they were, but I couldn't turn to them for comfort. I had to rely on myself, and as a young lad I just had no experience of life to comfort myself and tell myself it would all work out fine in the end. If I could just do my best and work hard, it would all work out in the end.

My neighbours and friends in Mullabeg remember me as a nervous boy who wouldn't say boo to a goose. I was constantly looking over my shoulder, trying to see if I could work out the next job that needed to be done. I jumped out of my skin if people came upon me unexpectedly. Within a year of moving to my foster home, even my youngest cousins had learned to dismiss me with "Ach sure it's only Philip." I was very different to the boy in St Joseph's who was showing off to impress his cousins. In the reports filed by social services, I was described as a boy who found it difficult to tell fantasy from reality. I couldn't agree more. When reality makes no sense to you, where else can you go but into your own fantasy world? It is healthy to have somewhere to escape to, even if it is only for a minute. In my fantasy world at that time, I was Philip Donaghy, with a mum and dad who loved me just for being who I was. I had brothers and sisters who loved me as Philip and I loved them too. In some ways I still have that fantasy; that need for unconditional love in my own family.

My uncle Francis used to call me the Mid-Ulster Mail, which was the name of the local newspaper, because of the stories he said I made up, and the gabbing he said I did about family matters. Everyone in the Donaghy household seemed to know by some kind of instinct not to speak about family business outside the four walls of the house. I didn't have that instinct. What could I have said to people anyway? Outside of school, I didn't have much of a social life in those early years. Although on the surface and to outsiders it looked like I was accepted as a member of the family, behind closed doors I never felt like one. I always felt like I didn't belong. I was put out of the room when family matters were discussed. When there were visitors, including social services, I was paraded in front of them like a new puppy and then put out. If a social worker arrived at the house when visitors were there, they had to speak to me and my aunt or uncle in the yard. I once had a meeting with a social worker in a car, parked round the back of the yard. My aunt and uncle didn't want anyone, even the family, to know I was fostered and had a social worker. I think people assumed my uncle and aunt adopted me out of St Joseph's. They did not. According to my files, they considered it at one time, but then came to appreciate the financial assistance fostering provided. To me, that said it all. I was not fostered for love. I was fostered for money. With a big family of their own, a half-grown extra one was cheap to rear, especially when social services paid for anything extra I needed. People say the fostering payments did not amount to very much. I say it was an income that my foster parents would not have had without me and they had to do very little to earn it. It was easy money.

I had lots of other cousins, besides my foster parents' children, but we were as good as strangers to each other. I knew who they were, and I would have recognised them if I met them, but we had no friendship with each other. It was not encouraged and as children we just accepted that. Today, I could pass people in the street who are my cousins and I wouldn't know them. A few times in recent years I have met people I think I recognise and I say to them, "I'm Philip Donaghy. Are you my cousin?" More often than not they are. I was in my late teens and living on my own in a flat in Cookstown before I got to know any of my other cousins. I don't hold any grudge against them for that. They followed the example set by their parents. When I was living out in Mullabeg as a child, I think my other uncles thought I was doing okay. They didn't give another thought to me. There were tensions between the uncles too, but that was their business, it was not part of my story. My uncle Francis was described by family members as "the big man, back in that time" or "the boss", even though he was not the eldest son. He seemed to have some sort of hold over his brothers and sisters that I didn't understand. They kept out of his way, much as I did as a child.

Before I came to live with my uncle Francis on the farm, my grandmother lived there too. My mother, Grace, used to visit at weekends, when she was well enough. She still had her own room there. My grandmother was gone by the time I arrived. She had left her home and was living with another of her sons, leaving uncle Francis and his family alone in the home place. Old Mrs Donaghy was unwell and nearing the end of her life. My mother's weekend visits stopped altogether when I was fostered. For two years, she was not told her brother had fostered me. It might have been upsetting for Grace, but there was plenty of time to prepare the two of us for finally meeting. There was no preparation done. When we were introduced to each other as mother and son, neither of us knew how to react. Grace treated me the same way as she treated all her nephews and nieces. She gave me no special notice or attention, and I responded in exactly the same way towards her. There was no emotional basis to our relationship. Nothing was done to help us to meet as mother and son for the first time. In fact, I rarely saw Grace, either before or after I found out she was my real mother. But I did start to wonder about my real father.

I remember going with my foster parents to visit Grace at the Willow Hill psychiatric hospital where she lived. It was a big, dark-coloured, stone building. It looked like a castle or even a prison. There were a lot of windows but they were narrow with small panes of glass. From the outside they looked as if they were barred, but they may not have been. They didn't look like they let in much light. Grace was in a locked up ward at the time when I visited. It was a frightening place for a young boy. I couldn't tell who were the staff and who were the patients and that's the truth. They were all bad looking, I mean really bad looking, and they were shouting and roaring at nothing that I could see. My mother, Grace, looked like the most normal person in the room. Although I didn't see Grace very often while I was fostered by her brother, I was always careful not to say too much and not to upset her in any way. I never called her "Mum" and she never asked me to. From time to time I would speak to her on the telephone, but we had very little to say to each other. My uncle was stingy with his telephone and I had to wait for ages on the end of the line, running up the bill, while a nurse went to find Grace. It meant nothing to me that she was my mother. It meant nothing to her that I was her son.

I have tried to remember some happy times from my childhood in my uncle's house. I remember playing with my younger cousins and I enjoyed that. But I was told by my foster parents to find boys my own age to play with. So even my happier memories were stained with the thought that I was doing something wrong or something that displeased my foster parents. Maybe my memory of that time has gone sour. I asked my friends and neighbours if they remembered any happy times for me while I lived there. The best anyone came up with was, "A walk up the mountain, away from the house, that would have been a happy time for Philip."

One of the neighbours said, "Whenever Philip came to our house, we always found it hard to get him to go home in the evenings. He enjoyed the craic and banter. Our boys are about the same age and he liked to knock around with them." I remember that feeling of wanting to stay in the neighbours' houses. It was comfortable and relaxed. There was no pressure on anybody. But of course I couldn't stay. Those were the kind of families I couldn't have.

I enjoyed my time at Mullabeg primary school. I enjoyed playing my football in the yard of the local pub with other boys. When I got a bit older, I went to a youth club. I played pool and handball. I remember doing a bit of wrecking one Halloween with other boys. We pulled up plants out of people's gardens and then hid out in the school until we were caught. The neighbours were raging, but that was the whole point. We were the Halloween spirits creating a bit of chaos. Sometimes I had my dinner in a friend's house. His mother said I had a good appetite but really I just preferred her cooking. My aunt Bernadette used to make a bread pudding with mouldy bread and custard. I hated it. The things I enjoyed were away from my foster home, but most of the time I was at home. Not in the house, but working on the farm. I wasn't encouraged to have friends outside the family. I didn't get pocket money. I had no nice clothes or trainers like the neighbours' children. I never got to see any of the money my foster parents were paid to rear me. Money was always an issue in the house. As soon as they were old enough to earn money, my cousins were expected to contribute to the family budget. There was a teapot in the kitchen for the wages, and there was a lot of pressure on the cousins to keep putting money in there, even though work was hard to find. I didn't know at the time that my foster parents were paid allowances to rear me. I thought I worked for my keep and reared myself. There was nothing left over for extras. I was always aware that I never had two pence to rub together. It was another thing that made me feel different and excluded. By the time I was 11 or 12, I had two Saturday jobs. I worked in the pig market in Cookstown early in the morning, and then I worked on a market stall selling shoes. I used to have a big Ulster fry for my breakfast between the two jobs. My friend, Tom Magill, worked on the stalls too, selling pictures, and I had a good laugh with him. I had to hitch a lift into Cookstown on a Saturday morning for my work and then back again in the evening. Very often I got no lift and had to walk the seven or eight miles each way. Tom Magill was selling a bicycle at the time, but my uncle wouldn't lend me the money to buy it. My wages went into the teapot, and I tried to keep a few pounds back for myself if I got any extra. It wasn't enough to buy the bike, but it was enough to tide me over.

Reading this back to myself it is hard to believe all this happened in the 1980s and 1990s. It could be 100 years ago or more.

In my last year of primary school, I reached a crisis point. Life had been difficult before, and it was only going to get worse. I was 11 years old and I was being confirmed into the Catholic Church. There was a lot of preparation to be done for the ceremony, and it was all managed by the school. One day, the teacher handed me my birth certificate and told me to bring it home. It was in an envelope and I could feel it burning a hole in my pocket. At this stage, five years into my foster placement, I was used to thinking of my uncle and aunt as my parents. Even though I had been told Grace was my mother, it didn't seem to count for me, as she wasn't there to look after me. I opened my birth certificate, which was a duplicate as my original certificate was lost when I was born. In the place where it says "Father's Name", I read the word "Unknown". I was very confused. *"What could this mean? My father must be somebody. Someone must know who he is. He must have a name."* When I got home, I started to ask questions about who my father was. I was fobbed off with answers like "Sure, what does it matter who your father is?" or "You don't need to know." One of my uncles said to me "Forget about it. What you need to be thinking about is trying to get yourself a decent job and work to get yourself a little house around the town." That was not the advice I wanted or needed at the time. I was 11 years old and I was looking to my family for support and for help in finding out who my father was. I didn't get it then and it would be more than 20 years before one of my uncles stepped up to help me. My social workers were told that I was asking questions about my father and they note that the family responded "sensitively". If telling me to forget about my father was the sensitive way to handle it, I would hate to see the insensitive way.

It is hard to explain to people who know where they come from just how much it matters to me to know who my father is. But I will try. On behalf of all the bastards out there, I would like to say we have a right to know our people and our history, on both sides of our family. To all the single mothers who maybe would rather forget who the father of their child is, for the child's sake, be open and honest about who he is. You don't have to force a relationship on the child, but you can at least tell the child who the father is. Even if you were drunk and it was a one-night stand, tell the child. If you don't, if you try to cover it up, I can guarantee it will come back to haunt you and it might even wreck the life of your child. The past will catch up with you. I am the living proof of that. It is not down to you to tell your child to forget about his father. That is the child's decision. It is your job to support your child through it, whatever he decides to do.

People who know who their father is don't understand the gap in your life when you wonder, "Do I look like him? Do I have the same personality? Will I do the same kind of work as him? Who are his brothers and sisters? Do I have grandparents? Do I have half brothers and sisters? Would he be able to help me in life or give me advice?" It is like half of yourself is missing, and I feel it even more deeply now that half my body is "missing". When I was 11, I knew my father and his history were out there somewhere, but I couldn't reach him. I don't think I expected to have a loving relationship with my father; after all I didn't have one with my mother. But just to see a name on the birth certificate would have been some relief to my heart. It would have been something to hold on to when life in my foster home became unbearable to me. I would have liked to think about my real father and wonder where he was. Maybe he never even knew about me. Or maybe he did know about me and didn't care. If only someone had stepped in at that time and helped me to understand my background, my life might have turned out different. What angers me still is that I have a family who could have helped me but they chose not to. They chose to keep me in the dark and to keep the secret of who my father is from me. They might have been ashamed. But one thing is for certain, they were not thinking about me and about what would be best for me.

It was all weighing very heavy on my mind as I prepared for my confirmation. I was the only child in the school who didn't know who his father was. At the service in the chapel, the bishop asked me "Who is your father?" I felt humiliated. Maybe I was meant to say, "God is my Father", but he asked me the question I had been asking myself for weeks, and I answered him truthfully, "I don't know, Father." Twenty odd years later, I am still trying to find out the answer to that simple question: "Who is your father?"

When I left Mullabeg primary school, I was very confused about my identity. I had always felt unloved in my foster home. I had never felt like I was part of the family. Now I knew why. I felt the weight of the family's shame on me. I felt Grace's disgrace on me. Now I knew what he meant when my uncle called me a wee bastard.

I went to a large secondary school in Cookstown. I was like a small fish in a big pool. Hardly anybody knew me there.

It was where I met my best friends Maurice Byrne and Tom Magill. I first saw Maurice with his mother in the uniform shop in Cookstown. Mrs Byrne remembers me as a small boy, smiling over at her and Maurice with mischief in my eyes. My school blazer was too big for me and Maurice's was too small for him, so we swapped. To this day I remind him that he was always fat. I thought it was great when I ended up in the same class as Maurice. The Byrnes didn't know me then. I used to take the bus to and from school. I liked school, although I was no scholar. For me, school was freedom. I could be out of the house all day. I didn't have to look over my shoulder. People took notice of me. It might have been for the wrong reasons at times, but at least I was noticed. I was like a pup off the leash, always joking about and looking for ways to get a laugh. It was easy to melt away into the crowd when I needed to. I am sure I drove the teachers crazy, but there was no real harm in what I was doing. My school reports were mostly not bad. One or two of the teachers definitely had it in for me, but most of them were encouraging enough. Some of the teachers remember me still. I suppose I was easily led as a young schoolboy. I would do or say anything to get a laugh. I suppose I could always be found with the lads who were wrecking and carrying on.

One of our classrooms was a prefab hut and it was stacked on bricks, like a mobile home, to keep it stable. We used to bash the bricks out of place so the building would start to cope when we were messing around inside. We smashed a few windows in that classroom, and then picked out the putty from around the replacement glass while it was still damp. Then we would wind the teacher up until he threw one of us out. The plan was to give the door a good slam on the way out so that all the new glass would fall out of the windows. Yes, I was a pain in the backside, but I wasn't the only one and every school had a bunch of lads like me and my friends.

There were times I never went to school at all, but got the bus in the morning and hung around Cookstown all day playing pool until it was time to go home. At home time, I would sneak out of a hiding place in the school grounds, jump on the bus, and mess around with my friends on the journey back to Mullabeg. Mrs Byrne used to go to the school to pick up her children and she sometimes saw me in the back of the bus making rude gestures at her out of the window. She was glad she was not my teacher, and she suspected that Maurice was no better than me. She was right about that. Back home, I would change into my work clothes and go out on the farm. I kept out of my uncle's way as much as I could. Looking back, I think my uncle Francis must have felt his grip on me slipping. When I went to the secondary school, I had other role models, and new friends who had nothing to do with my family. My uncle wouldn't have had a good word to say about any of my friends in Mullabeg, or their parents, who were his neighbours all their lives. If he wasn't fighting with the neighbours himself, he was blaming me for stirring things up with them. But he didn't know these new people and he had no influence over them, for good or for bad. When I was at the primary school, it was easy for him to rein me in whenever he liked. But at secondary school I felt different and I could express myself better there, even if it did mean getting on the wrong side of the teachers at times. Sometimes my uncle would keep me at home as a punishment. He knew I liked school so he used it as a privilege that could be taken away whenever he liked. The social workers didn't even challenge him on this when he told them.

I was growing into my teenage years with all the stress that brings into anyone's life. My hormones were all over the place. I was still anxious about my real father, although I knew better than to talk about it at home. I was developing my own personality and my own opinions on things. For the first time I was mixing with boys, no better or no worse than me, who were loved by their parents. I would go back to their houses sometimes and sit at the kitchen table listening to the banter between parents and children, the laughter and the jokes. I couldn't believe it. At home we sat in silence while my uncle ranted on about something or other. We couldn't wait to leave the dinner table. At night we would kneel down to say the rosary like a bunch of hypocrites. The atmosphere was so tense, I would rather have worked on the farm than spend an evening watching television at home. The odd time we would watch a football match or something on TV, but there was no pleasure in it. I began to want what my friends had, even though I knew I couldn't have it. I wanted to be in the middle of a loving family more than anything. It is what I have always dreamed of.

It was hard enough for me to find my feet at the big school in Cookstown for the first couple of years. I was small for my age and probably I was immature too. I got picked on by bigger lads. They told me I was born in the dung heap and I wanted to scrap them, but I always lost. Then I had a growth spurt and started to hold my own in fights. After that, I got a lot more respect. I never went looking for trouble at school, but I was often unlucky enough for it to find me. Mostly I just wanted to make people laugh and to hell with the consequences. I never for a minute worried about my education or my future prospects. I had enough worries living from day to day at home. School was just a place to have a laugh.

I rarely did PE at school and my friends couldn't understand it because they knew I loved football. I didn't want to change my clothes at school; I didn't want people looking at me and I didn't want to talk about it. My friend Tom Magill skipped PE a lot too because he was afraid of the bullies in the changing rooms. It was handy enough there were two of us skipping the class. I just pretended I was afraid of the bullies, the same as Tom. Nothing was ever done about it. It was just accepted that the two of us boys were rarely in the starting line for PE. The truth was, I didn't want to draw attention to myself in any way. I had got used to the idea by now that I should never talk about my foster family to outsiders. If the PE teacher ever noticed any bruises or marks on my body, what could I have said? It wasn't worth the risk and it was easier not to take part.

One day, there was a school trip planned and I didn't turn up. The bus waited and waited and eventually I arrived late at the school. I was hoping the bus would have left already and I just walked past it, as if it wasn't there. I had no money for that trip but I was too embarrassed to say it. I thought if I was late then the bus would go without me. I had not expected it to wait for me, and then I had to admit that I didn't have the money to pay for the trip. I stayed behind.

Life at home was getting harder. My uncle did not treat me well between the ages of 12 and 15, when I left my foster home. By the time I reached my teens, I had already been established as slow, retarded, a fantasist and a liar in the eyes of social services because of what my foster parents told them. I never contradicted that opinion because I was too scared. I would have needed a relationship based on trust with social services to even attempt it. The way things were, there was no chance the authorities would believe what I had to say. For years, I said nothing. When I eventually spoke up, it was too late. There was no physical evidence of mistreatment and I was not believed. My uncle spent years making sure that my word was not to be trusted, and he did a very good job of it.

There are many words that describe how I felt in my foster home. First, I felt unloved. Report after report says I was accepted into the Donaghy household and treated the same as the other children, my cousins. That may be, but they didn't love me. They didn't even want me. To be honest, I don't know how much the natural children were loved. But blood is thicker than water, I always say. I brought in money from the fostering payments, I worked in the house and on the farm and I had two Saturday jobs. Apart from that, I had no other use or value. I was also scared witless living there. Maybe I just didn't understand the unwritten rules of the house. Every family has its own way of going and you just learn what it is by being raised there. Like maybe you learn that if you want something you have to get round your mother first, and then she will work on your father. They are just small things, but if you don't understand a family's secret code, you just end up feeling confused and in the wrong place all the time. In my foster home, I never worked it out. All I knew was that whatever I did, it was the wrong thing. Whatever way I behaved, it would land me in trouble. No matter how hard I worked, I would be lucky to get even a word of thanks. I took orders and that was it.

After I was told that Grace was my mother, my foster family had another stick to beat me with. They told me constantly that I was mad, like my mother. Every time my personality asserted itself, and every time I did something that displeased my uncle and aunt, they told me I was mad, like Grace. It was bred into me and it is something I have fought against for most of my life. At the children's home in Belfast, my mother's mental illness was one of the reasons I couldn't be adopted. But at least the nuns accepted it. They never threw Grace's illness in my face. At my foster home, there was no sympathy for Grace. To her family, she was just mad and her son was mad too. If I have achieved anything, I hope I have proved my family wrong about that. But when I was living at my foster home, I think I even started to believe it myself. Sometimes I still do. My family still has the ability to make me feel like I am mad. In a heartbeat, I can send myself back to my childhood and remember it all. It was constant, mental torture and I felt the pressure of it every day. I would say that being put down all the time and told I was mad was the worst kind of suffering I have ever experienced. Sometimes I said to myself, "*It is not Grace who should be in Willow Hill, it is her brother Francis, he is the madman here.*" I remember my few visits to Willow Hill and I remember how scared I was of all those people, shouting and roaring out of them. Was that to be my future? Not if I had anything to do with it.

Teenage kicks

As a teenager, I was deeply hurt and unhappy in all areas of my life. I felt unloved and unwanted by the people who should have cared for me most: my mother, Grace, and my foster parents, uncle Francis and aunt Bernadette. I couldn't blame my mother. What could she do? She had her own troubles in the Willow Hill psychiatric hospital. Nobody knew or much cared about what her life was like in there. But I felt unsupported by her and her brothers and sister. I felt social services were blind to what I was going through, right under their noses. I couldn't hardly speak to the social workers. I said to myself, "*Whatever you say, say nothing*", but I still felt that someone should have recognised how troubled I was, without me having to spell it out, which I was too afraid to do. Social services described me in one of their reports as being incapable of having an emotional reaction. That was true in a way because I kept my emotions locked up inside and I still do. But they were wrecking my head. I did not live in a family that encouraged me to express my emotions. I did my work and I kept out of trouble as much as I could. There was no room for emotion in that routine. Except for fear. I had plenty of that. What I still don't understand is why my behaviour didn't ring any alarm bells. Children who are going through a rough time at home always behave in a strange way. Call it a cry for help, but they always find a way to draw attention to themselves, even if it is negative attention, and they usually don't talk about the real cause of their behaviour, at least not at first. The dogs in the street know that. But it seems the professionals who were responsible for me didn't. I knew I would have to take the matter into my own hands in the end. I had to do something. As time went on, and especially after I found out I had no father, I felt I had to get out of my foster home some way. I hated it there.

From about the age of 14, I would run away any time I couldn't cope at home. Sometimes I ran away because I felt I had been badly treated. Other times, it was just the pressure in the house. I will never know how the roof did not lift off that house with tension at times. There was constant pressure to earn money, but no encouragement. No-one ever said "That was a great job you did, Philip. Why don't you ask the neighbours if they would pay you to do the same for them?" No-one ever gave me any guidance on what I should do to plan for my future. Nothing I did was ever any good. I got the blame if anything went wrong in the house. If sheep died on the mountain, it was my fault. "Sure what could you expect from Philip? He's going to end up like his mother." People have observed that my uncle Francis was the kind of man who took pleasure from watching other people fall and fail. He was not the type of man who would help you to pick yourself up and start again. He would be too busy laughing at you and passing remarks on your failings. If I ever had self-confidence, it was knocked out of me by constant criticism. I was told I would never amount to anything in life. I was told I was slow and retarded. Throughout my teenage years I was told I was mad, like my mother. My relationship with Grace was never close, and it was no wonder. I never heard anyone speak about her in a positive way in my life. I developed a fear of mental illness. When they said I was mad like my mother, I believed I would end up in a locked ward at Willow Hill, stuffed full of tablets to keep me quiet. I had no idea what the future held for me, but I was convinced none of it would be good. It was as if I knew I was heading to a bad place, but I had no way to stop it.

When I ran away from home, my foster parents and social services explained it away by saying it was because of bullying at school and trouble with the neighbours. I would like to say for the record, I did not run away from school, I ran away from home. I did not run away from the neighbours, I ran away from home. Why would they look to the places and people I *did not* run away from for an explanation? Why did nobody look for a problem in the place I *did* run away from? I say to myself now, I should have spoken out and stood up for myself. I should have said something. Why didn't I? I know the answer. It had been bred into me from a very early age not to speak out my opinion and not to talk about family matters to outsiders. That included social workers. Especially social workers. I was shit scared of what would happen to me if I did speak out. One of my cousins, Ronan, the son of another uncle, said to me recently, "Why didn't you come to us, Philip, when it got bad up there?" I told him I was scared witless and I had been warned not to speak with family members about my home life. My cousin had no idea what was going on in the house at the time. He knew there was no love lost between his own father and uncle Francis, but other than that, he knew nothing. He never suspected the rough treatment I got although he often wondered how I stuck it, living with the "big man". Ronan had just started working when I was in my early teens. A few years later and he would have his own business. He says now, "If I had the business going sooner, I could have given work to Philip that time when life up there in Mullabeg was sore on him. That's the time when he would have needed a bit of direction and a bit of leadership. But it didn't happen. I was just starting out and I had nothing to offer him. It wasn't till a few years later that I heard about the rough upbringing he had up there."

One time, I ran away and broke into an abandoned house. I can't remember the exact reason for it. There were so many times when I felt I couldn't cope at home. It might have been the time I was ducked in the rain butt. Or it might have been the time I was lifted from the youth club in front of everybody and shoved into the back of my uncle's car. Something made me run, that much I know. There was no heat or electricity in the house. There were a few bits of old furniture in it. I lay in the house, out of sight, for three days. I would get up early in the morning and steal milk off the doorsteps of my neighbours. I survived by drinking the stolen milk and eating juicy leaves from the lane outside the house. The rest of the time, I hid out in the house and thought about my life. "*Why can't I have a family that loves me?*" I asked myself countless times. "*Why is this happening to me?*" I had no answers that were a comfort to me. I have never had anyone in my life I could take my problems to. There has never been anyone who can give me a different perspective. I only have myself, and I was no good to myself that time. I lay on the bare floor and cried my eyes out. The house was dark and musty and I was scared there on my own, but not as scared as I was at home. On the third day, my head was wrecked with loneliness and confusion. I was also starving hungry. I hid in a neighbour's shed. The Dunn family was always good to me. I used to hang about in their shed with Paddy Dunn, one of the local lads I played football with. Paddy met me in the shed and was going to sneak me out some food from the house. As we were talking, his mother, Ann Dunn, came to the shed door looking for something. I hid from her and tried to disappear into the darkness at the back of the shed, but Ann spotted me. She wasn't angry. Ann was never angry with me. She said to me, "Philip, what have you been at? They're all looking for you." I mumbled something in reply and I asked her if I could stay. She said, "You have to go home. I can't keep you here. I'm sorry, Philip, but I can't do nothing about it. You have to go home." Even today, Ann would be close to tears when she thinks about me that time, living in the abandoned house. She never said a word about the milk I took from her doorstep, even though she had a young family who missed the milk for their breakfast. Ann said recently,

"It broke my heart to send him away, but what could I do? It was the law. He never, never did anything bad, you know. It wasn't in him to be bad. He was full of life and a real good worker too. And, you know, he was very kind, he was a very kind cub. He would do anything for you. If he could help you, he would help you. And if he couldn't, you know, he'd be all disappointed that he couldn't help you. But he was … well, he had to work, and that's all."

Ann Dunn and her family have always been good to me and I am grateful to them because they saw me as Philip and not as a son of Francis Donaghy. Ann and her family never said a word against my uncle. They kept an eye out for me from a distance. I think they had a good enough idea what I was going through, and they supported me through it as best as they could in silence. They were not going to get into a row with my uncle about it. I spent as much time as I could with the Dunn's. They were a decent and caring family.

There was another time I ran away and stayed with my friend Tom Magill and his family in Cookstown. This time, social services had to get involved. I had stolen a couple of pounds out of my cousin's car. I was always in need of money and seeing it lying there was too much of a temptation. I would feel less of a scrounger at the chip shop the next day with my school friends if I had a couple of quid to buy chips. That was my thinking at the time. It was a wrong thing to do but, by God, I paid for it. I remember crying out when I was punished for stealing and my uncle was calling me for all the bastards of the day, and using much worse language besides. My aunt appeared at the door and said, "Keep down the noise". Then she left. I have that memory to this day. I try to imagine what

I would do if I saw what she saw that night. I think I would do more than worry about the noise.

I was to be kept from school the next day as punishment, but I got up early and ran out and caught the bus as usual. After school I went home with Tom. I spent the night there and went back to school the next morning. I came home with Tom again after school and hid out the back of his house in a shed. Later Tom's mother got a phone call from my uncle Francis asking if I was there. She didn't know I was hiding round the back of their house at the time, so she told him in good faith that I was not there. My uncle and aunt came round anyway. My aunt came to the front door of the Magill's house and my uncle went round the back, where he caught me coming out of the shed with Tom. My uncle grabbed me tight by the upper arm and my face went pale with fright. Then my aunt came out the back and they took one arm each and marched me through the Magill's house and out to their car. On the way out my uncle said to Mr Magill, "You're not too old for a good clip yourself." Mr Magill was so shocked he almost laughed in my uncle's face. He remembered that my uncle wouldn't help me to buy Tom's old bicycle. He wondered what kind of a man he was dealing with.

The Magills couldn't believe their eyes as they watched me being frogmarched out the door and into the car. At the time, Mrs Magill was being assessed as a foster parent herself. What she witnessed went against everything she was learning about fostering. She telephoned social services to describe what had happened and to ask for advice. Of course, social services knew all about me and what a liar and a troublemaker I was. The Magills were shocked by my foster parents' attitude to them and to me. My uncle telephoned them again when he got me home and gave them a load of abuse for "harbouring" me, as if I were some sort of a criminal. Mrs Magill telephoned social services again to say that she had received an abusive call from my uncle and she was very worried about me. I had told the Magills I was unhappy at my foster home, but I didn't go into the details. They knew it was hard for me to talk about my home life and they didn't pry. They had seen enough of my foster parents' treatment of me to guess the rest. All they could do was make me feel welcome when they saw me and that was all I needed at the time. I was sorry I got them into trouble with my uncle Francis. He has never had a good word to say about them from that moment. Even today he would say that they are only interested in me because I have money. All I can say to that is, I had nothing when they tried to help me.

Even though the Magills were concerned for me, the attitude of social services was to tell me my behaviour was unacceptable and I needed to improve at home and at school. It was no more than I expected. The social workers knew I had been "chastised" for stealing the money. But they asked no more about it. They reported that I was being bullied at school and it was making me disruptive at home. If the Magills had any idea I was soon going to be shipped off to a children's home, they would have stepped in and asked if they could foster me themselves. But they didn't know. No-one did. I told social services that I wanted to go back to St Joseph's Children's Home. This was coming up on nine years after I had left; there was no way I could go back. I was clutching at straws. Social services promised to look into alternatives for me. To give them credit, they did, and I was in touch constantly to find out what progress they were making.

Later that summer, my uncle Francis told social services I had been beaten up by a neighbour and his son. According to the report my uncle Francis gave, I was set upon up the mountain by the McGurks, father and son. They told me I was not welcome on the mountain as I was not truly a Donaghy, but only a foster child. Then they beat me up. This is a completely made up story. Being blood related to Francis Donaghy was no guarantee you would be welcome up the mountain or anywhere else. I have no memory at all of the incident and I can't imagine any of the Mullabeg neighbours teaming up with their child to beat me up. The whole idea of it is sick. What kind of a sick parent would do that? I asked the neighbours if any of them can remember the incident. Every one of them has said to me, "Philip, we never had any bother with you." One or two have commented that they can only think of one person who would come up with a tale like that, Francis Donaghy. Why would my uncle just make up a story? Could it be I had bruises that needed to be explained away? Was he as anxious to get rid of me as I was to leave? I don't know. One of the neighbours said to me, "Now I would have nothing to do with them up there, but I believe that nobody gets on with that man up there who fostered you Philip." The made up incident on the mountain was the last straw. Social services had to find me somewhere else to live.

My heart was lighter at the thought of moving away from Mullabeg. I even suggested going to a boarding school, but my school grades were not good enough. I just had to get out of that house, because if I had stayed one more day, I don't know what way I would be today. I probably would have been like Grace at the end of it. I probably would have gone mad. It doesn't sound like much of a plan now, but I decided to agree with anything the social workers and my foster parents cooked up between them if it would get me away. They went back to the old school bullying card. I was not bullied at school. I enjoyed my time there and the friends I made are still my friends today. But if claiming to be bullied would get me away from home, then I was happy to agree to it. I told social services that it upset me to be called a bastard and told I was born in the dung heap. I suppose nowadays there would have been some kind of counselling to help me and my foster family get over the issues of bullying together. Thank God, there was none of that back then. I would never have got away. My social workers looked into various work schemes away from Cookstown, but I was too young to qualify for a place on them.

Eventually they settled on Ballee Adolescent Unit in Ballymena, Co. Antrim. I would live there during the week and go to a new school, St Patrick's in Ballymena. I would spend weekends and holidays in Mullabeg. It was a shared care arrangement between my foster family and Ballee. It wasn't exactly what I wanted, but it would do. I was given a place at Ballee for a school year, on the understanding that when I left school at 16, I would return to the Cookstown area and find work there. As well as my social worker at home, I would have a residential social worker from Ballee assigned to me. The social work reports from the time said a stint in Ballee might bring some reality to my thinking and make me appreciate what I had at home. From reading the reports, it sounds like Ballee was to be my punishment for disruptive behaviour at school and at home. All I can say is, it was the happiest day of my life when I went to Ballee for the first time. The only cloud was the fact that I had to go back to Mullabeg at weekends.

The official reason I was in Ballee was because I was being bullied at school and this was making me disruptive at home and in my neighbourhood. The real reason I was in Ballee was because I had to get out of my foster home and it was the only place social services could find for me. I couldn't explain why I had to leave home at the time because I was too afraid. I didn't trust social services. To my mind, they were working for my uncle and aunt and not for me. There was never a bond between me and social services. When they came to the house, I was put out in the yard to get turf or coal or do some other job. As far as they could tell, I was healthy and happy enough. My uncle and aunt told them so. Why would they doubt it? I would never have contradicted anything my foster parents said. It wasn't worth the risk. I worked the system to get myself out of that house. That is one thing that kids in care learn how to do, work the system.

Ballee Adolescent Unit was a children's home for teenagers. At that time, there were about twenty of us living there. Ballee has been described to me as a "last resort" residential home for delinquent children with deeply troubled backgrounds. The next step is gaol. The prison system was full of people who had come through places like Ballee. Some of the other children had problems I couldn't imagine. They had no stability, no way of telling right from wrong, no positive way of communicating with the world. Some of them had been rejected by their natural family and had notched up several foster placement failures before they ended up in Ballee. Some of them had siblings and cousins in Nazareth Lodge, where I had spent my early years. My problems were nothing compared to some of the kids in Ballee. I probably knew that at the time, but the difference was that their problems were known to a certain extent and mine were hidden. It was probably the worst mistake uncle Francis made in his life, sending me to Ballee. He sent me to live with people whose job it was to listen to me. He was not there to comment on my behaviour or tell people I was mad. He could not wrap my new social workers around his finger all the time.

To the social workers at Ballee, I seemed like a decent, well brought up country lad with a supportive foster family. A lot of the Ballee staff couldn't understand why I was there at all. My "supportive" foster family did not tell anyone I was at Ballee, including my mother, and I was warned to keep it to myself too. I knew how to keep up appearances. My uncles were told that I was away at school. Some of them thought I was at Omagh Tech. Others thought I was at Ballymena Tech. Nobody outside my foster family knew the truth. At the time, I couldn't have cared if Ballee was Maghaberry prison. It wasn't Mullabeg and I felt free. That first night, lying in a strange bed in a strange room, on my own, about 30 miles from Cookstown, it felt deadly. It is still up there as one of the highlights of my life and one of my greatest achievements. People who know Ballee will be surprised to hear that a unit for messed up teenagers was far better than my home. But the way I looked on it was, I had succeeded in getting away. I had taken a positive step to change my situation. I didn't really know what I was getting myself into at Ballee, but I knew very well what I had got myself out of. Like I say, it was a deadly feeling.

The unit itself was a white u-shaped building at the top of a hill. It had been built in the 1960s, but the money ran out and it wasn't opened as a children's home until the '70s. By that time it was already outdated. It was kind of a depressing place really; more like a hospital than a home. There were long corridors with doors off and it was hard for the staff to keep tabs on residents. We could always get away fast when we needed to. My friend Maurice Byrne came to visit me once. He thought Ballee was very grubby and depressing. He said I was like a lost soul in the place and he didn't get a good impression of my friends. They were a much tougher crowd than the lads around Cookstown. But I had good friends among the Ballee crowd. We stuck together because not too many people outside the unit wanted to know us.

The staff at Ballee were fantastic. I realise now they were overworked and undervalued big time. I couldn't believe they were all there to support us and listen to us. I could have a good laugh with most of them. We traded insults and cigarettes and it was mostly good hearted and a bit of craic. My residential social worker was Bill McConnell, and over time I got close to him. Bill was young and steady. He had a wise look about him. You knew he would listen to you, but he also wouldn't take any crap from you either. He got my respect for that. He was a decent man, Bill, who did his best to help me. I think he would have done more for me if he had been allowed to. But at the end of the day, he had a job to do and more than one troubled youngster to work with. He had his bosses to report to and he also had his own family to look after.

I made friends and enemies at Ballee. There was always plenty of fighting and tensions could run high. But my strongest memory is that we all stood up for each other. Everyone there had some kind of trouble in their background. Some of the kids had been sexually abused by family members. That never happened to me, and I was grateful for it when I saw what that kind of abuse can do to a person. Other kids were the children of alcoholics and drug addicts. All of us had been abandoned or neglected in one way or another. You could understand why people might suddenly lose the head, so you just dealt with it. You expected people to do the same for you when it was your time to lose it. We all did, plenty of times.

Although the kids in Ballee supported each other, we didn't talk too much about our backgrounds. I can't really explain why that was. In my case I thought if I kept my problems hidden, they would eventually go away. I was sure that being away from my uncle was all I needed for life to be sweet. Each person spoke with their residential social worker, and problems were dealt with on a one-to-one basis. I think we were encouraged to keep these sessions confidential. The last thing anyone wanted was for their problems to be gossiped about, or thrown in their faces during one of the many rows we had. I had never had any encouragement to talk about my problems and my feelings openly before. It would be a long time before I could trust people enough to share what was on my mind. I also thought by leaving Mullabeg I was leaving my problems behind too. I didn't know at the time that you take your problems with you like a big bag of dirty laundry.

We had a lot of freedom at Ballee, far more than teenagers living at home with their parents. We had more pocket money too. I couldn't believe how flush I felt, for the first time in my life. Part of the money that had been paid to my foster parents was now coming to me. It was fantastic; I didn't even have to work for it. The Ballee staff acted as our bank and there were plenty of rows with them about money. We had to say what we wanted money for and we had to sign for it and produce receipts and the like. Alcohol was strictly forbidden, but we usually had enough cash between us on a Friday night to load up with cider and beer from the local off licence and hide it around the unit. We were in and out of each other's rooms, drinking and carrying on, taking care not to be seen by any of the staff, until we were so shit-faced, we didn't care. I must have snogged every girl at Ballee in my time. There was a big fuss when I boasted to my friends that I had lost my virginity. Up until that point, I had no education on the facts of life, just what I picked up from living on a farm and what the boys in school said. I refused to tell the staff, one way or the other, if my boasting was true. The only punishment if you got caught breaking the rules at Ballee was a lecture and the withdrawal of privileges, like maybe your pocket money would be docked. Compared to what we had all been through in the past, that wasn't punishment, it was a walk in the park. In any case, I wasn't planning on getting into any serious trouble. My plan was to be happy, to finish my education in Ballymena, move back to Cookstown to find work, and settle down to an independent life. I didn't plan to leave Ballee with a criminal record.

So, what happened? Slowly but steadily my behaviour started to deteriorate. Maybe I was mixing with the wrong crowd, although at the time I just thought I was having a laugh with my new friends. The monthly reports in my file get longer and longer as the details of "Untoward Incidents" and "Significant Interviews" are discussed. A favourite trick of mine was to set off the fire alarms when I got back to the unit after school. I used to break the cover glass and shout, "I'm home!" at the top of my voice as the bells went off around the building. I was very annoying in that way, but what harm was in it? The thing was, Ballee was not home. It was an institution. When you got back from school, there wasn't anybody waiting for you. You walked into that institution and the staff was off in the offices working. You might as well not have been there. Setting off the alarms was a way of breaking into the routine, of letting people know you were alive. "There goes the alarm," the staff used to say, "Philip's back."

I sometimes get angry when I read in my files about the stupid things I have done in the past, like setting off the alarms, drinking, swearing at people, or staying out later than I was supposed to. I'm not angry because I did those things, they are the normal things teenagers get up to, no matter what their background is. Most people go through a phase where their parents think "*What is going to become of him?*" and most settle down sooner or later. What angers me is that there is a written report on every stupid thing I did growing up. I have asked the parents of my friends, "Did you write it down every time your sons or daughters got drunk or stayed out late?" They laugh, "Of course we didn't. Why would we write it down?" I am not criticising the staff at Ballee. They were only doing their job, and most of the time they did a brilliant job. But what kind of a job has you writing reports on everything? October 1990: "Philip now does his washing twice a week". June 1991: "Philip's reports from work are very promising although he needs constant calling to get up in the mornings". April 1991: "[Philip] became involved in an incident … whereby a pair of underpants were set on fire and thrown from a bedroom window". Teenagers are scruffy, lazy and they get a good laugh out of setting pants on fire. So, what else is new?

I am not saying for one minute that I was an easy teenager to manage. None of us in Ballee was there for fun (although there is no doubt about it, we had good craic in the place). But the stupid incidents are given as much weight as the serious ones. Everything is buried in the reports and anybody reading them would think I was a bit of a madman. But the thing is, they might miss the things that were really bothering me. I was always on the lookout for a bit of craic, I was always joking about and acting the goat. That is the way I am. At Ballee I could be myself and express my personality. People who remember me from my foster home say I was very nervous and withdrawn and I wouldn't say boo to a goose. That pressure lifted the minute I walked into Ballee. It took several months for me to realise I didn't have to watch myself all the time. I could just be myself. Yes, I was noisy and crude. Yes, I got drunk and could be abusive. But I was also good company and thoughtful. The reports are not all bad. They record the times I apologised for bad behaviour, or volunteered to clear up any mess I made in the unit, or the efforts I made to improve my behaviour. They record the times I stuck up for other residents who were going through a hard time. I have always hated to see young people in trouble. I always try to take their side. I can't say what the reports of the other Ballee residents are like, but I know for a fact my behaviour was in no way worse than anyone else's. I also knew when I had overstepped the mark and I made the effort to make things right. I was generous with my money, my possessions and my friendship. Ballee was the first step towards an independent life for me. I made my mistakes, plenty of them, but I learned how to look after myself as well. I learned how to care for other people too and to help a friend in trouble.

When I look back now, I can see some aspects of my behaviour were crying out for understanding. I am not proud of some of the things I did. But setting fire to a pair of underpants is not one of them. I still get a laugh when I think of that one. I remember the social workers spending ages with me talking about it.

"Philip, do you realise," they said "How potentially serious that was?"

"Yes. I have one less pair of underpants." I said, trying not to laugh.

"No, Philip. You could have set the whole building on fire."

"But we threw them out the window." I really couldn't see the problem. I let it drop because there was no way I would be able to convince the social workers to see the humour in it. It was their job to put me on the right track, not to be distracted by my idea of a joke.

The people who lived near Ballee thought of us as criminals in the making. I once left a jacket into the dry cleaners and I forgot to pick it up. A letter from the dry cleaner to Ballee describes me as an "inmate". There could be half a dozen youngsters hanging around a street corner, and if one of them was known to be from Ballee, the police would be called. People's prejudices can wear you down. I had more than one run in with the police over behaviour most kids living at home would just have got a bollocking for. At Ballee we had no parent to bollock us and the ways we were punished were dictated by the law. Sometimes there was no alternative but to call the police, not because the things we did were so bad, but because there was no other legal way to punish us. I suppose what was missing was consistent leadership and role models. At the end of the day, the workers at Ballee went home to their families. They became parents to their children rather than professionals with their clients. We were left with the next shift of workers. While the staff were constantly rotated on shifts, it became easy to bend and break the rules. There was no-one, like a parent, who knew you deep down and who could reel you in when you started to get out of control. Some of the social workers would have been genuinely afraid of us at times. What could they do in that situation but call in reinforcements?

Within a few months of arriving at Ballee, I realised I had brought my problems with me. They were not going to go away just because I was no longer living full time in Mullabeg. My background and the people and events that shaped me growing up were still as much a part of me in Ballee as they had been in Mullabeg. The sense of relief and freedom I felt when I first arrived at Ballee did not reach deep enough to make my problems go away. All that had really changed was my foster family had less influence on me, day to day. I was still scared witless when any of my behaviour was reported back to my uncle Francis. I often dreamed of him, and once, when I was drunk, I thought the head of the Ballee Unit, Liam Toland, was my uncle Francis, come to take me back to Mullabeg. I struggled with Liam, "No!" I told him, "I'm not going back. I'm staying here." Liam could make no sense of what I was saying. He had always got on well with my uncle and he put my strange behaviour down to drink. He was a bit worried though, and he started to wonder if there was something in my past that I was keeping hidden.

I was brooding again about my family and my background. Even though I couldn't wait to get away from Mullabeg, I felt isolated. Nobody in Cookstown knew where I was at. Nobody had been told. I was always warned not to speak about family business to outsiders. My foster family kept a very tight grip on their secrets. They marked out their private lives the way they marked out the boundaries of their land, so that every last inch was fenced in. The way I saw it, my family was ashamed of me. Some might say they were ashamed of their failure as foster parents. But I don't remember my uncle ever admitting to failings himself. I have always claimed I was unloved and unwanted by my foster parents. The fact that I was hidden away in Ballee and nobody was told proved it. The fact that the shared care arrangement slowly but surely broke down in the course of my year at Ballee also proved it. I didn't want to spend any more time at Mullabeg than I had to, and my foster people didn't want me there either. Probably the payments they received while I was in their care full time were stopped. What was their incentive to see me once the money dried up? It was not love that is for sure.

One of the things I discussed with my new residential social worker, Bill McConnell, was my need to find out who my father was. At Ballee we were encouraged to have a "Life Book" project. It was a way to tell the stories of our lives and backgrounds, and to move on from the bad stuff that had happened to us. Bill did his best for me, but at the end of the day, I think he would have preferred for me to come to terms with the fact that I would probably never know the identity of my father. Even if I did find out who he was, what were the chances that he would accept me as his son? I would say Bill imagined what it would be like to answer the door to a stranger claiming to be his son. It would turn his life upside down, and it would be a difficult experience for everybody. I had often imagined that scenario too. But it only told part of the story. It didn't tell the story of the son who was eaten up inside because he didn't know who he was. It didn't tell the story of the son who was desperate to know the truth but couldn't find it. It didn't tell the story of the son who believed there were secrets about him that nobody was willing to share with him.

Bill worked with me as I tried to connect with my past. He made sure I had telephone contact with Grace, my mother, when I needed it. He contacted Sr. Paula about a visit to St Joseph's. I had an idea maybe my father was from the Belfast area, and that was why I was sent to a children's home there. By this time, Sr. Paula was living in Sligo in the Republic of Ireland. She didn't know that I was back in a children's home. My uncle Francis and aunt Bernadette visited her once on their way home from a break in Knock, Co. Mayo. Knock is a place of pilgrimage. It made me sick to think of those two hypocrites on a pilgrimage. I always remember a row of us Donaghys sitting at the top of the chapel on a Sunday, like a row of wee saints. We must be hypocrites too. We were there because we had to go, not because we wanted to and not because we had any choice in the matter. Sr. Paula asked my uncle and aunt for news of me and she was told I was fine. They didn't tell her that the fostering placement had broken down and I was living at Ballee Adolescent Unit. It was only when Bill McConnell contacted her out of the blue that she found out. Sr. Paula was shocked and hurt to learn where I was living. She had always liked my family and was disappointed that things had got so bad for us. She believed she might have helped if she had known. She had no idea the situation had gone beyond help.

I was grateful for Bill McConnell's support, but it was not bringing me close enough to the truth. There was another problem too. When I had a lock of drink in me, all the feelings I had spent years repressing came out in unexpected ways that always got me into trouble. I could be very ignorant and abusive to staff at Ballee. I could pick fights with my friends. Often I would be crying my eyes out and hitting my fists or my head off the nearest wall. Most of the time, the staff at Ballee would just do what they could to calm me down and sober me up. They would put me to bed and keep a watch over me through the night. Sometimes they had to take me to casualty at the local hospital where I would be monitored for overdoses, or the effects of sniffing glue and gas. Although the staff knew there was something behind my behaviour, they had to get me sobered up first. By the time I was sober, my feelings were all buttoned up again, and I wasn't able to talk about what was really bothering me.

Having been reared up and told, "You're mad, just like your mother", I had a fear of madness and mental illness. As soon as the social workers mentioned to me that I might like to talk to a counsellor or psychiatrist, I bottled it. No way. That was the first step. The next was I would be stuffed full of tablets. Then I would be just like my mother with a thick layer of cotton wool between me and the world. I never saw counselling as a way of finding new ways to look at old problems. I just saw it as a way of medicating problems and I wasn't going to fall into that trap. I have never been able to break the link that exists in my mind between counselling and madness.

I think I ended up confusing the social workers. There were reports of me getting into a tumble dryer, of pushing a pram around the outside of Ballee and claiming to be my own mother, of thinking every man who came near me was my uncle Francis. When I was sober and focused on school or work experience, I was a normal and reasonable person. I was thinking about what I was going to do in the future. I was interested in a caring profession, nursing or care assistant, and I got involved in voluntary work with Tower House, a day care facility for people with mental and physical disabilities. I was acting like two different people. No wonder the social workers thought I needed to see a psychiatrist. In the end I did go, but the psychiatrist just told me things that I already knew: that I was not mad but I had problems dealing with issues in my past; I had a lack of direction regarding my future; that I was scared about facing the future. It was not exactly rocket science, was it?

Within just a few months of arriving, Bill McConnell told me that he didn't think Ballee was the right place for me. He didn't yet know about the problems I had at home because for almost a year I never discussed them. But he knew about the problems some of the other kids had, and he believed mine were manageable with the support of my family. In Bill's eyes, I had the single biggest thing that he could not provide and that was a family. The thing about my family was that they gave the impression of being very caring. I knew different. Bill thought the longer I stayed at Ballee, the more likely I would be to fall in with a tough crowd. I could see his point. I was easily influenced as a young man, for good as well as for bad. I was lonely and isolated at the weekends when I stopped going back to Mullabeg. Ballymena was a big town compared to Cookstown and there was a lot of sectarian strife at the time. Bill probably thought it wouldn't be long before I got myself into some real trouble. I came close to it a few times.

At the root of all my problems was my need to know who my father was. Even though I didn't intend to, I upset my mother greatly by questioning her about my father. The Willow Hill authorities contacted me at Ballee to tell me to back off. I regretted distressing Grace in some ways, but I couldn't understand why she wouldn't tell me the truth. She told me something about my father one day, and then contradicted herself the next. She claimed her brother Francis and the nurses at Willow Hill told her what to say. But anyone who has met Grace would agree she is nobody's fool. I believed she could clear the whole matter up for me and I couldn't understand why she chose not to. Maybe I reminded her of my father in some way that she didn't want to deal with. Maybe she was afraid of the consequences of telling me the truth. Willow Hill might have looked like the worst kind of psychiatric institution to the outsider; it was isolated and creepy looking, but to Grace it was home at that time. I never thought Grace belonged there. I never thought it was the right place for her. But at the time when I was troubling Grace with my questions, Willow Hill had been her home for about 30 years. It was not in her interest to rock the boat or get on the wrong side of the people who had cared for her for so long. She didn't see, as I did, that the hospital had completely failed to care for her at the time she became pregnant with me.

I have to hand it to Bill McConnell, he did what he could for me. Together we approached the Willow Hill authorities for information. My question was a simple one. Since the hospital was responsible for my mother's care full-time, they must have known the details of her pregnancy. As I was the result of that pregnancy, couldn't they share the information with me? It was not easy for Bill to work with me on something so personal, and it was not easy for me to learn my mother had several boyfriends around about the time she became pregnant. The hospital was very vague about the whole case. They said there had been some kind of investigation at the time, but it did not reach any firm conclusion. Apart from that, the hospital told me nothing. They said it was down to Grace to share the information with me. Fine, I decided, if the hospital would not help me, I would get at the truth my own way. Bill McConnell advised me to be careful and I listened to him, to a certain extent, but I was not going to stand by and let Willow Hill treat me like a nobody. I abandoned my "Life Book" project and decided to do my own investigation into my background.

Life at Ballee got harder for me. I was drinking a lot and drink didn't suit me, it never has. I was sniffing gas and glue and taking any kind of drug that came my way. The staff at Ballee knew very little about this. There were strict rules about drink and drugs and I broke all of them. I got into fights at Ballee and in the town of Ballymena. I was increasingly angry and abusive. My work experience was not going as well as I wanted. I was often at a loose end at weekends when I had nowhere to go. Bill McConnell hoped that I could be persuaded to finish my youth training back in Cookstown. I thought different, and in any case, my foster parents were not that keen on having me back. They did not come out and say it until much later, but they put plenty of obstacles in the way to prevent me from returning to Mullabeg. My foster parents complained that I was less willing to help around the farm and to do what I was told. Damn right. I wasn't their skivvy any more. But maybe Bill was right. I was beginning to assert myself and my opinions much more in Ballee than I ever had in my life before. I felt my cheap labour was being taken advantage of at the care homes where I worked, and I was not slow to complain about it. I ended up leaving the caring professions for my youth training and going to work for a farmer. I enjoyed the work, and I got on well with the people, but I had no wish to be a farmer. In any case, the work was seasonal and Bill spent a lot of time looking for alternative projects for me. At night lying in my bed I got no rest from the thoughts spinning around in my head. I thought about my real parents and my foster parents. I thought about what I wanted to do with my life and I could not come up with anything that motivated or inspired me. I was adrift and I hardly even knew it.

Almost a year after I moved to Ballee, when I was due to go back to Cookstown, I made formal allegations that I had been physically mistreated by my uncle Francis during the time that he fostered me. In reality, the shared care arrangements between my foster parents and Ballee had just about broken down anyway, and I couldn't see a way back there. But it took that amount of time for me to feel strong enough in myself to tell the truth about why I was at Ballee and why I couldn't go back to Mullabeg. I told a couple of close friends in Ballee and then I told the social workers everything that had happened in Mullabeg to make me miserable. Then I had to tell the police. I understood that by making a statement to the police, I would be closing the door on any future good relationship with my foster family. I had mixed feelings about that. I worried about retaliation and I knew that I was really sticking my neck out by telling the truth about my life before coming to Ballee. I also knew that my uncle had made me out to be a liar all my life. I had to wonder if I would be believed.

When a child in care makes allegations of abuse, a whole process kicks in while the investigation takes place. This was the procedure I had to face. I was advised not to make any contact with my family during the investigation and I was guaranteed a place to stay at Ballee in the meantime. I was taken to Mullabeg by the police and I pointed out the places where I had been punished. That was a very tense visit as my aunt and some of my cousins were in the house at the time. They were shocked at what I had done and I was nervous about facing them. But then I thought to myself, they could have helped me. For whatever reason, they chose not to. I didn't blame my cousins, but at the same time, I think if I had been in their position, I would have tried to stop the abuse.

In my personal opinion, the investigation of my foster family was not done right. I had already been established as a liar in the eyes of social services. Family members who knew what was going on in their own home were not interviewed by the police. I quickly learned that blood is thicker than water. When it came to the bit, the family closed ranks and it made me look like the lying bastard they always said I was. The physical injuries I suffered were long healed by the time I made my statement to the police. It was no surprise that the case was dropped due to lack of evidence. But that was not the end of it.

I was left with a very sour taste in my mouth. On the one hand I felt there was no justice for me; I was just another abused bastard stuck in a children's home. Even though the Ballee social workers had supported me during the investigation, I felt that the case being dropped made me look like a liar in their eyes too. But I also felt relieved in a way. If the case had gone to court, I didn't know if I would have been strong enough to cope with the pressure. I didn't know if I could have faced my uncle in court. That didn't make me a liar; it made me scared. After the case was dropped, my uncle took every opportunity to quiz me about the allegations. He asked me which of the social workers had put me up to making them. He asked me to apologise to him. He asked me to withdraw the allegations in writing. Uncle Francis constantly brought the subject up in conversation with other family members present. I felt like a trapped animal. He wore me down. I made a personal, written apology to uncle Francis for bringing allegations against him that were untrue. I did that because I was afraid. Even that was not enough for him. He asked me to tell the police and social services that I had withdrawn my allegations. But I didn't give into that pressure. I stand by every word. If I had my time again, I would make sure the investigation was done properly.

I leave it to the readers of this book to decide for themselves if Philip Donaghy is a liar. There is a time and a place for everything and while there is no love lost between me and my uncle, this book is not about me trying to get back at him for events in the past. That's not the point I'm making. The point is that I have worked hard to overcome the problems I faced growing up to achieve a life I can be proud of. I never had a full grasp of all the information that would help me to make the right decisions in life. I never had the proper guidance. I never had full trust in the people around me. I never had love. I feel as if I had to make my way through life with my two hands tied behind my back. I did the best I could in bad circumstances. Nobody can change the past and I got a raw deal from day one of my life. I have struggled and fought and I have been nearly killed in a car accident. But I am still here. I am still Philip.

I was more lonely and isolated than ever after the abuse case was dropped. With drink or drugs in me, I started to mutilate myself. I talked a lot about suicide. I did some stupid things. One night I poured lighter fuel on my arm and set it alight, then I poured oven cleaner on the burn. I still have the scars. Why did I do that? I did it because I felt worthless. On other occasions I took overdoses of paracetemol. I must have an iron stomach, because they never seemed to do me any harm. I sniffed gas and glue. I would sometimes cry inconsolably and tell my friends that I would be better off dead. With the things I did, I probably came close enough to death, but I never really wanted to take my own life. I suppose it was a cry for help. A lot of us at Ballee would have harmed ourselves. We needed some way to draw attention to our hopelessness. No-one actually succeeded in killing themselves while I was at Ballee, but the threat of suicide hung over the place like a cloud. Sometimes it did seem like the only way out of sadness and misery. It was hard for us to see what kind of a future we would have when our young lives were so warped with bad experiences and memories. What chance did we have to make a good future for ourselves?

About five or six months before my 18th birthday, things started to go very wrong for me. Much as I hated being in care, I was scared about what the future would bring when I turned 18. I would be on my own in the world. There was some excitement about that, but also a lot of fear. I would be going back to the Cookstown area to find work and somewhere to live. I was terrified uncle Francis would retaliate in some way for the allegations I made against him. I had visions of myself being bundled into the back of a car by strangers. I had no qualifications and very few skills. I didn't know what kind of work I wanted to do. Jobs were few and far between at that time. Yet again, I had no-one to turn to with my fears for the future. There was no-one there to reassure me and tell me everything would be okay. I think even Bill McConnell was starting to get sick of me. He did a lot of work to find me training placements and I couldn't settle to any of them. I needed more than work experience. I needed reassurance, security and love. Those things didn't come from a youth training programme. They came from a loving family.

At one of my last care reviews, social services advised me they were not going to do any more to help me find out who my father was. When the hospital had refused to help me, I had done my own investigations and was getting very close to opening a whole can of worms. I felt social services were abandoning me just at the point when I could have benefitted from their support. Away from Mullabeg, and with Bill McConnell's help, I had tried to make a better relationship with my mother, Grace. I visited her regularly in Omagh and I got to know many of the hospital staff.

Grace finally told me about my father. She told me that he had worked as a nurse at the Willow Hill psychiatric hospital. She told me that she never saw him after I was born, and that he had died about three years later. He was a married man when my mother knew him, and a Protestant. She told me that she had been in a relationship with him and that she loved him. I was shocked and disappointed at the same time to learn in one breath that I did have a father after all, but that he was long dead. I also wanted to know what the hospital thought about a nurse having a relationship with a patient. And what about the families? What did they make of it? I didn't believe that Grace's family would have stood by and done nothing about it. It was a hell of a lot of information for me to take in.

But now it was all getting too messy for social services. There was too much dirt and they weren't going get involved in it any further. The hospital wouldn't confirm my mother's story and Grace didn't want to talk about it in the kind of detail I wanted. I just cracked up when I was told I was getting no more help. Bill McConnell was telling me to be very cautious. Social services advised me to get a solicitor. But what legal advice is available to a 17 year old bastard in a children's home? Let me tell you, not much. Today I have the finances to employ a legal team to help me. But back then, a useless Ballymena solicitor did nothing for me. I told the review panel they would regret their decision to stop helping me. I said to the senior social worker, "I'll show you who is boss here. I want justice done on this to find out who I am." The review was terminated because of my bad attitude. I was raging. On top of my feelings of insecurity about my future, I felt kicked in the teeth about my past. Social services took me a good bit of the way on my search for my identity and then they dropped me like a stone. It was more than I could cope with.

I got myself a criminal record in early 1993, a month or so after my disastrous care review. After a stupid row about pocket money or something, I wrecked Ballee Adolescent Unit. It was not the first time I had done a bit of wrecking, but it was the worst. Months of frustration and anxiety finally got to me and I just lost my head and smashed everything I could lay my hands on. The social workers who were on duty just stood back and watched me.

"Why don't you do something?" I shouted at them as I overturned furniture and smashed up light fittings. "Come on," I said, "Take me on." Nobody moved and it gave me a power rush. "If you don't give me the money I am asking for, I'll make sure I do plenty more damage. You'll pay for it." I took a brush handle to the ceiling tiles and walked through the unit smashing everything up as I went. The social workers phoned for assistance and were told to get the police. The police came and I went with them quietly. Bill McConnell couldn't believe the damage I had done when he arrived at the Unit for work the following morning. He didn't see the frustration building in me to that extent. "Philip," he said, "Why didn't you tell me that you were feeling so bad?" If he had seen it coming, he said, he would have done something about it. I had pulled down ceiling tiles and light fitments. I had smashed safety glass and upended furniture. I had broken chairs and dishes. I bulldozed my way through the unit in a frenzy of destruction and anger. Some of the girls were crying as they watched me. Most of the residents just got out of my way. I was arrested and held in police custody for several nights before being charged with criminal damage. I didn't resist arrest. I had no argument with the police. I think I realised I had burned my boats as far as Ballee was concerned. I was sent to Mullabeg, of all places, to wait for my court case. Ballee wouldn't have me back after what I had done. I was too young for gaol and the police couldn't hold me in the cells any longer. There was literally nowhere else for me to go except Mullabeg. The Donaghys weren't happy about it and neither was I. I was expelled from Ballee just a few months before I would have been discharged anyway. Looked at in that light, my behaviour was strange, immature even. But I had no context; I couldn't see the future, only the past. And while it was still unresolved and kept under the surface all the time, I had to get it out of my system. I had to let that frustration go. The only way I could do it and draw attention to myself, was to wreck the unit. Am I proud of what I did? Not now, I'm not. Now I see it as the stupid action of a very frustrated young chap. But then, yes, I was proud, I felt I was saying "I'll show you what happens if you try to sweep me and my life and my problems under the carpet".

I had my day in court. There were reports done on me and I was convicted of criminal damage. I was fined and placed on 18 months' probation. Although Bill McConnell offered me an aftercare service, I was finished with Ballee. Three months later, on my 18th birthday, I was shot of the lot of them and their reports and reviews and all the paperwork. They were left with a nice closed case and I was left unprepared for life as an adult.

Free at last

When I left care, I was an angry 18-year-old who wasn't ready for life as an adult. I wasn't mature enough to cope. I had very few skills and even fewer prospects. I had no home and I had cut most of my ties with my family and my social workers. I had a criminal record. I was unhappy and scared about my future. I had no plan, no next steps to follow. On top of all that, I still had the baggage of my background and my past to carry around with me. I felt let down by every adult in my life. I couldn't wait to leave them all behind, but at the same time, I had no idea how to face the future without them. I desperately needed someone to say to me, "Philip, I know you feel angry and let down. You might need a bit of time to cool off. But listen, you will find your feet. Don't let your anger wreck your life." There was nobody to give me that advice; no-one I would listen to and no-one I could put my full trust in. I was a disaster waiting to happen.

After I left Ballee, all I wanted was my freedom. Social services said there was an aftercare package available to me if I wanted it, but I rejected it. I was fed up going round in the same circles with the social workers. It was like a dance that was getting me nowhere at the end of the day. I have thought about aftercare services over the years. I remembered some of my Ballee friends and the problems they had. I said to myself, "*Those problems don't just go away when you hit 18. What if you are still struggling with the same problems at 40 years of age?*

What aftercare service is available for you then? You might be in gaol by then, and who is going to give a damn about what your childhood was like?" Those children in Ballee were not loved. That was all that was wrong with them. They were not loved as small kids, and they were not loved as teenagers. At 18, they were sent out into the world, and there was very little for them. It should come as no surprise to anybody that so many children in the care system end up in prison. And for the ones who managed to make a good life for themselves, they deserve a clap on the back. The ones who successfully reared a family of their own are like heroes to me. There are not too many of them. I haven't kept in touch regularly with my friends from Ballee, but occasionally I have met up with one or two of them. Of all the people I knew there, I would say that only one of them has what I would call a normal life: happily married with children and regular work. That is one of us out of the 20 who lived at Ballee when I was there. I would guess that one success story out of 20 is probably more than most children's homes achieve.

It was a terrible strain on me and on my foster family when I had to move back to Mullabeg to wait for my court appearance. It was like our worst nightmare. I felt like I was back where I started, only worse. I had finally got myself into real trouble and there was no possibility of a reconciliation with my family. They showed their true colours. Their worst predictions about me had come true. They couldn't wait to get rid of me for good, and I left them for the last time just after my court appearance and conviction. I lived in temporary accommodation for the first few months. I stayed in Shorts' bed and breakfast in Cookstown, which was good. Then I was offered a place in a hostel. I stayed one night. Social services were really pissed off with me that I didn't stick it for longer. All I could say to social services was that a hostel was not fit for an 18 year old to stay in. I might have been an adult on paper, and I might have been a criminal on paper, but putting me to live with aging alcoholics, long-term homeless men, drug addicts, ex-prisoners and paedophiles was hardly the best introduction to life after care. After the hostel, I went to live at Murphy's bed and breakfast. Somehow I have always managed to hook up with decent people in my life. Having had such a poor upbringing in a house where there was no respect for anybody, I am amazed that I have been able to bring out the good in people. The Shorts and the Murphys were both very good to me. They didn't have to show me any special attention. They got paid by social services regardless of how they treated me. But both of those families went over and above what they were expected to do.

Finally, with the help of social services and my probation officer, I found a flat in Greenvale Drive in Cookstown, which I made as comfortable as I could on a very limited budget. At Ballee, I had learned about cooking, cleaning, and budgeting. By the time I left, I was living in a sort of flat within the unit where we had to do our own shopping and cooking and all of that. But we never ran out of gas or electricity at Ballee. In the flat, when there was no money to replace the gas canister, that was it. No amount of skills could cook a decent meal without gas. At Ballee, I had plenty of pocket money and I could send out for a Chinese if I couldn't be bothered to cook. In Cookstown, I was on the dole. There was no money for Chinese takeaways. I used to boil an egg for my tea in the kettle. I would take the egg out and if the shell dried quickly, then I knew it was cooked.

But despite the hardships, and the lack of money, I loved that flat in Greenvale. If I could choose a time in my life before my accident to go back to, I would go back to Greenvale. I was at rock bottom in many ways, but the only place to go was up. I had my health, I was walking. Of course, I didn't put much thought into those things at the time. I took them for granted like everybody else. But I was beginning to realise that life had possibilities for me, even though my prospects were not great. Living in Greenvale gave me a base. It was a great party flat too and I remember nights on the beer with my friends watching football on TV and then heading out to the bars in Cookstown. I had hardly a penny to my name, but my friends subbed me when they could. Once I had got over the partying phase and got settled in work, I would have come good in Greenvale, I was sure of it. But by the time I started to get settled, I had other things on my mind.

At about this time, my cousin Cathal came back from working in England. Cathal was getting married and he asked me to be his best man. Cathal and his fiancée, Kathleen, were always a very decent couple and very good to me. They used to visit me at Ballee when they came home on holidays and they took me out for the day. They even arranged for me to work in London one summer, but the social workers weren't keen on the idea and in the end, I didn't go. There were strong objections in Mullabeg to me being best man at Cathal's wedding. I was not considered a member of the family. Cathal came to live with me in Greenvale for a few weeks before the wedding. We had some good times together, and some hard times too. There were lots of late nights and parties. I don't know how my neighbours put up with it. Cathal was very stressed when he came to stay with me. There was a lot of preparation to do for the wedding and a good dose of wedding nerves too I think. Plus, things were not going well for Cathal in the family. We had a few rows ourselves about stupid things, like football or what to watch on TV. In the end, Cathal buckled under the pressure from home and asked his brother Michael to be his best man instead of me. I was disappointed but I understood the pressure Cathal was under to choose his brother over me. I knew what he was going through having gone through it myself plenty of times in the past. Weddings are supposed to be happy occasions in a family and Cathal's was turning into one big fight. In any case, the best man business was a private matter between ourselves and I had no hard feelings about it.

But at the wedding reception, when the cards were read out, my cousin Michael passed the microphone to me. In front of the room full of guests and family he said, "I'll pass you over now to the man who can't read." He expected a big laugh. He didn't get one. It was an ignorant and untrue remark, but it was hurtful all the same. I went home shortly after that. I have never been comfortable at social functions since that day. I have always felt out of place, as if I was only there to be made a joke of and humiliated.

Years later, after my accident, Sr. Paula saw the video of that wedding. We were visiting my foster family with my cousin Elaine who was a nurse. Elaine was a regular visitor during the time of my rehabilitation. It was because of her nursing background that I was able to have days away from the hospitals and nursing homes. Sr. Paula wondered why I sped out of the room on my wheelchair when the video came on. I couldn't bear to revisit the scene of that wedding. Even stuck in a wheelchair, my family found a way to humiliate me.

Being back in Cookstown had one big plus for me. I met up again with the Byrne family. By this time, Danny Byrne ran a petrol station that he had bought off my uncle Joseph. It is a small world round Cookstown. For a time I wondered if I could trust the Byrnes as my friends if they had a connection to the Donaghys. But I have never known anything but kindness from them. Of all my uncles, Joseph was the one I had most time for and I got to know one of his sons quite well. As far as I knew, Joseph was the only brother who visited Grace regularly and he took her out for Christmas every year. I used to go up to Byrnes and help out at the petrol station. Very often, I stayed for my dinner. I had no great appetite and really only stayed for the craic in the house. I loved the feeling of being part of something, part of a family; even though I knew the Byrnes were not my family. Mrs Byrne would look at my plate and say,

"I cooked all of that dinner, not just the half you ate, Philip. Eat it up."

"Yes Mrs Byrne" I would reply.

"Can you not call her by her first name?" Danny Byrne would say.

"Old Humpy says I'm to call you by your first name, Mrs Byrne," I would say, all innocent. That is typical of the kind of chat that went on in the Byrne household. You could say I was cheeky, or you could say I gave as good as I got. Or you could say nothing and just enjoy the banter. It was all new to me and I loved it. I also knew that Danny Byrne would quietly let me know if I ever overstepped the mark. If I ever did, there would be no row, no shouting match and no scene. He would just let me know with a look and a quiet word. "*What a great life*", I said to myself.

I used to offer to make a cup of coffee after dinner and the Byrnes would always run a mile. My coffee was rotten and I always left the kitchen like a bombsite after making it. I never used a spoon. I just used to tip the coffee and sugar out of their canisters into the mugs, spilling as I went. Then I'd throw in the milk, making sure a good lot of it slopped out. I'd take two sips out of the overflowing mug and then leave the coffee sitting there in a sticky pool on the counter top. It used to drive Mrs Byrne crazy. I never even noticed what I had done until she told me and I would promise to make less mess next time. But by then I had forgotten my promise and the whole cycle started over again. I often ask myself "Why did the Byrnes take me in?" I don't really know why, but I am glad they did. I would be proud to have them as my true family. If I could ever have a father in my life, Danny Byrne is the man I would choose. But he is not my father, I know that. He has his own family to look after and support. Still, he is one of the few people in my life I would go to for advice.

Danny Byrne says today, "We never asked Philip to stay and we never asked him to leave. We passed no remark about it. He came and went as he pleased and he was treated no different than the other boys." Danny Byrne used to meet my uncle Francis at mass, and he would ask after me. Danny would let my uncle know I was doing all right. Maurice Byrne remembers my uncle coming into the petrol station. He always had a remark to make about me. He always warned Maurice to watch out and not to trust me. Maurice knew me better than that, thank God.

I spent more and more time at the Byrnes. I had to move out of Greenvale in the end because I had a crazy neighbour who played country music through the night. We used to call her "Lilo Lil". There was no harm in her, but I needed my beauty sleep and that bloody music used to drive me mad. I shared a flat on the Black Hill but I was still a regular visitor at the Byrnes. I loved it there. I loved the company, the work, the home cooking, and the craic. I was sometimes lonely in my flat, and there was always so much going on at the Byrnes. But I didn't want to outstay my welcome and I didn't want to be a nuisance. I always had my flat to go back to. In my head I could picture the day when Danny Byrne would tell me I was no longer welcome, that I was getting in the way of their family life. In my heart of hearts I know that Danny would never do that. But I have had an insecure life and I feared rejection every step of the way. At the end of the day, I knew I didn't belong anywhere, no matter how many times the Byrnes told me I was welcome.

I spent my first Christmas after I left care with the Byrne family. There was no fuss made about it. They just assumed that I would be there on Christmas Day and I was. I spend Christmas Day with them still. I have never in my life spent a Christmas with my mother. I think it was that first year, when I was invited to the Byrnes for Christmas dinner, my foster parents paid a visit. My aunt Bernadette handed me a blue plastic bag and wished me a happy Christmas. I opened the bag and inside was some slices of turkey. That turkey angered me more than I could say. It was an insult to me and it was an insult to the Byrnes who invited me for Christmas dinner when none of my blood related family would. Did my aunt think the Byrnes wouldn't have enough turkey to go round? Up until I opened the plastic bag, I had been having a good Christmas and I was feeling good about my life. The bag of turkey was like a kick in the teeth, a reminder that I was a worthless bastard with no proper family of my own. I fed the turkey to the family dog.

After Christmas I put my mind to getting some proper work. I was still helping out at the petrol station, and I had found a temporary job in a meat-packing plant, but I needed something more permanent. Danny Byrne always said to me that hard work would keep me out of trouble. He certainly kept me hard at work and out of trouble. I used to change wheels, wash cars, serve petrol, mind the shop and drive the forklift. I was the best forklift driver he had. But then I remembered all the times I crashed the thing and the time I let it sink in the muck behind the petrol station. Danny would watch me at work. Some days I would have a desperate hangover, and would be looking to skive off. Other days I would be more interested in chatting up the women who came to get their cars washed. But all the time, I would feel Danny's eyes on me. He never had to say anything. I would just feel his eyes burning into the back of my head. I would get on with the job, and call him "Oul' humpy" under my breath.

Working at the Byrnes was the best aftercare package I could have hoped for. It was hard work, but I was starting to feel secure and useful, plus it kept me off the streets and out of trouble. Best of all, there was nobody writing reports on me, month after month. For the first time in my life, there was no official record of what I was doing. Nobody had to write down what I did with my money, or how many times I got drunk, or who I was socialising with, or what I had done at my work. But at the same time, for the first time since I left St Joseph's children's home, I felt there were people who genuinely cared for me. I hope that someone from social services will read this book and think about that. Mr and Mrs Byrne were not professionally trained to write reports and look after other people's unwanted children, but they provided me with everything I needed to turn my life around and to prepare for my future. I have a lot of respect for the entire Byrne family who took me as Philip and not some kind of problem or case.

I saw a job in the paper that I decided to go for. It was as a gravedigger with the local council. There was a big application form for it and Clare Byrne helped me to fill it in. I must say she was very creative about my achievements, back then when I really had no achievements. It did the trick and I got the job. I learned a lot from that application. I learned that there was no point in being too modest about what I had achieved in life, even if I didn't think I had achieved much. Nobody else was going to care about my achievements if I didn't. To be honest, I wasn't the best gravedigger. I kept crashing the digger into the gravestones. There was no worse job than digging graves when it was raining. It was so miserable it made me want to jump into the hole and cover myself up. My flat was near the graveyard and I used to nip off for a cup of tea when it rained. But, it was a permanent job and I was still able to help out in the petrol station in my spare time. For a while it felt like I had the best of both worlds. I had my own place to live and my own job and I was welcome at the Byrnes any time.

Mrs Byrne always said, from the first time she met me in the school uniform shop in Cookstown, that I was like a lost boy. She noticed that the more time I spent with her family, the more settled I became. I seemed happier in myself and a bit less lost. Then, all of a sudden, I would go off and do something really stupid. She never knew what the trigger was, except that when I seemed to be settled, that would be the time I would lose the head. The times when I felt like I really was part of the family, I would say to myself, "*This isn't your real family, Philip, you know*". That would be enough to knock me off the rails. The Byrnes never, ever made me feel this way. It was just my old insecurity getting at me again and telling me that I didn't belong anywhere, and especially not in this family that I would have loved to call my own family. Mrs Byrne gave me a nickname, after a kind of bun they used to sell in the shop that I loved called Donkey Lugs. She used to call me in from the petrol station, "Come on in, for a cup of tea Donkey Lugs." I used to fight away with Maurice and Ciaran Byrne. They weren't my brothers, but they felt like brothers at times. They would go completely mad at me when they caught me out washing cars wearing their best shirts that they were keeping for going out at the weekends. They complained about my stinking feet, the smell so bad that it would wake them up in the night. To this day, I tell them it was their own feet that were stinking, not mine. It was a real, loving family and I felt part of it in a way.

But then I would lose the head. There was one night I arrived back at the house, soaking wet and covered in muck from head to toe. I had been out drinking with Ciaran, and took a notion that there was a shortcut back to the house through some fields. Ciaran argued with me, but I wouldn't be told so he left me to it and was not surprised to arrive home before me. He went to his bed and fell into a deep sleep. I had forgotten that the river lay between my short cut and the Byrne's house. I waded through it, but I was forced back, slipping and sliding on the riverbank. I had to go home the normal way, soaked through. I could have drowned that night, or at least caught pneumonia. I must have dropped my key in the river so I had to knock on the window to get into the house. I got the whole family up and I was some sight standing there shivering and filthy.

"What possessed you, Philip?" Mrs Byrne said, getting me a towel. I tried to explain what happened.

"There's no talking to you, Philly, when you take a notion," she said. I just stood there dripping wet and feeling very foolish. I made a promise to myself to wise up and for a while I did, until the next time I felt that my luck was too good to be true.

One thing about being 18 years old and back in Cookstown was that I had a great social life with my old friends. One of my mates got his first car and we used to spend a lot of time cruising in that beat up old car: four big lads piled into it. Back then, the army had a checkpoint on the main street in Cookstown and we mooned at the soldiers on the way past in the car. We thought we were deadly, and then we spotted some girls we knew walking down the other side of the street. We did a quick U turn and followed them, passing remarks out the window at them and laughing away. The next thing we knew, we were being pulled in by the soldiers we'd mooned at just a few minutes earlier. "Get your hairy arses out of the car, boys," they said.

Maurice Byrne and me used to fancy ourselves with the women. One night two women came and sat beside us in the pub and started chatting. We weren't too interested in them for some reason, I can't remember why. We were making signals at each other behind their backs about getting away. "Leave it to me", I said. One of my front teeth was capped and I removed the tooth and smiled over at the girls, then I dropped the tooth into my pint. Maurice was laughing so hard he almost choked on his pint and sent froth all over the table. No big surprise, the girls left, totally disgusted with us. The next morning, I couldn't remember what I had done with the capped tooth. I wondered if the barman found it lying in the bottom of a pint glass. I am sure he has found much worse things.

By the time my probation was up, I had been back in Cookstown for nearly two years and things seemed to be going really well for me again. I had my work and my friends and a great social life. I had stayed out of trouble since leaving

Ballee. Life was looking good. With the help of the Byrnes, I was beginning to find my feet in the world. And then I announced that I was giving up the gravedigger's job and moving to Omagh. Mrs Byrne in particular was not too happy about it. "Why would you do that, Philip?" she asked me, "Look at all you have here. Don't be giving it all up. There is nothing up in Omagh for you." Now that I had proved I could earn a wage and support myself, I went back to thinking about my father. The way I looked at it, I was in a better position to find out more about him. I was no longer in care, I had kept out of trouble, and I had an independent life. I thought all those things would stand to me and that I would get more respect from the Willow Hill hospital than I had when I was in the children's home. Since leaving Ballee, I had done no more work to find out about my father, but that didn't mean that I had put him out of my mind. Far from it. I dreamed about him all the time. I thought that if I moved closer to where Grace lived, I might have a better chance of finding out from her, or from the people who knew her, about how I came to be in the world. My relationship with Grace was not good at the time. When I was in Ballee, I could telephone Grace regularly, using the office phone. But once I left, I had no telephone of my own and I found it hard to talk to Grace on a payphone. In any case, Grace was not good on the telephone. She wouldn't tell me what I wanted to hear over the phone. I thought if I lived closer to her, I would be able to go and see Grace, build a trust with her, and find out what I wanted to know. When he saw my mind was made up, Danny Byrne said "Well Philip, you'll learn from your mistakes."

Danny's own father had been orphaned very young. He was split up from his brothers and sisters and was sent to St Joseph's, the same children's home in Belfast that I was reared in. At the age of 12, Danny's father was hired out to a farmer. He was 30 before he knew he had a family. Danny met one of his cousins recently. Her mother and Danny's father were brother and sister. The sister had been adopted and reared in England. She raised her own family there and her daughter was able to tell Danny more about his background than his own father ever knew. With that experience, I think Danny wondered just how I would cope with finding out who my father was. He was right to be concerned but I did know how I would cope. Whether I would be happy or sad, delighted or disappointed, I would cope alone.

Was it a mistake moving to Omagh? I didn't think so, but it didn't go well for me there. I found work in a petrol station and I made new friends. I lived in a bed-sit in the town and it was very lonely there at times. I went back to Cookstown and stayed with the Byrnes on my days off. My relationship with Grace was as bad as ever. Moving to Omagh didn't change anything there. One day she wanted to see me and talk to me, the next day she complained that I vexed her with all my questions.

Grace had nothing more to tell me about my father. For her it was all in the past, a closed book. My dream of a loving family could never be. But at the back of my mind, I was not sure if I could put my full trust in what Grace had told me. Inch by inch, I was slowly getting closer to a picture of the man she claimed was my father. But there was no proof. A few more people working at Willow Hill got to know me, and I had hopes that they would remember something about my father. They told me that he was a good man, and I was pleased about that, because there were times when I wondered what kind of a man he was. I had no social worker this time to help me to talk to the hospital authorities. I just dug away on my own, finding out as much as I could.

My father became something of an obsession for me. On good days, I wondered if my ambition to work as a carer came from him. On bad days, I wondered if he had taken advantage of my mother. At other times, right up to the present day, I wonder if Grace is telling me the truth. Maybe he is the man she wanted to have a relationship with and my real father is one of the other boyfriends it is claimed she had at the time. In the back of my mind, I still think it is possible Grace was seeing somebody in Mullabeg on her weekend visits. Back when I was at Ballee and the hospital told me that Grace had more than one boyfriend, I could feel the embarrassment in the air. But at the end of the day, my father could only be one of Grace's boyfriends. It didn't bother me how many men I had to ask. But no other names were ever mentioned and the hospital told me that it was up to Grace to share or withhold information, as she saw fit. The man Grace described to me was the most likely candidate.

Being around Grace distressed me as much as it did her at times. I didn't like the way my mother was being treated at Willow Hill. She was still in a secure ward at the time and I thought she would be better off living in the community. She didn't like me saying those things, especially when I gave my opinion to one of the nurses. She asked me to leave, and when I refused, she would ask the nurses to get me out. Then I was angry and I wouldn't go to see her for a while. When I eventually went back again, it was like starting all over again with Grace. I told her that some day she would move away from the hospital and live with me. Looking back, I should have been more sensitive. It was like telling a child that she would be taken from her home, her friends and everything she was familiar with and put in a place she didn't know, among strangers. Then again, that is exactly what happened to me when I was fostered at the age of six. How would I know any different?

While I was working at the petrol station in Omagh, I met the man who was to become my solicitor, Feargal Logan. At the time, he played Gaelic football for Co. Tyrone. I was filling his car with petrol and I gave him a touch about a lousy performance his team had put in at the weekend. He stopped and looked at me. Feargal is a big lad and I had a moment when I thought I had gone too far. But Feargal came forward, shook my hand and introduced himself. I think I got the measure of the man that time. Later, when I needed a solicitor, it was Feargal Logan I contacted. He was working with me to find my father before I had my accident and he said to me once, "You know Philip, if I had a nephew in your position, I would do everything I could to help him find out who his father is. And I would support him, whatever he finds out." Feargal Logan was more or less a stranger to me when he said that. It was more than my family has ever said to me. My cousin Ronan said to me, "Look Philip, I might not agree with it, but as far as the family is concerned, the big man took you in and it is down to the big man to tell you who your father is. He knows and your mother knows." The big man is my uncle Francis. In the back of my mind, I have always wondered if it was him who planted the story of my father in Grace's mind in the first place. The dead can't speak up. I wouldn't trust that man, Francis Donaghy, as far as I could throw him.

One day in the petrol station in Omagh, I met a girl who could be my half sister. She came into the petrol station and one of my colleagues said to me, "Philip, if what you've told us is true, that's your half sister out there in the forecourt." My heart jumped. I have always wanted a sister or a brother. I recognised the girl because she was a regular customer at the petrol station. But until that moment, I had no idea that she might be related to me. I am not proud now of the way I approached her, but I believed she would be as desperate for answers as me. I was wrong about that. She probably knew nothing about me. I was too direct and I scared her witless. I just didn't think about how she would feel being approached by a complete stranger, out of the blue. I didn't think about how upset she might be about the information I had relating to her dead father, that in any case might not even be true. I had lived with the uncertainty of my situation for so long, that I wasn't embarrassed or shocked by it any more. I shouldn't have assumed the same thing for the girl in the garage forecourt. But I did. I ran out and just told her who I was and that I thought her father might be my father. I told her I was sorry that he was dead. I asked her if she had a picture of him. I told her I would love to see what he looked like. God, but that was a big mistake I sorely regret. The girl just rushed past me and paid for her petrol. She drove away without a second look at me. I was standing there feeling like crap, knowing that I had blown it with her. I have tried to make amends in the years since that first meeting. I have tried to explain more calmly and sensitively what I have been told about my background. But the damage is done and she wants nothing to do with me. I don't blame her, but I wish she would change her mind. If she thinks I am wrong about her father, she could take steps to prove it and I really wish she would. If it turns out that I am right, I wouldn't try to force any kind of a relationship on her, although she might come to like having a brother, in time. At this stage, I just want to know the truth.

I contacted my alleged father's brother in a very direct way too. I found out about him from nurses at Willow Hill. He used to drink in a bar in Killyclogher and I went to see him there. He had me thrown out. Shortly after that I had a visit from the local police who told me to back off or face court proceedings. I was wrong to just turn up in Killyclogher, but I didn't agree with the police being called on me. The man could have spoken to me himself. If he had nothing to hide then he had nothing to fear. While I was at Ballee, I tried to do everything the right way, the official way. It got me nowhere. It looked as if taking the matter into my own hands was going to land me in a lot of trouble. Since my probation, I really didn't want to get involved with the police. I knew that if I got charged with anything, no matter how small, I wouldn't get away with probation again. And I still was no further forward. Why would nobody help me? The way I saw it, when I was living in Omagh, two families knew what I was looking for, my mother's people and my father's. Either one of them could have stepped in and told me the truth. Grace stuck to her original story and offered no further proof. From the other side I was threatened with court proceedings. The Willow Hill hospital also knew more than it was willing to admit, and continued to hide behind my mother's right to give or withhold information. Where did that leave me? It left me wondering what everyone was so scared about. It also left me more frustrated than ever. I desperately didn't want to repeat the kind of behaviour that had got me arrested at Ballee, but I could feel the anger building in me. I was prepared for the worst.

On Christmas Eve that year I was in Omagh, I paid a visit to the Byrnes back in Cookstown. They were delighted to see me and asked me to stay over for Christmas dinner. But I said no. I told them I had to work on Christmas Day. That wasn't true, but I felt that I just couldn't face being in the middle of a happy family when I knew what a mess I was making of my own family up in Omagh. The Byrne's petrol station was busy with people getting their cars cleaned and filled for the Christmas holidays and I offered to help out. After work, Mrs Byrne told me to take a shower and while I was in there, she took my clothes and put them in the wash. Then she said to me, "Now you have to stay, Philip. You've no clothes to put on you. We are going up to Omagh tomorrow night to visit relatives. We'll give you a lift back then if you want it. You are staying here for Christmas dinner and that's that." Well, what choice did I have? It was another great Christmas at the Byrne's house. They took me back to Omagh on Christmas night and I spent a lonely time sitting in the dark, thinking.

I decided I had to get out of Omagh. Cookstown was too near. I felt I wanted to be miles away. I turned to the only person I could think of who would help me, Sr. Paula in Sligo. She must have got the shock of her life when she heard from me. What was she going to do with a 19 year old man in a convent in Sligo? Although I kept in contact with Sr. Paula, it was not what you would call regular. Sometimes she heard from me and sometimes she didn't. She hadn't seen me for about four years. But when she heard how miserable I was in Omagh and how I had messed things up with Grace, she told me to pack a bag and come down straight away.

Going down to Sligo was probably the best thing that could have happened to me at that time. In one way, I was running away from my problems. But in another way, putting the miles between myself and the hopeless mess I had left behind me in Omagh gave me the courage to try and build a future without any of that stuff sticking to it. Sr. Paula found me accommodation in Sligo and I had work delivering coal for a man who did a run from Cookstown, Pat Hagan. Pat is the brother of one of my old neighbours from Mullabeg. It is a small world. I got on the best with Pat Hagan and later, after I had my accident, and I was staying at St John's hospital in Sligo, Pat was a regular visitor. As well as the coal run, I was a volunteer at the Nazareth House nursing home for elderly people. I helped out as a porter and general assistant. Everyone knew when I was around because I had all of the old people up on walkers. I have never liked seeing elderly people just staring at the four walls of a day room. The Nazareth House is a very good nursing home with a good reputation, but I still thought the residents could do with a bit of exercise and variety in their daily routines. I was the same when I had to live in nursing homes after my accident. I couldn't get up on a walker myself, but by God I could encourage the old people to get up and get out for a short time every day.

I started to make friends in Sligo and I was really enjoying myself. I had a few pounds in my pocket at the end of the week and I had proved to myself again that I could earn a living and make a life for myself. I made a decision then to tell the new people I met that I had no family, if they asked. In time, all of my good friends met Sr. Paula and I told them that she was as close as a mother to me. Everybody accepted that. Nobody passed any remark about it. It was like disowning my family and it felt strange to me at first, but then I got used to it. Nobody knew my background and it made me feel lighter in myself. In Cookstown, I would meet people in the street who would say to me,

"Aren't you Francis Donaghy's son?"

"I am not," I would say, "I am Grace Donaghy's son. Francis only fostered me."

"Grace?" they would say, "What is she doing now? I haven't seen Grace in years."

"She's living up there in Willow Hill this past 30 years or more."

"I didn't know that. God luck to her. I didn't know that at all."

Sometimes it felt like betraying Grace by telling people where she was living and that I was her son. It had been kept quiet for so many years. But at the same time, I had nothing to be ashamed about and I didn't want people going round thinking that I was Francis Donaghy's son. In Sligo, nobody except Sr. Paula and Pat Hagan, who I worked for, really knew me or my family. I didn't have to explain myself to anybody. I was just Philip and that was that.

I began to lose touch with my old friends in Cookstown. We met up a few times. I went to Cookstown once, and Tom came down to Sligo to see me. But after a while, the arrangements dwindled down to nothing. Just one of those things. Brian McGovern was my good friend in Sligo. We used to go out drinking together and we had some laughs. Late one Saturday night, he put the clock in my flat back by three hours. When I woke up on the Sunday, the clock said a quarter to eleven, and I jumped out of bed to get ready for 11 o'clock mass. I had a desperate hangover and could tell I was stinking of drink, even after a shower. I arrived at the church just after two, still thinking I was heading for 11 mass.

The church was empty except for a few old people praying and Sr. Paula. I was totally confused and wondering what was going on. Sr. Paula gave me one of her disapproving looks. She copped on more quickly than I did that someone must be playing a prank on me. She shooed me up to the Nazareth House and gave me a strong cup of coffee to drink, all the time giving out to me about drinking too much and carrying on. Me and Brian McGovern were mad men together, but I'll say this for Brian, he was a good and a constant visitor when I was in rehabilitation in St John's in Sligo. It was not much of a laugh being with me then, but Brian was there every day. He is still a good friend.

Soon after I arrived, McDonald's restaurant opened in Sligo and I went along for an interview. I got the job and I loved it. I was quickly promoted and I think McDonalds tapped into something in me the care system and my foster parents hadn't a clue about. I am the sort of person who can live for a long time on just a little bit of encouragement. At McDonalds, I got loads of encouragement and it inspired me to work harder. The more I got from McDonalds, the more I gave. It was that simple. I had so little encouragement in my life when I was growing up. In my heart of hearts, I thought I was no good at anything, except acting the goat. I got a lot of self-confidence through working at McDonalds and it was great for me. I met Rachel Desmond in McDonalds, and when the manager, Peter O'Neill, got the job to open the Castlebar branch, he took me and Rachel along with him. It was a new start for me, in every way.

Castlebar in Co. Mayo is about 45 miles from Sligo. For me, it was a world away. I found my feet in Sligo, but I found my wings in Castlebar. I had my beautiful girlfriend, Rachel, and a good job with prospects. I was playing my football and going out dancing at the weekends. I was making new friends and I had a lovely place to live. My next door neighbours, the Flynns used to do my washing and ironing for me. I was never any good at ironing. As I said before, I have never had a problem finding good and decent families who are happy to help me out when they can, and who can take my old cheeky chat. The Flynn family was that family for me in Castlebar.

I was the Customer Service Manager at McDonalds. I used to have to interview new staff and I loved that. I got very good at spotting the ones who would fit in and work hard. One of the last things I did before my accident was to arrange for a group of children with spina bifida to visit McDonalds. I made sure the restaurant had the whole party atmosphere and I gave discounts to the group. I might have thrown in free ice-cream as well. I think the McDonald's bosses over in England were a bit pissed off with me at the time. But if they thought about it, what would those children remember about McDonalds? They would remember that they had a good time and the staff (that was me and my team) put a smile on their faces. What better publicity could you buy for the price of a few burgers and ice-creams?

I got my first mobile phone in Castlebar and I had my number printed up on stickers. I went back to Sligo for the weekend to visit my friends and Sr. Paula. I gave her one of the stickers and told her to ring me on that number from now on. Her first reaction was to get all annoyed and say she wasn't made of money and she wouldn't be ringing me on any mobile phone, but I knew she would. In fact, Sr. Paula was the last person I heard from before I had my accident. I rang her one time from the back of a friend's car. We were on the road, going to a concert in Dublin and I rang to tell her about it. "Be careful, Philip," she said to me, "I hope you are with a good driver." Sr. Paula worried that a crowd of young lads in a car on the way to Dublin was risky, an accident waiting to happen. But we got back, safe and sound. I called Sr. Paula to let her know. On my last visit to Sligo, before the accident, Sr. Paula thought to herself that I had finally grown up and turned into the young man she always hoped I would. "I remember standing out the front there," she said, "And you know when you suddenly see a young lad, he seemed to just become a man that summer." She was right. I had everything to live for. I was with Rachel and Sr. Paula really liked her. It felt like I was getting a seal of approval when she told me that. I had my work, my friends, and, for the first time in my life, I had a plan.

I had heard about a car wash franchise that was for sale in Castlebar. I knew the car wash business from my time working in the Byrne's petrol station and I knew I could make a go of it. I could also fit it in around my work at McDonalds. I set about negotiating for the work and I was thrilled when it came off. I had flyers printed up advertising the business and I was really proud of myself and looking forward to getting started. My idea was to put away a bit of money every week to pay for legal services. I was talking with Feargal Logan about getting information on my father the legal way. It was something I kept to myself, but I had to do it. Having my own business seemed like the only way I would be able to afford it. Feargal came up with a few ideas that would help us to get cooperation from the Willow Hill hospital. This time, I was sure, I would get to the truth. I told Feargal I would come to see him as soon as I could get a few days off to travel north.

I had my accident the night before I was due to take over the car wash business. Even Feargal thought I would not make it. When Sr. Paula got the call, she immediately thought the worst. She remembered the concert I had been to in Dublin. She held her breath, expecting to hear that I had been with a group of lads and the driver lost control of the car. She was waiting for a body count. Sr. Paula contacted my uncle Francis, so relieved that I was alive, and he cried. The news flew around Cookstown and Sligo. Grace was not told at first. I don't think she was ever told how critically ill I was, and I was glad of that in a way.

All my plans, all the hard work, just ended that night. Sometimes I think to myself, I might as well not have bothered. I should have just become the waste of space I was expected to become when I left care. All the signs were pointing in that direction. What was the point in making all that effort when it came down to a smash on the side of a road? Maybe my foster parents were right about me. Maybe I would amount to nothing in life. But then I get a grip on myself. Who says my life is worthless? I started out in this life with nothing, no name and no family. I was brought up the rough way and every step was a struggle for me. I had to overcome being thought of as retarded. I had to fight against the stigma of my mother's mental illness. I had the self-esteem knocked out of me. I was insecure about my background. I had a family who were ashamed of me. I have had to prove myself time and again. Nothing ever came to me on a plate. By the time I had the accident, I was starting to make my way in the world. I was proving my family wrong who said I was mad and nothing and nobody. I had no help from them to find my direction in life. I found it myself. I found friends who would help me. I found families, like the Byrnes, who were an example to me of love and support.

To this day, I wish I had a family that encouraged me and recognised my achievements. Nothing has come easy to me my whole life and for once, I would like my family to say, "You know what Philip? You are an inspiration after all you have been through. You have done well for yourself." I am not talking about financial success. I had to have a nearly fatal accident and then wait five years before money came into my life. I am talking about the effort I make to build a life for myself and to get through each and every day. Instead, my family say, "Philip? What has he achieved? He has achieved very little, poor lad. If that was me, I would rather be dead." And how does that make me feel? It makes me feel like a useless, dirty bastard, as usual

Grace

When news of my accident spread and I was lying in a coma in hospital in Dublin, family members gathered round. I was not expected to live. It was a six week waiting game. Six weeks for the family to think about all that had happened in my young life, to have regrets, maybe, and to say goodbye. Who knows what went through their minds as they watched and waited? Uncle Francis and aunt Bernadette were there. Sr. Paula was there. Rachel Desmond was there. Friends who could not be with me waited on the end of the telephone for news. Visitors came and went, relieving each other from the burden of waiting, and then coming back again to sit and watch and wait. I was there, but I was in my own world, down inside my own head, healing myself the best way I could through the deepest sleep. My mother, Grace, was not there. She was kept from the truth, as usual. She didn't see me until months later when I was in rehabilitation in the Musgrave Park Hospital in Belfast. To this day, I don't think my mother has a clue how close to death I was following the accident.

I sometimes think of myself lying unconscious that time. It feels like a whole other life, like life in the womb; alive, but not really alive; completely dependent. In hospital, I depended on machines to keep me alive. In the womb, I depended on Grace. Back then we knew and understood each other; we existed together and nothing else mattered. Real life couldn't be more different. Since the time I was born, Grace and me have never really known each other. We don't understand each other. We have no real connection. I can hardly even imagine what kind of a life Grace has had, and I know very little about her really. I can only see all the things Grace lost out on in life. There are only a few stories and even fewer shared memories of Grace that I can rely on. There are a lot of secrets. Grace doesn't want to share her experience with me. She doesn't want to be a part of my book. But there is no Philip without Grace. The life I am going to describe is made up in places, because I have no other way to tell my mother's story. I have to fill in the gaps some way and I do it as honestly as I can with the facts that I know. I might be wide of the mark sometimes. I make no apology for it because I have been going around Grace in circles for years with a blindfold on. The truth has always been just out of my reach. But, on the other hand, I might know more about Grace than anybody thinks I do.

My mother's name is Grace Donaghy. I call her "Grace". I never call her "Mother" or "Mum" to her face because it feels too strange to me. Grace is my mother but she never got the chance to be a mother to me. I was taken from her just after I was born. It is hard for me to accept that. For me the word "mother" holds so much. I know if things had been different, I would be the type of man who puts his mother on a pedestal. I would probably have expected a lot from her too. I would have wanted my dinner on the table when I came home from my work and my shirts ironed for me. I would have relied on her for good advice when I was growing up. I would have expected her to be there all the times I was lonely or confused as a young man. I probably would have turned her hair grey with worrying about me at times. If I had been lucky enough to have a family of my own, I would have wanted my mother to babysit her grandchildren. But most of all, if things had been different, there would have been a strong bond of love between us. I would be the proud son taking his mother out, giving her presents on her birthday and at Christmas, and sending her flowers on Mother's Day. I would be privileged to take her away on holidays with me. She would have wanted for nothing.

The relationship I have with Grace today is nothing like that. I do my best; I take her out, give her presents on her birthday and things like that, but we have never had a connection. I am not comfortable with her, especially since my accident. I don't think that a present from me means anything more to Grace than the price tag. That's harsh, but I think it's true. These days, I don't even expect even a phone call to say "Thank you". It hurts sometimes but I have got used to it. Grace is Grace and I have learned to expect nothing from her. I have learned to accept her the way she is. I understand that the life she has had didn't teach her about the give as well as the take of normal family relationships. It is not her fault. Grace never got the chance to care for me or for anybody else in her life. Who can blame her if she doesn't know how to do it?

In some ways, I have had too many mothers in my life. I would see Sr. Paula as the mother of my very young life. She was the one who reared me as a baby and a small boy. Mrs Byrne is like a mother to me in my adult life. She is the kind of mother I would have liked to have. She is strong and also loving. My foster mother was the mother of my childhood and teenage years, but she was no kind of mother to me at all. One thing I have never had is the unconditional love that people say you get from your mother. None of my mothers has been able to give me that, especially not Grace. It vexes Grace to talk about herself as a mother. It is as hard for her as it is for me to talk about being an abandoned child, an accident. I can really only guess at what Grace thinks about our relationship. She has told people that she is proud of me and all I have achieved since my accident, but she has never told me. Maybe she thinks her opinion has no value to me. Maybe she has got used to thinking of herself as worthless. Maybe she is afraid to give her opinion without someone there to tell her it is okay. She wouldn't understand that I am motivated by encouragement. She has no way of knowing that. I ask myself at times, "*Is my mother proud of her son?*" I hope she is, but I really don't know. If I had a son who achieved all that I have achieved, I would be proud of him and I would tell him.

Grace was the second youngest of six children. She had one older sister, three older brothers and a younger brother, Joseph. Her father was a farmer and he died young in 1949, when Grace was about 6 or 7 years old. That left her mother to rear the family and manage the farm in Mullabeg by herself. There was no help from the government at that time. Money was very tight. A lot of families would have struggled to make ends meet. There was no work and just small farms to scratch a living from. Mrs Donaghy and her older sons did the best they could to make a living. The children worked hard; they were all known as good workers. But they knew that the farm couldn't keep all of them as they grew up. When they were old enough, a couple of the sons emigrated to find work. The eldest daughter got married and moved away to a nearby town. By the time Grace was a teenager, she was living at home on the farm with her mother and just a couple of her brothers. It was a hard life. The 1950s in Ireland was a harsh time to grow up in. People had no expectations of life. They worked hard to keep a roof over their heads and food on the table and that was about as much as anyone had. Some people had a lot less.

Grace was a quiet child growing up. She lived in the shadow of her mother, who was known as a sharp woman. They visited among the neighbours and Grace sat quietly taking everything in while her mother talked about the news of the day. Grace can remember details about houses she visited as a child that nobody else can. She remembers the pattern on carpets and curtains that are long gone. Some would say she has little else to think about, but Grace has a brilliant memory. Today, she can name people she has not seen in 45 years. She doesn't see age on them. She sees them as they were, frozen in time, as she is herself in some ways.

When Grace left the local school in Mullabeg, she found work in a clothing factory, but she was not suited to the work. It was piece work and she struggled to keep up. She became more disruptive at home and was prone to childish temper tantrums. Her mother couldn't control her. There was no talking to Grace once she lost the head. The brothers all married and one of them brought his new wife to live at the farm. Another brother, Francis, who had emigrated, came home to the farm with his wife. It felt very crowded at home. Grace felt in the way at times. She always looked to her mother as the head of the household, but now her brothers were there with their new young wives. Grace was part of the family in one way, but she felt like an unwanted stranger at times too. Grace didn't have too many opportunities to get out and about and meet people her own age. It was too far to walk to the nearest town and there was no public transport. Fuel was scarce and people were not in the habit of driving to the town unless they had to. Grace was often left behind to look after her mother when the goods were brought from the town on a Saturday evening. When she wasn't able to find work and earn her own money, Grace felt under pressure in the house. She wasn't bringing money in; she was put to work in the house and on the farm. She was dependent on her brothers and their families for everything, down to a packet of cigarettes as a treat at the weekend. Grace was lonely and frustrated. She had nobody to talk to when things were getting her down. There was no time for talk of that nature. Who could she tell that she needed more in her life than Mullabeg? There was nobody for Grace to turn to and her problems welled up inside her.

As time went on, Grace became more unpredictable. Her mother's health was failing and she couldn't cope with her daughter's behaviour problems. A couple of the brothers said, "If only Grace had a younger sister living at home then maybe she could have sorted out her problems at home." Grace's only sister lived in a nearby town and their relationship was not close. She was no help to Grace at all. She never has been. Even now, with her family all grown up, Grace hardly ever sees her sister. Grace did her best to get on with her sisters-in-law but there was tension in the house. Children were being born and there was less room and less time for Grace. Her social life was mostly friendless. There was nobody close for her to share things with and confide in. She sometimes went to the local bar on her own, but it wasn't really acceptable behaviour for a young woman at the time. She suspected that there might have been talk among the neighbours about her being a bit wild. There was a bit of banter among the local men about what a fine looking girl Grace was. There were rows in the house about what Grace was getting up to.

One of the brothers and his wife moved away as soon as they could afford to, even though it meant giving up their influence on the farm as well as the house. One brother and his family stayed. That was Francis, Bernadette and their young children. Although Grace got on well with Francis and Bernadette, she was not treated as a full member of the family. Grace had as much right to be in the home place as any of them, probably more, because she was the unmarried daughter of the house when Francis moved back. But from 1961, when she was just 19, Grace started to spend short periods of time at the Willow Hill psychiatric hospital in Co. Tyrone. She was a voluntary patient, at least at first. She was often at home and the neighbours around Mullabeg didn't know that she spent time away in hospital as far back as 1961. It was kept secret from them. Nobody knew where Grace was at when she wasn't at home.

The first time Grace set foot in Willow Hill as an inpatient, she was scared witless. The rages that had driven her there were gone. There were hundreds of patients living on the wards back then. Men and women were segregated. The hospital was old and built from dark stone like a kind of haunted castle. It was on the edge of the town of Omagh, and the local people spread rumours about straitjackets and padded cells. The place had a terrible reputation, and ending up in Willow Hill was the last word in punishment to small children. It was said that inpatients, forgotten by their families, were buried in communal graves when their time came. Grace was not from the town but still she knew what the Willow Hill hospital meant to people. She had a small suitcase with her. She wanted to know where she would be sleeping. She wanted to unpack her things. She was relieved to see that there were no padded cells, just secure wards at that time.

The hospital had a strict routine but there was a kind of freedom in it for Grace. She didn't have to do any farm work or housework. Nobody shouted orders at her. Nobody made her feel like a nuisance. Nobody made her feel like she was getting everything wrong. For the first time in a long time, Grace didn't feel out of place. The medication helped and so did the strict visiting times. Grace could nearly forget that she had a family as she settled into her new routine, Monday to Friday. Willow Hill started to feel like home to Grace. She had been lonely at Mullabeg. At Willow Hill, she met new people. Nobody singled her out as being mad or different. She was accepted by the staff and patients just as she was. Grace was a very good looking young woman. She liked to have her hair done and her nails done. This was available to her at Willow Hill. She liked to take part in social events, like any young girl. She had company if she wanted it 24 hours a day. People listened to her in hospital. For the first time in her life, Grace had her own friends who were not related to her or connected to her family. She began to feel more secure at Willow Hill than at home. Grace still had her problems with dark moods and sudden temper tantrums; she could be very childish. But sometimes she lay in bed at night listening to the sounds of the ward as her medication took hold and sleep came. She felt comforted.

At the weekends, Grace found it hard to get back into the old routines on the farm in Mullabeg. There were nieces and nephews there now, growing up before her eyes. She played with them and fought with them. She had more in common with them than with their parents. Grace was still close to her mother, but she could see that her mother was becoming feeble. She was told not to vex her mother with bad behaviour and she did her best. But it seemed like the slightest thing Grace did upset somebody in the house. She went out as much as she could, but there was nothing in Mullabeg. Grace would have been a familiar sight to the neighbours as she walked the lanes and the countryside. She would become anxious as the time came for her to return to Willow Hill. She was as glad to leave Mullabeg on a Sunday evening as the family was to see her go.

Years passed and Grace was finally diagnosed as schizophrenic. She spent time in locked wards and had no freedom to walk unsupervised in the hospital grounds. She was said to be incapable of managing her own affairs. She was on powerful doses of medication to keep her calm and quiet. Occasionally, she would make a break for it, just to get out into the fresh air. But most of the time, Grace did what she was told. She kept her appointments with the doctors. She took her medication. She didn't want bad reports of her behaviour getting back to her brother Francis. He visited her regularly. He told her that their mother was getting weaker and she was losing her hearing. He told her that her brothers had made a bloody mess of the farm and he was working all the hours God sent to put it right. He told her that money was tight and he had nothing to spare for her this week. He handed over a box of 10 cigarettes. He told her to do what she was told and not to give any trouble to the nurses. He told her he would take her out for the weekend as soon as the locked ward restrictions were lifted. He never asked her anything about her life at Willow Hill. He never paid much attention to her friends. But at least he came to see her; that was the main thing for Grace. She got used to looking up to her brother. She tried to remember everything he said to her and to do everything he told her. It wasn't easy, because he wasn't there all the time to remind her. But she did her best.

The times Francis didn't come on a visit, Grace could nearly forget about him. She chatted with her friends and when she was well enough, she went on outings to the town. She enjoyed going to cafes for coffee and cake. She liked to look in the shop windows. She was hardly even aware of people staring at the Willow Hill patients. She would have been nervous on her own, but with all her friends around her, she felt confident. On her good days, nobody would have guessed that she was mad. She was very good looking and she knew it. She had a trim figure and she looked after herself. She especially liked to look good when she went into town. She would catch the eye of a local man and flirt, like any young woman. It made her feel alive. It was hard to get to know men at the hospital. The patients were kept apart most of the time, and there were rules about mixing. But still, Grace managed to attract the attentions of a few of the men around the hospital. It didn't bother her that some of them were considered mad. They were no madder than she was, and most of the time Grace was fine.

When Grace was unwell, she got depressed in herself. She was drowsy and sluggish from the medication. She got used to having everything done for her. She became very dependent on the nurses. Even when she was feeling better, she would ask them to brush her hair, or read to her from the newspaper, or go to the shop for her. Most of all, she wanted their company. She wanted to know if they were going out with anyone, who their families were, if they were going on holidays. If any of the nurses got engaged, Grace would get very excited. She loved to talk about their wedding plans and to admire their engagement rings. She would have loved to get married herself. Now and again, she was allowed to go to the church to see a wedding. Grace became a favourite with the nurses. She was demanding of their time, but they were very fond of her. The nurses meant more to Grace than her own family. Their lives were more real to her.

News came to Mullabeg that Grace was pregnant. She had been a patient at the Willow Hill hospital for about 12 years at the time. She came home for Christmas, 1974, expecting to share her good news. The family was shocked and their reactions split them down the middle. Some of them wanted to hunt down the man who was responsible. Others wanted to let the matter lie. They fought bitterly amongst themselves. They must have realised how little they knew about Grace and her life; out of sight, out of mind, as the saying goes. It was like Grace had a life that was separate from her family and they didn't want to know a thing about it. If she had a boyfriend, nobody in the family knew about him. As far as they were concerned, Grace lived at Willow Hill and the hospital was responsible for her, not her family. The hospital also claimed not to know. The nurses Grace made friends with said they didn't know if she was going with somebody. If he was seeing Grace at the hospital, it should have been easy enough to work out who he was. If he was seeing Grace in Mullabeg, a family member or a neighbour must know him. What other opportunities could Grace have had? Nobody said a word.

The family argued backwards and forwards. At first Grace would tell them nothing. Things were not working out the way she wanted. Nobody was happy for her. Everybody was confusing her with questions.

"Who was it, Grace?" they said, "Who left you like this?" and then they would rant and rave.

"If I could get my hands on the man," they said, "The dirty bastard." She wanted to tell them "No, he's not like that. We love each other." But nobody was listening. In any case, Grace hadn't seen the man since she found out she was pregnant. She wasn't sure if he did still love her. Mrs Donaghy cried when she heard the news. Grace had upset her again when she had not meant to. Grace got distressed and in the end she told her mother and her brother Francis everything. Francis called the family together.

"Nothing," he said, "is to be done about this. My mother wants nothing done about it." The brothers could hardly believe it. Someone had to be held responsible for what had happened to their sister.

"My mother doesn't want to wreck two families over the head of this," Francis told them, as if the pregnancy was nothing. "Grace is going to the nuns. There is to be no more talk about it." Several of the brothers objected, but they were shouted down by Francis. It was none of their business. The decision had been made by their mother and it was final. Francis let it be known that the man responsible was a Protestant. This was what had upset their mother the most, he said. The mid-1970s were the darkest days of the troubles in Northern Ireland and sectarian feelings ran high. It would be better all round for Grace to be sent away and for the family to forget all about it. Nobody asked what was to become of the baby. Francis told Grace never to talk to anybody about the father of her child. If anyone ever questioned her, she was to come to him, and he would tell her what to say.

Some of the brothers were fuming, but they didn't stand up to the "big man" and they didn't want to distress their mother any further. They thought more should have been done for Grace. They suspected that another patient was involved and the hospital should have been held to account for it. They had no doubt that their brother Francis knew the truth of the matter. "Well," they said "If he knows the truth, it will be down to him to handle the truth, whatever way it turns out." They never strayed from their opinion.

Grace's mother spent a lot of time in the chapel, praying for forgiveness for her daughter. It brought shame on the family that Grace had got pregnant outside of marriage. But if the father of the child was a Protestant, the whole family was in disgrace. Mrs Donaghy had turned to her religion in her old age. It was her only comfort in a hard life. She spoke with the nuns at the Good Shepherd Convent in Newry. She arranged for Grace to be discharged from the Willow Hill hospital and taken to Newry. The nuns told her that they were used to handling single mothers. So long as Grace herself was a Catholic, they could overlook the matter of the father of the child being a Protestant. They sympathised with Mrs Donaghy and told her they felt her pain and her shame. Grace would be well looked after and she would work in the laundries during her time with them. The Catholic Family Welfare Society would be on hand when the baby was born. Everything would be taken care of. Mrs Donaghy had no need to worry. They would handle everything and the child would be baptised and reared as a Catholic. For Mrs Donaghy, this was the best that could be expected from a desperate situation.

After Christmas, Grace packed up her things and went to the convent in Newry. She wanted to send word to her baby's father that she would be thinking of him and that he could maybe write to her there. It would be impossible for him to visit. Her brother Francis had told her she was never to see him again. Grace was too frightened to argue. She spent the next six months in Newry, working with other pregnant girls in the laundry. Some of them were right smart girls, who knew everything and who made Grace laugh. They made the pregnancy easier for her. All of the girls were some way in disgrace. Some of them, like Grace, never really had a proper chance in life. Others had big plans for after their babies were born. None of them was going to be allowed to keep her baby.

In the last month of her pregnancy, Grace had high blood pressure. The baby was breach and the doctors decided to deliver it early by Caesarean section. Their medical history of Grace went no further than to say that she was mentally subnormal before and during her pregnancy. She saw her baby and held him for only a minute or two. She said that he was to be named Philip when he was baptised. When she left hospital, she went back to Mullabeg. The baby was never discussed at home. Grace was expected to drop back into life on the farm in Mullabeg. Nobody asked her how she was feeling. The problems that had driven Grace from Mullabeg 13 years earlier returned. The family couldn't cope. One day, a nurse came and brought Grace back to Willow Hill. She was back in the secure wards. Some of her old friends were still there and she was glad to see them. Nobody asked her where she had been. They had got used to Grace coming and going. Nobody even knew that she had had a baby. She never spoke about him. She didn't know where he was at or who was rearing him. She never saw her baby's father again. It was like a dream. Sometimes she believed it had never happened. But at other times, it wrecked her head and she was given more tablets to keep her quiet. This was the shape of Grace's life for years. She was kept from reality with drugs and lies; thousands of tablets over the years to keep her quiet, thousands of lies to keep her from the truth. In time, Grace could hardly tell the truth from fiction. Having a baby was not real for her. It was like reading about it in a book or a magazine. When her baby's father was dying, he sent word to Grace to ask what had become of the wee lad. Grace had nothing to say.

Suddenly, about six years after her baby was born, Grace's visits to her home place stopped. She was told there was no room in the house for her, that the family needed her old bedroom. Her mother had also moved out of the home place and was living with another of her sons. Now and again, Grace would spend a day with her mother. Sometimes she would go for a walk and end up at the home place. She never got over the door on these unexpected visits. The brothers were told by Francis to keep Grace away. It was for her own good, he said. About two years after her visits home stopped, old Mrs Donaghy died. Then, one day, Francis and Bernadette brought a small boy to see Grace at Willow Hill. He had brown hair and big blue eyes, just like Grace's.

"Who is this?" she asked.

"This is Philip," Francis told her "We have adopted him out of the children's home. He is living with us now." The little boy was too shy to speak. Grace tickled him under his chin and he drew back from her. His eyes never left her face, but she paid him no more attention. When she visited Francis and Bernadette, the little boy, Philip, was there. He was among his cousins and he looked just like them. Grace thought that was a good thing. She wasn't involved in any decisions about Philip. She rarely saw him in the years he lived with her brother. When the relationship between Philip and Francis broke down, Grace wasn't told at first. Philip telephoned her from a children's home and Grace told him he was wrong to vex his uncle who had been so good to him, and who had provided a home for him. She wouldn't listen to any stories of harsh treatment. She told Philip to say no more about it. She hung up when he started to ask her questions about his father.

Philip came to see Grace in the hospital. He came with a social worker from the children's home. He was nearly 16 and had grown up tall and healthy. She thought he was very good looking. But she was suspicious of him. He was always asking her about his father and she didn't want to remember any of that. She complained to the nurses and to the social worker. She asked them to keep Philip away. He would get very angry with her and she couldn't deal with it. She would refuse to see him for a while and then he would make contact again. He would promise to behave himself and for a while they would have a nice time together. He always brought her something when he came to visit. But then the old questions would start up again and she thought Philip was very cheeky to her. She fought with him like a child. She refused to tell Philip anything about his past. Her doctors said that was up to her. She contacted Francis and told him about Philip's questions. She always relied on Francis and she would always have been closer to her brother than to her son. The next time Philip visited, she was ready; Francis had said it was okay. Grace told Philip that his father had worked as a nurse at the hospital. Grace said she was in a relationship with the man and that she used to meet him in one of the hospital outbuildings because, she said, he was a married man. Grace had not been able to tell her baby's father that she was going to the convent in Newry. When she got back to Willow Hill, he was gone and she never saw him again. About three years later she got news that he was dying. Philip wanted proof that the man was his father. But Grace had no proof and she got angry with him and sent him away. She told Francis what had happened and Francis said she had done the right thing.

But Philip wouldn't let the matter drop. He kept on and on at her. He wanted to know how a nurse could be in a relationship with a patient. He wanted to know who the man's family was. He wanted to know what the hospital had done about the pregnancy. He wanted to know why Francis was in the middle of it. He said there was some kind of cover up going on and he would not rest until it was all out in the open. Grace felt under pressure and she couldn't cope with all of the questions. She fought with Philip constantly. They stopped seeing each other and then they made up and the whole thing started up again. Grace wasn't happy when Philip told her he was moving to Omagh so that he could find out for himself if she was telling him the truth about his father. She had nothing more to say to him about it. One day she wasn't allowed to leave the ward. A nurse sat with her and told her there were some very cheeky posters somebody had put on the walls of the hospital. Grace just knew it was Philip. Later, she found one of the posters sticking out of a bin. It said "Nurse Rapes Patient and Willow Hill Covers It Up". She was very upset and she told the nurses not to let Philip in to see her for a while. The next time she saw him, she was living in her own flat in sheltered accommodation and Philip was paralysed in a hospital bed.

That is the story of Grace's life, the way I see it, and from what I know. Whatever way you look at it, it is a sad story. I would not like to be in Grace's position in life. I wouldn't swap my life for hers, even if it meant I could be up on my feet walking. Grace never had a chance and she never got the proper support from her family. She is institutionalised having spent the best part of 45 years in a psychiatric hospital. Even though she has her own place in a fold now, she is not suited to it. She gets very lonely and she would rather be back on the wards with company around her than in her own flat with her own things about the place. She has an intercom in her flat and she can call the nurses on it 24 hours a day. Grace depends on them for everything. She would hardly speak out her own opinion without a nurse telling her what to say. I have to go through the nurses any time I want to speak to Grace on the phone. I have to get their permission any time I want to take Grace out for the weekend. They are Grace's family, more than her brothers and sister, more than me.

I feel sorry for Grace in a way. What would it have been like for her if she had the love and support of her family instead of an institution? Grace had a mother and brothers and a sister. Between them, you would think they could have managed to look after one of their own. The doctors might have said that Grace was schizophrenic back years ago, but I think that is a wrong diagnosis. As far as I know, there is no cure for schizophrenia, but they tell me Grace doesn't have it any more. Her brothers say that she used to lose the head and it was deadly. They say she would throw things and break things and become very demanding. They say there was no talking to her. As far as I can see, they are describing normal enough teenage behaviour. I did a bit of wrecking myself in my teenage years, and thank God I was not thrown into a mental hospital for it. I paid the price through the courts and then the slate was wiped clean. Grace was not so lucky. She was thrown into a mental institution for the rest of her life for shouting the odds and breaking a few dishes when she was a teenager. I might have got a criminal record for wrecking Ballee, but it is nothing compared to what Grace has been through. She might as well be in gaol. My behaviour was no better than Grace's at times. My uncle Francis was only too happy to let people know that I was mad, like my mother. Lucky for me, I did most of my wrecking at Ballee Adolescent Unit, otherwise I might have had the same life as Grace. Her mistake was to do her wrecking at home. Once Willow Hill became her home, she had no chance to mature into an adult and to find ways of dealing with her emotional problems. That is why today Grace can still throw a tantrum like a child. She knows no different.

I have heard all I want to hear about things being different in the past. That is no excuse. Far too many people in Ireland were dumped in mental homes by their families and forgotten about. In a loving family, Grace could have continued to live at home until she sorted out her problems. If she never managed to sort herself out, then the family could still have looked after her with a bit of support from the health service. Grace might have needed to be hospitalised from time to time. But she didn't need to spend her whole life in an institution. She didn't need to find herself pregnant in an institution. I know from my time in a children's home whatever problems you go in with stay with you. Grace was a disruptive teenager when she went to Willow Hill, as I was when I went to Ballee Adolescent Unit. 45 years later, and there is still something childlike about Grace. Physically, she has hardly aged. Her skin is clear and pale, with only tiredness around her eyes to tell you the hard life she had. Emotionally, Grace is still a teenager. She is quick to laugh and quick to cry. She can lose her temper in a heartbeat; she can complain and sulk. But she comes round quickly too, she is easily distracted and she loves a bit of banter and joking about. It is as if her emotional clock stopped in 1961 when she went to Willow Hill for the first time.

By the time I was fostered by uncle Francis, Grace had lost her old bedroom at the farmhouse. That was the moment when Willow Hill became her permanent home. I shared Grace's bedroom with my cousin Cathal. Once I came to Mullabeg, there was no room for Grace, even if she had been welcome in her own home. The way I see it, Grace was not welcome. She should have had the chance to live out her days in her home place, but she never got that chance, and she never got the love and support of her family when she needed it most.

Over the years, I have tried to imagine what it must have been like for Grace growing up in a hospital with problems she couldn't fix herself. I have a picture of her hanging in my living room. I think it must have been taken not long before she went to Willow Hill. She is a beautiful looking young girl in the photograph. She is slim and wearing a smart summer dress. She has a shy smile. She looks a bit like me around the eyes, I think. I am sure Grace was the best looking young woman in the hospital. What man wouldn't have wanted to flirt with her and get to know her, maybe take her out for a coffee or something? That is nothing for Grace to be ashamed of, and I like to think of her having a bit of a social life when she was young, even if she was in hospital. But at the same time, she would have been very innocent. Without the support of her family, living up there in Willow Hill, stuffed full of tablets, it would have been easy for strangers to take advantage of her in some way. There would have been nobody to look out for her.

No matter what way I look at it, even on her best days, Grace would have been a very vulnerable woman. I think that should have been obvious to any man, whether she met him at the hospital, or at home on a weekend visit. I wonder if she was really in a position to give her consent to a sexual relationship. If she was not, then I am the product of sexual abuse or even rape and that is a very hard thing to live with. When Grace got pregnant, did she keep it to herself for as long as she could? Did the man wonder where she was at during the time Grace was sent away to the convent in Newry? Did he try to stay in touch with her, or did he forget all about her? One thing I do know, my father never tried to contact me. If he is the man that Grace has told me about, he had a couple of years before he got sick to find out about me. Grace said she was in a relationship with this man. Maybe she was in love with him. But if he is my father, he was not free to be in a relationship with my mother. First, he had a duty of care towards her as a long-term patient in the hospital where he worked. Second, he was already married to somebody else and he has a daughter the same age as me. Since the man is dead, I sometimes think to myself that it was very easy to pin my mother's pregnancy on him. He has no way of defending himself. There is no proof other than the word of Grace and her brother Francis. No other man's name has ever been mentioned to me. If my father is somebody else, then it is a very closely guarded secret. If he is a neighbour from around Mullabeg, he must have seen me all those years when I was fostered. Maybe I was harshly treated in my foster home because I reminded the family of someone in their own community who had taken advantage of Grace. Whoever he is, my father never bothered about me. At the end of the day, I was just an accident.

Grace was left to bring a child into the world on her own, with no man in her life and no family to support her. She had her mental illness to deal with and she had no proper home to rear a child in. My uncles have said to me, "Look Philip, there is no way Grace could have reared you. She wasn't fit to do it. She was hardly able to look after herself." But what support did Grace get to reach that decision? She was sent away to a convent to live with other single mothers. All of them had to give up their babies. They were not given any guidance whatsoever about rearing children. There was no point to it. None of them were going to get the chance. But for Grace, and for some of those other girls, maybe it was their dream to have a child. How many of them are sitting today wondering about the son or daughter they had to give up 30 years ago? Some of those girls might have gone on to get married and have families later in their lives. But Grace didn't. I was her only chance to be a mother and I wonder what kind of a mother she might have been.

I hope that all those other babies had a better upbringing than I did. Probably all of them were adopted. I say to myself, could it have been any worse if Grace had tried to rear me herself? I don't think it could have been worse. I am sure I would have been in care during the times Grace was sick; it would not have been an easy life. I would probably have had some of the same problems. But when Grace was well, it might have been a good life. I would definitely have got to know her better if she had been around me more when I was a child. I would love and trust her more than I do now. I might have known the truth about my father. I might have found out about him when I was a young boy and it would not be wrecking my head now. But I am lucky in a way; at least I got to meet my mother. Our relationship is not really a good one, but I do the best I can and I will never abandon Grace. I will make sure that she is looked after for the days that are left to us. We have not gone through life together, but we have been through too many hard times to give up on each other now.

I try to understand the position Grace found herself in all those years ago when she was pregnant. I can't blame her for giving me up. She had no choice in the matter. If I have lost out by never being loved by my mother, then so has Grace. She never had the chance to love and rear her own child. But I think Grace could have been more involved in my life. The health service and social services could have helped her even if her own family would not. There must be plenty of women like Grace now who are given the chance to rear their children, even if they do need extra help. I was not given up for adoption, so Grace would have had the right to come and see me in St Joseph's Children's Home. But she never did. She should have been consulted about her brother Francis fostering me. She would probably have agreed to it, even though I think it was the biggest mistake ever made in my life. But she was not consulted. She was not even told about it until two years later, after her mother died. I was 8 years old at the time, and probably Grace hadn't given me a thought for most of those years. All of a sudden, there I was at the hospital visiting her. She must have got the shock of her life. She had no preparation for it. When I think about it now, it seems like a very heartless thing to do to a vulnerable patient in a hospital, to bring in her 8 year old son, who was taken away from her at birth. You wouldn't do it to a dog. All through my life, there were times when Grace should have and could have been involved in decisions about my care. I might have been able to turn to her and confide in her when I was in trouble. She might have been able to help me with love and support. Instead, I was taught to keep things from her and not to upset her in any way. She never got involved.

It has made for a very unnatural relationship. In some ways, Grace is the child and I am the parent. I am the one who makes decisions and plans in life. I am the one with financial independence. I am the one living in my own home with bills to pay and staff to manage. I am the one who makes contact with Grace for a chat or a visit. I am the one who makes arrangements with the hospital to take her out for the weekend. Grace is the dependent child that all these things happen to. Her life has a shape and a routine that she is used to. She has practically no responsibilities. Willow Hill and the fold are her home and her family. God knows, she has more contact with the doctors and nurses than she has with her blood relations. The world outside Willow Hill is more of a threat to Grace. At the end of the day, her security is in hospital and it is likely that she will see out her days there. I used to think that I would like to take Grace out permanently and set her up in her own place in Cookstown or Moneymore or Magherafelt, some place familiar to her from her young life. I think it is too late for that now. It would be too stressful for Grace. All that I can do now is to make sure she is well looked after and comfortable and as happy as she can be. She might complain that I could do more for her. Her brothers tell her that I am the man with the money and she should ask me if she wants anything. I hope I would never leave Grace in need of anything, but at the same time, I am not Santa Claus. She treats me like an entertainment or a distraction sometimes, and not like a son. I also think that Grace's brothers and her sister could have done far more for her over the years than I can ever do. It is not just about having money. It is about investing the time to love and support a sister who has had more than her fair share of troubles.

When Grace comes to my home for a visit, it has to be carefully planned. I need to get permission from the hospital and arrange suitable times to pick Grace up and leave her back. As well as that, I have to make my own preparations. I need to be in the best of health. I would not want Grace to be there if I am sick in my bed. I have to make sure I have a driver available. Somebody has to be there to cook Grace's meals and make her cups of tea and coffee. Somebody has to help her to settle for the night and to have her breakfast ready in the morning. I am not able to do any of those things for Grace and I need to work them out with a staff member well in advance. At my home, Grace is more or less housebound, because that is how I live. She can become quite anxious and I think she would like to be taken out into the town more. She doesn't seem to understand that I can't just get up and go. It is not that easy for me. It comes back to the same old thing: me and Grace don't understand each other because we never had that early connection in life. It comes down to the same thing that has been with me all my life. When I need support and advice on what to do with my life, I am on my own. I am no more the son that Grace wants than she is the mother I need.

What can a disabled bastard do?

When Dr McCann in the Musgrave Park Hospital told me that it was down to me how I was going to live my life, it really affected me. I had been feeling like there were no choices open to me. I was paralysed. I would never walk again. I couldn't hardly talk. I couldn't do anything for myself. I needed nursing staff to look after my most personal care 24 hours a day. I was also bored out of my head. I had nothing to do, and nothing to keep my brain active. What choices did I have? How was I going to live my life? I looked around me at other patients in the hospital and I saw that some of them had just about given up. They were defined by their injuries and disabilities. They allowed themselves to be poked and prodded by nurses. They were smothered by the pity of family members. In the end their whole world was contained in a hospital ward. That was not for me. Every ounce of strength I had left said "no" to that kind of life. I thought of my mother and her life sentence in an institution. I thought of all the times I had been told I would end up just like my mother. Lying in hospital in Belfast, I felt close to it and it scared the wits out of me. I wanted more from my life than that.

Some people with disabilities are embarrassed of themselves, and don't want to speak out about the conditions they have to live in. You never see those people. Some people with disabilities have families who are embarrassed of them, who keep them hidden away and don't speak out on their behalf. My own mother, Grace, has been hidden away all her adult life because of mental illness. Some people with disabilities are so protected by their families that they become helpless and don't speak out for what they want to achieve in life. They feel too grateful to their families for the care they receive and they end up being smothered and can hardly think for themselves. I have no family to fall back on for my care. That is a fact and in some ways, it is a good thing. A loving family might just wrap me up in cotton wool and make me too afraid or too helpless to try anything for myself. The way I look on it, I probably wouldn't have taken on the challenges of trying to live an independent life if I had a family to look after me. I always try to increase the number of things I can do for myself. A supportive family might have taken that fighting spirit away by doing everything for me and I wouldn't want to live that way. I always have goals and dreams to aim for to keep me motivated. I also speak out my opinion on how I have to live. I do get embarrassed of myself, plenty of times, but I think it is more important for people to know what disabled people have to go through. I don't mind using myself as the example if it will help somebody.

I remember living in a nursing home and being hoisted, half-naked, from my room down the corridor to the shower. When the nurse got me there, there was already somebody in the shower and we had to wait outside until they were finished, me hanging there in the hoist and a wee nurse talking to me. Anybody could have been passing through that corridor, staff, residents, visitors, delivery men. I was that embarrassed of myself and I could do nothing about it, except wait for an elderly person to finish in the shower. Ask yourself this question, "I*s that how you would like to take a shower every day, queuing up in a corridor and hanging half-naked from a hoist in full view of passers-by?*" If the answer is, "No", then why would you accept those conditions for your elderly and disabled neighbours? How are their needs any different to yours? The way I see it, the accident took away my dignity but how I am treated in public as a disabled person takes away my humanity at times. If people want to know why I put myself out in the public eye, it is to remind people that there is more to me than my disability. Being paralysed doesn't make me any less of a human being.

As I was trying to come to terms with what my new life as a disabled person would be like, I requested a move from Belfast to St John's Hospital in Sligo. I wanted to be near Sr. Paula and near my friends in Sligo again. I wanted to take myself back to a time in my life when I was happy, I suppose. To a certain extent, I was running away from my problems. I knew what I didn't want from my life, but I still couldn't face the future. I planned to make Sligo my permanent home. It was the town where I became an independent young man and I thought it would work its magic on me again. While I was trying to think about what kind of a future I would have, I kept getting distracted by friends and family members who could think of nothing better to say than, "You'll walk again, Philip, if you put your mind to it." That was just oul' crap and I knew it. It was doing my head in to listen to it. I had to start thinking of a future where walking wasn't an option. I was hopeful that one day there would be a medical breakthrough for people with spinal cord injuries, but there was no point in lying around waiting for it. It was a long way off and what was I going to do in the meantime? I had to think of things to do that would bring me a sense of achievement in my life now, the way it is, not the way it was or the way it might be. I definitely didn't want to turn into some kind of a vegetable, waiting for the miracle cure and dependent on other people for everything. There was nothing wrong with my brain and I knew I would have to use it or lose it, as the saying goes.

Although I was living among elderly people in Sligo, St John's was a brilliant hospital. It prepared me for the good and the bad aspects of needing 24-hour nursing care. I was no longer sick. I didn't need any particular medical treatment. I just needed to build up my strength and immunity and then get used to a life being paralysed from the chest down. I had to get used to all the things people would have to do for me that I used to be able to do for myself. It was the hardest thing, having to rely on strangers for everything. I think it was especially hard for me who never had anyone to rely on when I was growing up. I never got into the habit of depending on people. It was not easy for me to put my full trust in people. But here I was in St John's, watching a wee nurse half my size getting ready to hoist me out of the wheelchair and I was terrified at times she would let me fall. She never did, but it was hard for me to trust that she wouldn't drop me the next time. Being anxious about it probably made me harder to hoist than if I had just relaxed and let the girl do the job she was trained to do.

One day in St John's, I just broke down. I had spent weeks after Musgrave trying to be positive, and trying to take heart in the tiny little things I could do by myself. I kept pushing myself to work harder and achieve more. But it wasn't easy. This particular day, I was being hoisted out of my wheelchair and into the shower. The nurse helping me was Harry Gallagher. I caught sight of myself in the bathroom mirror, suspended in a thing that looked like a sumo wrestler's nappy. My thin legs were just hanging there, useless. I could hardly believe the pathetic looking creature in the mirror was me. I had been a fit young lad who enjoyed his football. I looked like a wasted pipe cleaner in the mirror. There was no strength in my legs to kick a football the length of myself, even if I still had the ability to do it, which, of course, I didn't. I was suddenly filled with despair. "*Look at the shape of me!*" I said to myself, "*What can I do that will make a difference to anybody or anything? There is nothing I can do, nothing. I was a bastard before, but now I'm a dirty, disabled bastard."* Harry just let me cry my eyes out. He didn't say a word. He knew what was going through my mind. He could see for himself what my physical shape was like. He gave me the space and the time to get it out of my system. Then, when I was done, he lit a cigarette, handed it to me and I smoked it. It was the best cigarette of all time. Thank you Harry Gallagher. I don't smoke any more, but I often think of that cigarette when I am feeling down in the dumps. I am not a one for tears, especially in front of people. In fact, I think that time in St John's was the first time I broke down in tears since the accident. But I will always remember Harry Gallagher and how he just knew exactly the right thing to do for me when I was at one of my lowest points. I have had many moments of despair since my accident, but something or someone always appears to make me feel better about myself. That time, it was Harry Gallagher.

Sometimes, in Sligo, I would sit in my wheelchair watching the cars speeding by on the Ballytivnan Road. I would think to myself, *"It would be so easy to just pitch myself out into the road under the traffic and end it all."* One day a group of nurses was watching me. They were worried enough to come rushing down to get me. But the very next day, I was back on the side of the road watching the traffic and thinking things through. There was another patient in St John's who had been in a crash, a married man, who took to the drink after his accident. He couldn't cope with being disabled and feeling useless to his family. In the end, he wrecked his family with drink, not with his disability. When I looked at myself, I thought *"Well, I have no family to wreck and I have a massive disability, but my brain is still working. There must be something I can do."* I knew I was better off than that poor alcoholic man. I thought of all the people in my life who expected me to come to nothing. I had to prove those people wrong, even though it might have been easier to just play on their sympathies for the rest of my life.

I decided I had to stick around long enough to show them that I am somebody. I had to see the look on their faces when mad, bad Philip became a success story. I had that fighting spirit even in those dark days in Sligo. Suicide would have proved nothing. People would just have shaken their heads and forgotten about me. Don't get me wrong, there are still days when I think "*What am I still doing here?*" The day I can't answer that question is the day I will do something to end my life, but Sligo was definitely a turning point for me. Maybe the town was working its magic on me again after all.

I experienced something of a miracle when I was in St John's, but I couldn't really tell anyone about it. I am sure Sr. Paula would have loved to be close to a miracle, but when she reads about this one, she might change her mind. One day my friend Tom Magill came down from Cookstown to visit me. Although I was feeling quite strong and healthy in myself, Tom didn't think I looked that great. He was a bit worried about me as he took me outside for a smoke. My neck was giving me a lot of trouble at the time. I wasn't able to control it properly and my head flopped over like a flower; my neck just wouldn't support it. Me and Tom went outside and smoked a marijuana joint, quickly, for fear of being caught by the nurses. It felt good, but we smoked it too fast and I felt a bit light in the head. When I had finished the joint and didn't know if I was feeling mellow or sick, I raised my head and tried to straighten up my neck. I heard and felt a massive click. I thought the whole town must have heard it. For a minute I thought I had snapped my neck in two, but no, my neck clicked back into position and that is where it has stayed ever since. You can understand why I kept quiet about my wee miracle.

My solicitors, Logan and Corry, back in Omagh, were working with me at this time to prepare a case for the insurance claim we had lodged because of my accident. It took the best part of four years to get it all settled, and that was with me constantly harassing the legal teams to get moving. It kept me busy and motivated and it felt good to see progress being made, knowing that I was part of the team pushing the thing on. Although the case was about my disability, working on it was the first thing I did where my disability didn't hold me back. What I mean by that is, sitting on the wheelchair didn't stop me from ringing up the solicitors to discuss the case and tell them what I was planning. A lot of cases like mine take much longer than four years to settle. I was living in limbo during that time, not knowing what way it would end up. When the settlement was finally made, all the nursing homes lined up with their bills looking for their share. I had to go to court in Dublin to explain and defend the estimated costs of my care. Line by line, we had to justify every cent. I remember we were even questioned about the type of toothbrush I used, and what it cost. I was well able to speak up for myself, but the worst thing about being in court was that the judge didn't look at me or talk to me directly. It was as if he thought I was not all there, as if I couldn't speak up for myself. I have learned a lot of disabled people are treated like that. But it was my body that wasn't working properly, not my brain. It didn't take me long to let the judge know that. I was not about to be ignored by someone in authority. This was my future life he was passing judgement on. If the judge had any idea of my background, he would have known to look me in the eye and talk to me, man to man. But I was a stranger to him, just some poor bastard in a wheelchair. I think a criminal on a murder charge would get more respect in a court room than I did. It was hard to believe that I was the innocent victim of an accident, the way I was treated. The central part of the court case was about where I would live. I had been living in hospitals and nursing homes around the country ever since I had the accident. I had already decided that I wanted my own home. That was a hell of a decision for a man who never had a proper home in his life. I knew it would be hard to achieve, but it was the first of many dreams that kept me going for five years or so after the accident. In my mind, I saw my mother living on a hospital ward all her adult life and what that had done to her. I didn't want that kind of a life for myself. I told myself that living in a nursing home was okay for a short while, but I fought against becoming institutionalised. I think that is why I moved around so much, from nursing home to nursing home.

In court, one argument stated that I should make a nursing home my permanent home, since I seemed to be well enough settled and I would get the right level of care. If a deal could be struck with a nursing home, it might have worked out cheaper for the insurance companies. It was all I could do to stop myself shouting out, "No way!" But Feargal Logan put his hand on my arm and told me to sit tight while the counter-argument was made. In the end, we agreed on a settlement which meant that I could start looking for a home of my own.

People say to me "Ah, Philip, you're the man with the money." I say to those people, "How much money would you want to take my position in life?" That fairly shuts them up. Yes, I got a financial settlement; a reasonable sum of money that has to last me the rest of my life. It's not linked to inflation or a pension plan. It's not protected in any way, other than by me being careful about how I use it. I am not like a lottery winner who goes on a spending spree. What use is money to me at the end of the day? What can I buy that is any use to me? My money is for my care. That is my only priority.

The first thing I did was go looking for a home of my own, where I could learn to live my life as a disabled man. Although I met some great people in the nursing homes, both staff and residents, a nursing home was not the right place for me to make my home. I needed to get out and about. I needed a bit of craic in my life. I wanted visitors at any time of the day or night. I wanted to go to the pubs once in a while and come home roaring drunk. I wanted to play my music really loud. I was still a young lad in my twenties, after all, and I was living with 90 year olds most of the time. In a nursing home, I had to abide by their rules and think of the other residents all the time. I was able to do that, but everybody needs to let go now and again. It was very restricting to live my life under the rules and routines of a nursing home. Plus, they didn't have the specialist equipment I needed and they couldn't justify the expense of buying it for the benefit of only one person. I understood that in a way, but I was paying £400 and £500 a week to stay in places that weren't properly equipped to care for me. I had to buy my own shower chair in the end, and while I am on the subject, the general public has no idea how expensive equipment for disabled people is. In my opinion, disabled people get ripped off, big time. When I needed intensive physiotherapy and massage, I had to look elsewhere because it was not part of the care package offered by the nursing homes. I was paying for care and I was paying for all the so-called "extras" that I needed to keep me fit and healthy. I was paying for taxis to take me out so that I could meet friends and have some kind of a social life. A nursing home was not the place for me. It might have worked out cheaper for me to live in a nursing home, but cost was only part of it. It was about quality of life too and having as normal and independent a life as I could.

In the nursing homes, I met some great people. In one of the places, my key worker was Michelle Brown, who I got on really well with. Michelle is English and I used to call her the UDR woman. But on the days Michelle was not working, my key worker could be someone I didn't really know. That made life difficult for me and for the staff at the nursing home. I was a lovely cooperative chap with the people I knew well, and a pain in the backside with the people I didn't know. Michelle was my key worker for two years. We became good friends and we used to go for a drink together. I knew Michelle's partner, Paul, and her children too. Michelle understood me, and she knew how I felt on the days I was down in the dumps and didn't want to talk. She got on with what she had to do and she just accepted it if I was in bad form. Michelle also helped me with personal things, like buying presents for people, or writing letters, or helping me to organise a holiday. I still keep in touch with Michelle and we see each other when we can. People are busy these days. Some of the people I met in my time at the nursing homes said they would keep in touch, but it never happened. I might see them the odd time in the street and they are friendly and that, but they don't come to visit me, or ask me to go out for a coffee or a drink. It makes me appreciate the ones who have kept in touch even more, like Michelle.

After my court case, I moved up North again to Mid-Ulster. I had thought I would settle in Sligo, but when it came to it something pulled me to the North. Sr. Paula said to me, "That is where your family is, Philip, of course you would want to be in the North." But that wasn't the way I saw it. It was more to do with the fact that there was unfinished business relating to my background and I was only likely to get it cleared up by being in the North. I have to admit though that some members of my family got a bit closer to me while I was in rehabilitation in the North. Some of my cousins that I grew up with in Mullabeg were good visitors. Sr. Paula reminds me of that now and again and I have to thank them for that.

Sr. Paula was still a regular visitor herself. She encouraged me to go to the shrine in Lourdes, France, on a pilgrimage. I couldn't go on my own and I asked Karen Mitchell from the nursing home to go with me. It felt like I was asking her on a date and I felt very nervous about it; what if she said no? Plus, going to Lourdes would be the first time in my life I had ever been on an airplane, and I was worried about that too. Karen was another lovely worker and I was good friends with her. She said she would come with me and I was right and glad she was sitting next to me on that plane. I knew I wouldn't like flying and I was right. We had a great time in Lourdes. I stayed in a hospital that had the right facilities for me and Karen stayed in a hotel down the road. We went out for dinner in the evenings and I felt like a normal person. When Karen had got me settled back at the hospital for the night, she would go back to her hotel and then phone me to tell me she had arrived back safely. She was a lovely, thoughtful girl. Karen wouldn't get into the holy water spa, but I did. I didn't expect a miraculous cure or anything like that, but I also didn't expect to be as moved as I was by the experience. There were people in the water at Lourdes who would soon be dead. I could see it in their faces. Lourdes was their last hope. By comparison, I was healthy. The experience, once again, made me appreciate what I have in life, rather than getting down in the dumps about what I have lost. I hope those people got some comfort. I only went to Lourdes because Sr. Paula was giving me grief, but I am very glad I did because it gave me new hope for the future.

When I came back from Lourdes, my mind was made up. The search for a house was on. I had never had a home in my life. I thought of all the rented flats and bedsits I had lived in since I left care. I thought of my foster home and the children's homes. I thought of the nursing homes and hospitals. I was done with all of that. I wanted a home of my own. I was sitting in the nursing home with the clothes on my back, a CD player and a heap of equipment for a disabled person. That was the sum total of my worldly goods. Who knows how things would have turned out if I hadn't had the accident? I like to think I would have married Rachel Desmond and we would have bought our own home and raised a family. That didn't happen, but the dream was still alive. I was a familiar sight in Mid-Ulster, spinning round on my wheelchair, looking at houses and planning how they could be converted to become a dream home for a disabled young person.

As I went round different places looking at houses, I started to notice other disabled people struggling in manual wheelchairs. There were a good few hilly places in the towns of Mid-Ulster and some of the footpaths were very uneven. It was okay for me, I could drive the wheelchair on the roads if I had to, but people in manual wheelchairs couldn't do that so easily. As well as that, some of the shops and cafés in the towns were in older style buildings with no decent access for disabled people. I had a state of the art electric wheelchair and I found it tricky enough to get about the town. It really angered me to see disabled people struggling in manual wheelchairs just to get their bit of business done. Sometimes I saw an elderly parent pushing their disabled son or daughter in a manual wheelchair, and they looked worn out. Why can't the health service provide electric wheelchairs for all disabled people? A manual wheelchair might be fine for getting about the house or into the next door neighbour for a chat and a cup of tea. It might be good for building muscle tone in some disabled people. But it is no good for going down the street and around the town. The disabled person has to work so hard on getting from A to B that there is no time or energy left to stop and say hello to the people passing by. That is one of the reasons why people get used to ignoring the disabled and not passing the time of day with them. They see them struggling and they think, "God luck to them" and walk on. That's the kind of attitude I have got used to fighting. There are not too many people who get away with ignoring Philip Donaghy.

I spotted my dream house by chance. I was looking at the house behind it, when I saw a for sale sign through the hedge. I went and introduced myself to the people who owned the house, accidentally knocking over the for sale sign with my wheelchair on my way in. I took that as a good omen. I realised straight away that the house could be perfect for me. The family had converted the garage into a granny flat and I could see a lot of potential in that. At that stage, I was still waiting for the insurance settlement to come through, so I hadn't a penny to my name. It makes me laugh now to think of myself going round looking at houses to buy, knowing that my pockets were empty. Anyway, with the famous Philip Donaghy charm, I managed to persuade the vendors to hang on for a few months until I had the money to buy their house. I have to give them credit and thanks because they took their house off the market for me, and waited without a deposit or any kind of guarantee until I was ready to move. But I had given them my word, and they trusted that I would honour it. That was the important point about the deal, trust.

At first, I didn't tell anyone about my plans. Danny Byrne used to say to me "Watch and listen, Philip, watch and listen." That is very good advice. When I started to focus on my plans for the future, everyone had an opinion. "Do this, Philip, do that." I don't think anybody thought it was a great idea for me to live alone in my own home. "What if something happened to you in the middle of the night, Philip?" they said, "You would be better off with people around you." My foster family visited me regularly at the nursing homes. In the early days of my rehabilitation, I appreciated them being there and it relieved the boredom for me too. One of my cousins was a nurse and she was very good about taking me out for trips and visits and making sure that I was properly looked after. It was good in a way to get closer to my cousins. But I was still very wary of my uncle Francis. As I started to get stronger in myself, I took Danny Byrne's advice to heart. I was watching and listening, big time. I think my uncle Francis seriously thought I would go back and live in Mullabeg. He even broke down crying on one of the visits and told me he had a great pity for me sitting in a wheelchair. He said he was sorry if he had treated me harshly in the past, and that he treated me no different than his own children. He offered to sell me a site to build on near the home place in Mullabeg. That way, I would have my own home but with family members close by. I admit I let him think I was interested. But the alarm bells were ringing in my ears. I don't know what it was, but I knew

I would be like a fly stepping into a spider's web if I went back to Mullabeg.

Some of my old neighbours from Mullabeg used to come to see me in one of the nursing homes I was in. One of them was talking to me one day about my injuries and I was describing what it was like to be paralysed. He said to me, "But what about the head injury, Philip?"

"What head injury?" I said.

"They say you have a head injury, you know, like your brain."

"Who says that?" I had a pretty good idea who said it. "Listen," I said, "Just so you know. I don't have a head injury or a brain injury. There is nothing wrong with me behind or above the eyes. You can tell that to anyone who says I have a head injury, alright?"

There is a saying I like to follow that goes, "Keep your friends close and keep your enemies closer". I realised I would have to keep my plans for the future very close to my chest and make sure that nobody could interfere. What if the people selling the house got wind of the idea that I was brain injured? Would they trust me then? Who would blame them if they decided to pull out of the deal? The next time uncle Francis came to visit me, I was ready for him.

"How much are you looking for the site?" I said to him.

"Don't worry about that til the house is built," he said to me, "We'll sort it out later."

I think the man must have really believed I had gone soft in the head. As if I would hand over money to live next to him. He probably would have put his two oldest sons on the building work and taken money from me for that too. The thought of being a neighbour of Francis Donaghy made me laugh. He had no time for his neighbours and he had never had any time for me. But I went along with the scheme to a certain extent. All the time though, I had an offer made on a house. It put uncle Francis off the scent. I was acting on good advice: I was watching and listening. His tears were not enough to make me trust the man, let alone forgive the man or forget about what he had done to me in the past. You can forgive, but you never forget. That is my experience. Once I knew I had the house I wanted, I told uncle Francis to shove his site and I threw him out of the nursing home. I have hardly seen him since. He is not welcome in my home. I am sure he was ripping to think he lost out on a pile of money from his brain damaged nephew for his oul' site, and I thought to myself, "*Just wait and see. I'll have the last laugh.*"

When I bought my house, I signed up an architect to do the conversion work, Collie McGurk. I knew exactly what I wanted to do. I turned the granny flat into my bedroom. I built on a steam room and a shower room to the back of the house. I had an electric hoist put in. All the doorways were made extra wide for the wheelchair. The overall design of the house was open plan. There was a room for massage and exercise. There was a living room, bedroom and bathroom for a full-time carer. There was a sitting room for visitors. I had a beautiful landscaped terrace and garden. I had a computer system installed that provided CCTV and security. I could control my gates, front door, TV, music and intercom using a PDA. My good friend Rodney Stewart designed and installed the system. I spent a fortune on it but it was worth it for the independence it gave me and the control I had over my living space. Doing the electronics in my home was a first for Rodney. He was used to installing sound and lighting systems in nightclubs and cinemas. He had never had a residential customer and he had never had a paralysed customer. Rodney worked with me and the architect and we hit it off straight away. I didn't know Rodney before my accident, so he never knew the "old" Philip. But he is another friend who just takes me as I am, as Philip. If I pass a remark on him, he passes it right back. He is straightforward and he treats me like a normal person. We have an ongoing joke about tea. I drink

Earl Grey tea because it doesn't clog up the catheter. When Rodney comes round he calls me Earl Gay and I call him my boyfriend.

It makes me feel good to be able to open my doors to my visitors and to welcome them into my home. I can see them arriving on my TV screen. As soon as they get out of their cars, my front doors swing open. They walk into my house and if I am not there to greet them, I hear them calling me, "Philip, where are you at?" and they walk through the house on marble floors and everything is modern and tidy and brand new. I have furniture in that house I can never use, so it is in mint condition. I didn't want a home that looks like a hospital. I keep my disabled equipment out of sight when visitors are there, except for the wheelchair. My house is like a normal home, better than a normal home, because I spared no expense on design and interiors. I think of myself boiling an egg in the kettle when I lived in Greenvale Drive. I think of the lumpy old second hand furniture I had back then. Who would have thought that I would be able to oversee the building and furnishing of my own home? I had to prove to myself and everyone else that I was capable of leading as normal a life as possible. It costs a lot of money, but it is worth it to see how people react when they first walk into my home. It makes me feel proud of myself to know that I achieved all this myself.

It took just 14 weeks to complete the conversion of the house and I was on-site regularly making sure the work was being done right. I had a new roof put on the house and new windows were put in. Very few people knew what was going on. The staff at the nursing home in Magherafelt knew I was planning a move, but they thought I was going back to Sligo to St John's. I was happy enough for them to think that. The last thing I would have wanted was social workers crawling all over my house telling me, "You can't have this, Philip. You can't have that." Just a few days before I moved into the new house, I contacted the local newspaper and radio station, and they were there when I officially opened the doors to my new home. When I left the nursing home for the last time, I said to the receptionist,

"Margaret, I'm off to my new house now. I am finished with nursing homes for good."

"Philip," she said, "You are a shrewd man. Good luck to you."

"I kept you all going and you know I'll always have the last laugh," I said

I hosted my house-warming party on the first year anniversary of moving in. It took me that long to get fully settled and to know in my own heart that I had made the right move and that it would all work out. As well as being a sound and systems expert, Rodney Stewart was in a band called Juice, and they did the music for me at the party. I invited everyone I knew, except my uncle Francis and aunt Bernadette. A lot of people thought that was a spiteful thing to do. By not inviting them, I was sending a clear message: "You are not welcome in my home." To this day, they are not welcome in my home. I am not ashamed to say it; I would not even call them my family any more.

My mother, Grace, came to my party and met neighbours from Mullabeg she hadn't seen for 40 years. She remembered them all. She remembered things about them they had forgotten themselves. Grace is sharp and she has a nearly photographic memory for details. Sr. Paula came and met some of my family, including my mother, for the first time. Sr. Paula has always liked my family and it is her wish that I could be reconciled with them all. The Magill and Byrne families came. Uncles and cousins came. I had been to school with a local chef and he did the catering for me. There was champagne on ice and I got blocked on it. I had a great time and it was an unforgettable party. I am glad I invited the neighbours because it was a long and noisy night. Best of all, I organised every detail of it myself. I was quickly learning that my disability was not holding me back in every way. There were plenty of things I could do.

All the time I was planning my home, I was also involved in another aspect of my life that has become important to me since my accident. I have been active in road safety work. Sometimes I would be sitting in a nursing home watching the traffic on the road outside and I would get so angry when I saw people speeding or driving like lunatics. I had got over the feeling I had in Sligo that it would be easy to just fall into the road and end it all. That feeling had become anger and also concern that people were just so ignorant when it came to road safety. I could see them taking stupid risks, never thinking of the consequences. Sometimes I would go out on the road in my wheelchair, put the hazard lights on, and literally challenge the cars to slow down or run me over. People just don't think when they get into a car. They're late, they're busy and they think it will never happen to them. I thought it would never happen to me, and look at me now. People say, "It is a blessing you are alive, Philip" and it is a blessing I am alive, I never forget that. But take a look at my life. How many people would think life is a blessing if they had to live as I do? I have fewer friends than I had when I was walking. Some of the old crowd just can't take me in a wheelchair, and who could blame them? My social life has gone down the pan because there are so few places I can get into now. I don't have a girlfriend because I think most women are embarrassed of me and don't know what to say to me when I am out. I have to rely on strangers to wash me and clean my shit. It is hard to live this life, no matter how grateful I feel, it is damn hard. But still there are people drink-driving, speeding, stealing cars, killing and disabling people on the roads. I just want to make people think about what they are doing when they get into a car. I want them to think about the injured victims and what way they have to live day-to-day. It annoys me when I hear that a drink driver gets banned off the road for a year or two years. They should be banned off the road for life. They should feel it every day when they are standing at a bus-stop in the rain waiting to go to their work. They should feel it every day when they have to rely on their friends to take them places, what fucking idiots they were the day they decided to drink and drive.

On the rare occasions that I do get out for a night I look around me at all the young boys in their fancy clothes meeting their friends and looking for women in the bars about the town. I am jealous in a way, because I was exactly like them until it was all taken off me. I see those young chaps in their fancy cars, out for their good times at the weekends and I feel like saying to them,

"You think you have it all, don't you, young lads? Well let me tell you something. I have something you can only dream about. I have women all over me every day of my life, and all they want to do is to take the trousers off me. Think of that, young lads. Do you like the idea of that? I'll bet you do. And you are well on your way to getting it too. Just you carry on into that bar and have a few drinks. Find yourself a nice woman and smash up your car on the way home. If you're lucky, you will have the life I have. And let me tell you, you will hate every minute of it. The women are only pulling down your trousers to clean your ass. You will never be able to take a shit the normal way again. You will never be able to piss right. You will need someone to take your clothes off you and your shoes. You will need someone to put the shampoo on your hair and the body wash on your facecloth. You will need someone to dry you and put on your deodorant and after shave, and clean out your ears with ear buds, and put toothpaste on your toothbrush. You will need someone to put your clothes back on you and hoist you into your wheelchair to sit for 10 hours a day. That is the ordeal I live with seven days a week. Think about it young lads, is that what way you want to end up when you go out drinking at the weekend? And if it's not you that is left paralysed, maybe it will be one of your mates or your girlfriend whose life you wreck with drinking and driving. Could you live with that, young lads?"

That is what I wanted to say to people, but the only problem was I had no way of reaching people to make my point. I had to find a way.

It is a terrible thing when people die on the roads. It is terrible for their families and friends left behind, wondering why this has happened. They become obsessed with "what ifs?" What if their son or daughter hadn't gone out that night? What if their husband or wife had taken a different route? What if their father or mother had set off just 5 minutes earlier? What if everyone wasn't in such a damn hurry all the time? I have met the people left behind on many different occasions. I understand what it is like for them.

I sometimes think, and it is not a popular opinion, that people like me are forgotten about. We are the living victims of road carnage, not the statistics. Unlike the dead, we can talk back and speak out about what we are going through. Everyone wants to shake their heads about the terrible waste of a life cut short. It seems to be harder for people to accept the idea of a person, still living, but with serious injuries to deal with and no hope of making a full recovery. People like me, who were walking for so many years of their life, and who are now sitting paralysed on a wheelchair with strangers coming in every day to clean their shit. I know what they are thinking half the time: "He'd be better off dead, poor chap." I have had that thought myself, plenty of times since my accident. But I would say to people, just because you think I have no quality of life, it doesn't mean you are right. Just because you wouldn't like to be in my position in life, don't write me off. I don't like it either, but there it is, that's life. Don't just stare through me when you meet me in the street in my wheelchair, as if I was already dead or a ghost. I am not dead. I am still a person with a life and with opinions. I am just the same as you when I go down the street or into the town. I would like for people to say hello, to talk about the weather, to ask me how I am. You might be thinking to yourself "God luck to him, poor chap". But at least give me the chance to pass the time of day with you, maybe even surprise you by putting a smile on your face.

When I go into the town on the wheelchair, I say hello to everyone I meet. That way people get to know me, and I don't feel like such a freak when I go out. Some days I might not be in the form for talking. Some days I am just embarrassed of myself and feel everyone is staring at me and thinking "Poor bastard". But most of the time, if people are friendly to me, then I am friendly back. The staff in the places I go to in Mid-Ulster know me now and most of them go out of their way to help me or chat to me when they see me coming into their business. I always have a good line of chat for the female assistants in the shops. I haven't met a young girl yet who doesn't like to hear a man telling her she is beautiful. But as soon as I see that look on someone's face that says, "Is he alright? Is he mad in the head?" I couldn't be bothered with them. You have to face prejudice against disabled people most days. Sometimes in a busy shopping centre, I catch someone looking at me as if to say "What's wrong with him? He doesn't look right." I will catch their eye and let a big mad roar out of me. Then I spin away in the chair, laughing to myself. Sometimes it does me good to confirm the prejudices about people in wheelchairs. That's right, we are all mad and dangerous and we are here to make you afraid. That is what a lot of people think. They are wrong, but I don't mind scaring the wits out of them from time to time, shake them up a bit, make them think.

But it is not just about getting myself noticed when I am out and about. I have lost count of the number of places I have been in where I just felt like a nuisance: shops and bars, cafés and restaurants, cinemas and theatres, all places where people go to spend their time and their money, but that are not welcoming to disabled people. My time and my money are worth just as much as anybody else's. I always feel that my wheelchair is in the way. Instead, I should be thinking that the place I am in is badly designed or badly laid out, and I should be talking to the manager about it. Why should I feel like I am the problem? I am a paying customer at the end of the day, just like everybody else in the place. When I see the blue sign on a shop door of a stick person sitting in a wheelchair, it means nothing. It is there to make the general public feel good that the business is welcoming to disabled people. It is there because the business got a grant off the government to put in a disabled toilet or some hand rails. But you try getting into that shop in a wheelchair. You try moving around between the racks of goods in a wheelchair. A lot of businesses have no permanent ramps for wheelchairs and they have no staff ready to put out temporary ramps. They have no internal doors wide enough to take the wheelchair. They have no automatic doors. Their counters are too high for them to see you waiting there to be served. They have the goods you need on a high shelf, or a low shelf, and no-one available to help you get what you need. Everything is self-service, but what happens when someone like me comes along who can't serve himself? You sit there like a lost soul trying to get some service while the rest of the world walks by, and they don't even look you in the eye. These businesses get grants off the government to put in facilities for the disabled, but they haven't a clue about the whole experience for a disabled person. It is a disgrace and our politicians are doing very little about it. Disabled people have a vote too and the politicians have a duty to serve us the same way as they serve other members of the community. None of us asked to be disabled, so I would say we deserve more than the average person for all we have to put up with. As well as better access for disabled people to all the amenities, I would like to see heavy penalties for those businesses and institutions in the private sector that are not disabled friendly.

The politicians need to think that it could be them sitting on a wheelchair some day. It is time to come down hard on the private sector. The businesses in the private sector are quick enough to take our money, but they aren't providing a good enough service for the disabled.

The more I thought about it, the more I wanted to get out in the public eye and make my points. Road safety seemed like the best way to get through to people about how the disabled are treated, not just accident victims, but people disabled since birth and people with disease, and elderly people. The first person I got in touch with was a journalist called Martin O'Hagan, who worked for the *Sunday World* newspaper in Belfast. Martin did a great write-up on me for the paper and he was a really decent man and an excellent journalist. Martin O'Hagan was shot dead by loyalist paramilitaries in September 2001. It is a great loss. Martin came up with the headline "Crippled for Christmas" which he used to tell my story in the *Sunday World*. I liked that because it got people thinking.

After the *Sunday World* coverage, I started to contact local TV and radio stations. At first, they didn't want to know. But I kept harassing them. I told them it was important to have a survivor of road carnage who was willing to talk to the public about his experience. You can't argue with that, and in the end I got my chance. Over the years, I have appeared on several TV shows both North and South of the Irish border. I've been on *UTV Live*, *Country Times*, *The Kelly Show*, *The Late Late Show* and *Home Sweet Home*. I enjoyed being on the television. I liked being in the limelight. I must take that from my father's side of the family, because the Donaghys are embarrassed by me appearing on TV. They wish I would just hide myself away. That is what the Donaghys are like. If you have a disability, whether it is mental, like my mother's, or physical, like mine, you would be better off to hide yourself away. You are easily forgotten about then, and left to rot. I was the first living victim of a road accident to appear on TV in Ireland to talk about my life and road safety issues. I didn't have a script. I speak as I find. Lots of people have come up to me in the street since I was on TV to talk to me about road safety. They are usually people whose families have been affected by road traffic accidents. They want to know more and I am happy to share my experience. What good does it do to hide that experience away? It does nobody any good at all. Why not help people with as much information as you can give them? That is how I see it.

I was talking about the impact of road accidents on *The Kelly Show* one Friday night. I was speaking from the heart and I didn't hold anything back. A few miles away from the studio in Belfast, George and Tracey Doherty were watching me and thinking, "*This is exactly what we need. I wonder would Philip work with us.*" Sergeant George Doherty of the Police Service of Northern Ireland (PSNI) and his wife Tracey were working on a project to increase awareness of road safety among young drivers. Practically every weekend young drivers are involved in crashes, some fatal, some not. George and Tracey came to see me to ask if I could help them. I was in the Ulster Hospital in Dundonald at the time, being treated for a pressure sore. I always say I have the sorest ass in the country, and, by God, I definitely did that time. Although I couldn't feel it, I knew it was bad by the expressions on the faces of the nurses when they had to treat it. The sore was open to the bone, and that is not a pleasant experience. George and Tracey walked in to see me in the hospital and told me they were very impressed by the way I talked on "*The Kelly Show*". They told me about their own road safety project idea and I was keen to get involved, but at that time I didn't have my own transport and it was hard to get me around. My health wasn't as good as it is now, and I wasn't able to commit to the project 100%. George and Tracey didn't want to lose the opportunity of working with someone like me, who was willing to talk openly and honestly about the effects of road carnage. They put their heads together and came up with the idea of the Roadsafe Roadshow. It is a collaboration between the police, AXA, the insurance company and Cool FM, a local radio station, which they take around colleges, leisure centres and theatres. That way, large numbers of people come to see me at the roadshow, rather than me travelling around to see small groups. The roadshow is aimed at 17 to 20 year olds who are just starting out as drivers.

The Roadsafe Roadshow brings together the emergency services, a hospital doctor, a bereaved wife, and someone like me, a living victim. It tells the story of a young man who has just bought his first car and is ready to hit the road with his new girlfriend. He hasn't a care in the world. Within a few hours, the car is a write-off, his girlfriend is dead, and he has a spinal cord injury. It isn't my story, but it is a very familiar one on our roads today, and it gives out part of the message I want to say to people. Each person in the roadshow talks about their own experience of road carnage and everyone has a tragic story to tell. When I come on stage, I represent the young man in the prime of his life who has been taken off his feet by a crash. I am like a shock to the system and you can hear a pin drop when I appear on stage. I have had the surgery, the rehabilitation, the counselling. There is nothing more that can be done for me. I will never recover more than I have already recovered. This is me. I sit in my electric wheelchair and silently move to the centre of the stage. I describe my accident and how I live today, with 24-hour nursing care. I ask the audience to stand up, and they do, immediately. It is a very strange experience to look at 800 or 900 young people silently telling their bodies and legs to stand up, and watching them do it. What I wouldn't give to be able to stand up on my own two feet after sitting in this damn chair for so long. I watch them; some of them stretch, some of them grip the seats in front of them, some of them drop something and bend down to pick it up. Some of them lean across to nudge one of their friends sitting in another row. Some of them jig about, moving from foot to foot. I see it all from the stage. The faces of those young people tell many stories. Some of them are not going to take any more lifts with their friend who drives like a madman. Some of them are going to pay more attention on their driving lessons. Some of them are making a promise to themselves to be safer drivers. A few of them don't seem to give a damn about what they've seen at the roadshow, and I worry about them. Sitting there, in my wheelchair, I ask them all to sit down. They sit.

I worked regularly with George and Tracey and the roadshow team for about four years from 2001 to 2005, when I was well enough. They have another young victim helping them now, but I still occasionally step in when they need me. We have reached tens of thousands of young people throughout Ireland. In 2003, the team was presented with the International Prince Michael Road Safety Award. This was a big achievement and I am proud to have been part of it. I thought we could have gone further by producing a hard-hitting road safety advertisement for TV, using me in the role of the victim. At that time all the advertisements used real policemen and paramedics, but they used actors for the disabled roles and I didn't agree with that. It is something I would still like to do in the future. The injured victims, you see, don't go away. We live on, sometimes in terrible conditions, and it is living with dreadful injuries that I want to draw attention to. Maybe some day an agency, North or South, will take me up on my offer to work on an advertisement. The public needs to understand that road carnage is real; it is not faked up by actors. And it could happen to them.

When I do road safety work, I feel embarrassed about telling strangers that I need 24-hour nursing care. The easiest thing to do would be to say nothing about it. The easiest thing of all would be not to bother doing the road safety work. But it is important to me to get the message out there, and if it makes even one person change their behaviour, then it is worth a bit of embarrassment. Every day, I make my own decisions and assess my own achievements. Some days my achievement could be something as small as putting toothpaste on my toothbrush. But that is something I couldn't do before, so to achieve it is a milestone for me. I never sit back and say to myself, "*Well, I think I have done enough. I will just stop trying and hand responsibility over to somebody else.*" When that day comes, it will be time to meet the Man up above. It is a long way off yet. This is my one and only life and, by God, I have a lot left to do in it. I have achieved everything I set out to achieve so far since my accident, and I am proud of myself. But there is still more to be done.

I always say, if I can save just one life, or if I can influence just one person to stop them taking stupid risks on the roads, then it is worth it. It is worth the inconvenience of transporting me in my chair for miles around the country. It is worth the nervousness I sometimes experience when I present myself to a huge room full of people. It is worth the embarrassment I feel about myself most of the time, as if the "real" Philip is trapped in my useless body. But there are a lot of young people out there who just haven't got the message. These are the car thieves, the joyriders, the underage drink-drivers. The lucky ones get caught before they do any permanent damage. They are convicted car criminals, and some of them are as young as 14. Too young for prison, part of their probation is to come and see me in my home.

Some of these young lads think they are right hard men. And I am sure they are, in their own territory. But my house is my territory, and I am the only hard man allowed. They come into my house and sometimes they are with their parents, or sometimes they are with their probation worker. We get over the softy chit-chat very quickly. I am not here to make them feel good about what they have done, and I am not here to offer any kind of forgiveness. I treat them as criminals in a way, because that is what they are. But at the same time, my number one priority is to make them think. I said to one young chap recently, "Would you ever get drunk and smash up a stolen motorbike again?" and he said to me, "I never say never." He was a cheeky wee shite, but not all of them are like that. I tell the young chap, and it is usually a male, to sit in my shower chair. It is a manual wheelchair with a hole in the seat, so that your backside can be cleaned out in the shower. They don't know that. Not yet. They sit in the chair and even the biggest of them looks small and hunched in the sloping seat of the chair. I give them an enema bottle and a catheter tube to hold.

"What's this?" they say.

"Are you easily embarrassed?" I say. They shrug. "Well, you'll find out later." I say. I ask them about what they have done, about how they feel about it now. I ask them if they have families, parents, and how their families are coping with what they have done. I haven't yet come across a young person whose upbringing was as rough as mine, and that's the truth. All of these young kids have at least one parent, and usually two parents, in their lives. And yet I never got involved in car crime. In fact, I never drove a car in my life. About now, I am starting to see a change in the young chap's attitude. He is starting to wonder about me, but he is too much of a big man to ask. So I tell him a bit about myself and my accident. I ask him how he would feel if his best friend got paralysed in a car that he had wrecked. I ask him how he would feel if it was his best friend who was driving and he was the one who got paralysed. I don't wait for the answers to these questions. I just leave the young chap to think about them for himself. I am not here to tell him what to think, but I want to make sure that, for once in his life, he does think about the likely consequences of his behaviour around cars.

With one of my carers pushing him in the shower chair, I take him on a tour of my house. At this stage, he is probably thinking "*Nice house*" and he is right, it is a beautiful house. Extra wide doors, for the wheelchair. Marble floors, for the wheelchair. Open plan, for the wheelchair. Plenty of wide open spaces, for the wheelchair. I gave my wheelchair total respect when I built my house. I had no choice in the matter. That is the way it had to be. We go into my bedroom, where another carer is waiting. At my signal, the two carers manoeuvre the young chap into a sling while he sits in the shower chair. The sling is like an adult version of one of those papoose things that people carry their babies round in. You feel like a baby when you are wearing that sling. In fact, you feel like a baby most of your life when you are paralysed. The carers then switch on the electric hoist above my bed. They hook up the young chap in the sling. I can see the panic in his eyes "Don't worry, boss", I say, "You won't fall. It is built to take your weight". I say to the carers "Put that young lad to bed, will you". He is hoisted out of the wheelchair in the sling. He hovers there for a moment, his limbs dangling, and then slowly, steadily, he is hoisted over the bed and dropped gently down. My bed is a work of art. The mattress alone cost £10,000. It looks like a normal enough bed, but it is specially designed to prevent pressure sores and it can be raised and lowered electronically. I tell him all this. He doesn't look too impressed. In fact, he looks terrified. The carers hoist him up again, and hoist him over until he is facing the mirror on the wall above my chest of drawers. It reminds me of the time I broke down in Sligo and Harry Gallagher gave me the life-saving cigarette. But I am not offering any comfort. Through the mirror, the young lad can see himself in the sling, up on the hoist, hovering there. His feet in their expensive trainers look like a child's feet, dangling. He is still holding my enema bottle and my catheter tube, as if they were his favourite toys. "Take a look at yourself, boss" I say. We sit in silence for a minute or two. And then I tell him if he is paralysed in an accident because he was driving illegally, a stolen car, drink-driving, no insurance, he won't have an electric wheelchair. He won't have his own home. He won't have an electric hoist to help his carers to get him in and out of bed. He won't even have a shower chair. He will be stuck in a nursing home, taking up a bed intended for an elderly person, a burden to the state and his family. He will stare at four walls all day long. The carers release him, and I take him to the bathroom. All this time, he has been holding the enema bottle and catheter tube. I tell him what they are, and he nearly drops them in disgust. I tell him to put on a pair of surgical gloves. I show him my supra-pubic catheter: a tube surgically inserted through my abdomen directly into my bladder. I show him how to help me have a pee. He lifts the leg of my trousers, the catheter tube ends at my ankle. There is a small tap to release the flow of urine, which he directs into a jar. He closes the tap and flushes the urine down the toilet. When he has dumped the gloves and washed his hands, we go back to the sitting room and have a cup of tea.

There are no traces of hard man left in the young chap. Usually, he is white as a sheet. I ask him what the hell he thinks he is doing with his life. I ask him what he wants to do. I tell him he only has one life, to grab it with both hands, to face his problems, to accept help, and to get on with it. I have been criticised for being too blunt with the young kids who come to my house. But the way I see it, I can say things the professionals can't say. I can tell them to forget school if it isn't working for them, and to find other ways to get their education in life. I always remember Danny Byrne saying to me that hard work would cure the badness in anyone and I pass this advice on. Boys who are dog tired in the evening after a day of physical work are not going to steal cars in their spare time. Boys who have earned a few shillings in their pocket at the end of the working week, every week, are gradually going to get some self-respect. That is the way I see it and that is what I tell them.

The cheeky lad who said to me "Never say never" was no different to any of the others, except I thought he was going to faint by the end of the tour of my house. He had a big white face on him and he said to me, "I was wrong. You have scared me out of my wits. I won't be drinking and driving again." I know rightly he won't.

In 2008, I received a Criminal Justice Award for my work with young people on probation for car crime. I was up in Hillsborough mixing with all the snobs of the day. To be honest, I downplay the awards. I am not the kind of man who gets nominated for awards. I have been up in court myself, who am I to be receiving an award? But then, I look at it in another way and I say to myself, "*Philip Donaghy, you have achieved this yourself and you have made a difference in this world. There's probably a good few young lads who have learned a hard lesson from your life. Maybe you have even saved some lives. Why not accept a bit of recognition for it?*" Who would have expected that from me, the bastard in a children's home? Not my family, not social services back in the time before I was 18, not even myself in the time before my accident. I might have admired other people for getting involved in road safety or work with the disabled, but I was on the sidelines. I never expected that I would put so much of my time and energy into it. It is important work and I am proud of myself. It makes me want to achieve more, do more, make an even bigger difference. I would like to get involved in more road safety work south of the Irish border. I had my accident in the south and in some ways I see it as my way of paying back the care I received during my recovery. It is good to have goals and to keep myself motivated to achieve them. The hardest thing is passing the time on a wheelchair, but if there are new ideas to think about and new people to meet, the time passes quicker. In 2009, I have been discussing work with adult car criminals as part of their rehabilitation after serving prison sentences.

But sometimes I say to myself "*What is the point in what I have achieved?*" Yes, I have a bit of money and I have put it to good use. But what use is money to me? What "future" am I investing in? Yes, I have a beautiful house, but it can feel like a prison because I can't even get up in the morning by myself, I have to rely on strangers to get me up and washed, to cook and clean for me, even to make me a cup of tea. Even though I have a fighting spirit and I have proved to myself time after time that I can achieve things, I get down in the dumps sometimes. I get to feeling a bit sorry for myself and I hate to have self pity. But when I look back, I see that every time I have been knocked down in life, I find some way to get back up again. All the plans I made in the past, before my accident, might have come to nothing. But I have made new plans and I have achieved them too. Being paralysed in a car crash is my biggest challenge yet, but I will meet it. It would be easy to lock myself away from the world and just live out my days being nursed around the clock. But that is not the life I want for myself. I spent enough time in my childhood hidden away because my family was ashamed of me. I know what that is like and it is not the life I want. I say to myself "*Why shouldn't I have the life that I want? And if that life can be an inspiration to other people in wheelchairs, that is all the better.*" I remember being in the Musgrave Park Hospital and Dr McCann telling me that I had choices in life. I could hardly believe it at the time. What choices? But then I realised Dr McCann was right. I am not a freak of nature, I am not helpless, I am not brain injured. What I am is a young chap who is paralysed because of an accident. It doesn't make me invisible or incapable of living my life. I realised the most important thing to me is to have a normal life: a home of my own, friends, a social life, something to work at, a wife and children. I remind myself that those dreams are a lifelong project. They can be adapted and changed; they can always be improved. But every day I still put in the work to achieve that normal life.

A normal life

I say to myself, "*What is a normal life, Philip? And what would you know about a normal life? You never had one.*" That is true. I had a very insecure childhood and before my accident, I was just starting to find my feet in life. I look back on the times in Sligo and Castlebar as some of the best times of my life, but it was so short. I was out at my work, playing my football, taking my girlfriend out dancing, having a pint with the lads. I was busy, too busy to sit back and ask myself if I was happy and enjoying my life. If I am honest, I would say that I never really enjoyed my life. I never had the chance. I was insecure and that takes a lot of the pleasure out of life. I had good times, but I also had times when I was wrecking my own head with worries. I always had it in the back of my mind that I was a bastard from a children's home. For just a few short months in Castlebar, I started to get the idea that maybe I could be happy, some day, and then I had the accident. So what is a normal life?

I look around me and I see my good friends, the Byrnes and I say to myself, "*That's the kind of family I would have liked to have.*" But I can't have it. Wishing for it is not achieving it, I know that much. For me, a normal life means buying a house, getting married and raising a family. It means having friends about me that I can trust. It means taking part in life and not hiding myself away from it. It means keeping myself busy. If I was on my feet, I would be out at my work all day. I try to have the same attitude on a wheelchair, although some days it is very hard to pass the time. It can be the loneliest thing in the world, sitting on a wheelchair. I go out when I can and I try to have a social life. It is not easy for me or for my friends and I don't have the same number of friends I had when I was walking. I don't have casual friends that I might run into on the street. I don't have any new female friends, apart from the women who care for me. Everything in my life has to be planned, more than most people's day-to-day lives. That's life. My life might not look too normal to strangers, but if they had any idea that I was expected to live out my days in a nursing home, they would see how far I have come.

Moving into my new house was a big step on the path to a normal life for me. I had a home of my own for the first time. Having spent five years in hospitals and nursing homes, the feeling of opening my own front door for the first time was unbelievable. I never had to buy furniture before, or linen or appliances. I never had to decide what colour to paint the walls. I never made that kind of decision in my life. It was all new to me. I couldn't wait to see my name and address in the telephone book. I felt like I had finally made it when I saw that listing. It gave me a real buzz. I was officially a house holder and it felt great. I was not part of the routine of a nursing home. It was down to me to decide how to organise my days. At first, that felt like freedom, but the feeling didn't last. At the end of the day, when my front door closes, nobody knows what it is like to live my kind of life.

When I first moved into my house I had constant visitors coming to see me. I got my face in the local papers. Some people just came round to be nosy because they never came back to see me since. I gave that many guided tours, I could have done it in my sleep. I was also getting used to the electronics of the house that Rodney Stewart installed for me. He got used to being on the end of the phone at all hours of the day and night when something got stuck.

"Hey Rodney," I would say, "This system you installed is for shite."

"What have you done to it now, Philip?" Rodney would say.

"I've done nothing. I pushed the button and nothing happened."

"Then what did you do?"

"I did nothing. I just went over to the computer and footered about a bit."

"I thought you said you did nothing."

"Aye, that's right. I did nothing. I just tried to fix the damn thing."

"Hang on Philip, I'd better check it out myself. I'll see you in half an hour." He would jump in the car and come up to the house to see what I had done to his beautiful system.

After the first few weeks of living in my new house, I realised that I had fallen into my own routine, and it was not all that different to a nursing home. I still needed 24-hour care and that puts a routine on your life, whether you like it or not. Needless to say, I don't like it at all and I find it hard to share my home with strangers. I have visits from home helps twice a day. They get me up in the morning and put me into bed at night. But the only problem with home helps is that you get used to them and then the health service changes the shifts or changes the teams, and the routine gets messed about. The health service should ask the people who rely on the home helps first, before they mix up the arrangements. Community nurses come to see me three times a week. They are my first contact with the health service if I am sick. They write it all down if my catheter gets blocked, or they write "Philip had a good bowel movement today," stuff like that. Just think, reports have been written about me by strangers all my life. I have a social worker again too, Deirdre Loughran. I can hardly believe it. Deirdre writes reports on me, the same as the other social workers had to do, back when I was a child. But she is on my side and not on my case all the time. Deirdre says about me, "It was clear to me that Philip could have given up on life a number of times, but he uses adversity to motivate himself. He has such confidence and determination. I can't help but be inspired by him." I wish someone had recognised this spirit in me when I was a young child too scared to speak out. The way I see it now, I suppose I have nothing to lose by speaking out. The social services treat me as an adult now. Back then, when I was a young child without love in my life, it was a different story. They treated me as a wee bastard for they knew no different.

On top of all that, I privately employ people to come in during the day to cook and clean for me, and to do the shopping and that. Linda Little does that for me and she is a good worker. I get on very well with Linda and her daughter Lisa. I am comfortable going into the town with Linda. She says to me, "Philip, I'm nothing but the skivvy around here," and I suppose that is true in a way, but I was the skivvy once and I think I treat Linda a lot better than I was treated. I sometimes sit out at the back of the house and look in the patio doors at Linda, working away in the kitchen. But then she finishes her work and leaves to collect her daughter from school and go home. I am left looking in at a clean, empty kitchen, all the noise and chat gone from it. I have a van, customised to take the wheelchair, and my carers are trained to drive me about in it, to medical appointments, social events and the odd weekend away. I have someone covering weekend shifts and holiday and sick leave. Sometimes I think I employ the unhealthiest people in Ireland! I lie awake nights wondering who it will be getting me up tomorrow morning. There are nights when I just don't know, another stranger, and I find that very stressful. I lash out at my carers at times, because I have no other way of letting my worries and my frustrations go.

Some days I might have a meeting with my solicitor, Feargal Logan, or my accountants, McAleer, Mullan and Jackson. They come to the house to meet me because the disability access at their offices is pure shite. The people from the Youth Justice Agency call round every few weeks with another youngster for me to educate on car crime. My friends visit and we watch the football or sit around and chat. Martin McKenna might call in with my prescription medicines and pass the time of day with me. He is a good lad, Martin. I run a busy home and it takes a lot of my time and energy to keep things running well. And would you believe it, it is so lonely at times that I just shut myself in my bedroom and cry. I say to myself "*This house is full of strangers. It doesn't feel like my home at all.*"

I look at the 10 years I have been sitting on the wheelchair and there has been no improvement in service for disabled people in that time. The health service provides the minimum and if you have the financial support, you can pay for extra service yourself. That works for me because I got an insurance settlement. I can invest the finance in my care. But what about the people who don't have the finances to employ people to look after them, or to have an electric wheelchair, or a van to get them about? What about the people who never knew what life without a disability was like? They have to rely on what the health service offers and let me tell you, it is not very much. It is even less if you don't harass the hell out of them. It is not right that the people who shout the loudest get the most, but on the other hand, people with disabilities shouldn't hide themselves away or live life like they expect to be ignored. There are people out there who have been disabled since birth, and people who have been disabled through disease, like spina bifida. Really, the only positive image you see of disabled people is at the Olympics. Those athletes are an inspiration for everybody, with all they have achieved. But they are just the tip of the iceberg. Most disabled people will never get to the

Olympics and never get noticed. Not everybody can be the best, but everybody deserves proper care and attention and they shouldn't have to fight for it.

Bernie Boyle, Pat Jordan and Clare Monaghan are the home helps I see regularly, and I owe them a lot. I have a good bit of oul' chat with them every day. It takes my mind off the embarrassment I feel about all they have to do for me. Some days, when I am down in the dumps, I can hardly bear to look at them. "What's wrong Philip?" they say, "You're not in the best of form today." I feel like saying "Have I not got the right to be in bad form?" But I don't. Here's the thing. I have to watch what I say in my own home. If I was to lose the head with the people who work for me and tell them to fuck off and leave me alone, the chances are they would, and they wouldn't be back. I'd be left; angry, alone and helpless. Not only that, but the health service and the agencies I use would be down on me telling me to improve my attitude or lose the support they give me. Sometimes I feel it is my main job to make my home more pleasant for the workers than it is for me, and it does my head in. I realised writing this book and speaking my thoughts into a bloody Dictaphone, I really have nobody to talk to about my problems. When problems build up, there is no way to let them go without putting my future care at risk by lashing out at the workers. I have said more into a Dictaphone than I have said to any living person since I moved into my house, and that's the truth. The Dictaphone is like my psychiatrist at times. What kind of a way is that to live? Is that normal? I don't think so.

For the first seven months in my new house, I thought I could do without care during the night. Although I respect my home helps for all they do, I get fed up with strangers all over me every day of my life. Once I am in bed at night that's it. Nothing happens until my carers come in the morning to get me up and showered. I thought I would be able to manage on my own during the night. 24-hour nursing care for the rest of your life is a terrible burden to carry. I thought to myself that life would seem more normal if I could reduce the care to about 14 or 15 hours a day. If I could manage on my own at night, it would be another milestone I had achieved. Feargal Logan was worried about me that time.

"Philip, what if there is a fire in the house during the night? What if you have an intruder?" he said, "You would be lying there helpless. It doesn't bear thinking about. It could be a disaster. I just don't think it is worth the risk." I said I would take the risk. But when I thought about it, I got anxious. When I lay in my bed at night listening to the sounds of the house, feeling nothing, I came face to face with everything I had lost in life, my mobility, my independence, my social life; but still I thought I should challenge myself to manage on my own. If I need anything during the night, I can only get it if it is on the bedside table. If my PDA were to fall on the floor, I would lose access to all the controls of the house that would help me to raise the alarm if anything happened. One night I tried to empty my catheter on my own, and ended up with a huge pool of piss all over the floor and nothing to be done about it until the home helps came in the morning. I had a big smile on my face that morning, to hide my embarrassment. They are brilliant, the home helps, they just get on and do their work and don't make me feel any worse than I already do. The more I thought about it, the more uncomfortable I got about the things that could go wrong in the hours I spent alone. What if I fell out of bed? What if I took sick? I finally gave in. I had to resign myself to the fact that I would need a live in carer. I was just too vulnerable on my own.

I kept saying to myself "*The last thing I need is more strangers about me.*" From the day I was born, strangers have looked after me. From the staff in the maternity ward, to the nuns in St Joseph's, to my foster family, to the social workers at Ballee, to the medical staff and the care assistants in hospitals and nursing homes. Look at me now, a whole team of people coming and going through my house seven days a week. But I say to myself, "*It's only a job to them It's the job they are trained to do. They never chose to look after Philip Donaghy, they are paid to look after me.*" In the 10 years since my accident, I have met some people, I can tell you. Some of them have been brilliant, and I have a brilliant team around me now. But some of them have been ignorant, and some of them have had more problems than me in ways. Some of them are just plain unreliable, and I can't have that kind of person about me. If someone doesn't turn up for their work, it is down to me to arrange cover and to worry about what all needs to be done. I have employed people who don't even think that letting me down at the last minute could put me at serious risk. It's not like a normal job where someone else takes up the slack, or the work can wait a while. There is no slack and the work can't wait. I have got very good at spotting people who have a heart and who really care for me and those who are just doing a job and couldn't give a damn. At the end of the day, I rely on strangers, and that is the hardest part of being Philip Donaghy.

When I agreed to look for a live in housekeeper who would be there in the house with me all night, I knew I would have to feel some kind of trust with the person straight away, otherwise I wouldn't be able to have them in my home. I tried to be positive but I was scared. I knew nothing back then about hiring staff and Feargal Logan helped me to find somebody. I told him to find me a rare looking girl and he did. Katarzyna Potocna, or Kate as I called her, was from Poland and she was my first live in worker. I knew as soon as I interviewed her that we would get on. She was straightforward and modest in a way. She was good looking and had a good strong personality. We just connected on some level and it worked out. Kate stayed with me for eight months and we became good friends in that time. Kate had never stripped a disabled man and showered him before, and I had never had a woman living in my house before. It was a bit awkward at first, but we became comfortable in each other's company. Kate would say to me, "Philip, just be yourself", but it was hard for me at the start. I would lie in my bed and hear Kate moving about the house. I would be wondering what she was at, but soon the sound of her was a comfort to me. I felt more safe and secure knowing she was there and I could call her any time I needed her. I was happy to share my home with Kate and I hadn't expected to be. I had spent so much time fighting against the idea of a live in worker. I had made up my mind that it would be terrible and that I would have no privacy with someone looking into my business 24 hours a day. I decided that it would make me feel like a useless bastard. But when Kate came, I saw that it didn't have to be the way I imagined. It could be a much better experience. I would have care if I needed it 24 hours a day, and the rest of the time, I could build a trust and a friendship with a beautiful Polish girl. That is exactly what happened. We laughed, we fought, we went out for dinner together, we sat at home and watched TV. It was great and I can honestly say that for most of the eight months Kate was with me, I thought to myself, "*This is it. I have achieved it. I have a normal life.*" That is how good Kate made me feel about myself and I have to thank her for that. I have always said that Kate would make a great business partner. She is very smart and she has good ideas and a good head on her shoulders. She would be a credit to any company that employed her.

When Kate came to me first, I was still getting used to living in my own home. Kate gave me a bit of a buzz and she challenged me to lead the life I wanted. Sometimes it was just easier to sit in the house than to go out. There were all sorts of arrangements to make with taxis and venues. It was a lot of hassle at times. But Kate would say to me, "So what, Philip. Let's just go." We went to restaurants together, to the cinema and to the pub. We had a good laugh. I would have loved to take Kate dancing, but of course I couldn't. When I was walking, I used to love dancing. If I was walking again, the first thing I would do would be to take a beautiful girl out for a dance. Even before I burned the wheelchair and the hoist. Going out to these places with Kate was much easier than going on my own. I didn't feel so self-conscious. I used to wonder what people thought when they saw me and Kate together. Did they think we were a couple? Or did they assume Kate was my nurse or my care assistant? I always introduced Kate to people as my friend; I never said that she worked for me. We weren't a couple and we didn't have a romantic relationship, but maybe that's what we looked like to some people and it made me feel good. It also gave me hope. Maybe there is a beautiful girl out there who could be my girlfriend some day. Sometimes me and Kate just sat in the house, watched a DVD and opened a bottle of wine. Just like any other couple. We had our rows too. We have similar strong personalities and sparks flew plenty of times. But it felt normal. It felt like the sort of relationship men and women share all the time. I didn't have to hide anything and I didn't feel such a strong need for privacy when Kate was around. I trusted Kate and she motivated me. That was a great combination for a partnership. Sometimes it felt like she was kicking my ass, but if she did, it was because I needed it. Kate had strong opinions and she would argue her points. I looked to her for advice. I didn't always take it, but I always listened to her, and I was always interested in what she had to say.

At Christmas the year Kate lived in my home, we went to midnight mass together. I could tell that Kate was missing her family back in Poland. She asked me if I would like to try some Polish Christmas food and I said I would. To be honest, they eat some funny things in Poland at Christmas. I didn't know what I was eating half the time and I told Kate it was all lovely, but really it wasn't. I preferred Mrs. Byrne's Christmas cooking any day.

When Kate was with me, and for all the good times that we had, I didn't tell her the full story about my background. I felt that Kate had got to know the real Philip, and I thought that if she knew the rough upbringing I had as a child, she would change her opinion of the man. I hope when she reads this book, she will understand and accept why I am the man I am. Living with Kate in my house was one hell of an experience. Kate was the first woman I ever shared a home with in my life. When I was going out with Rachel Desmond, and we moved to Castlebar, she had her place and I had mine. I never even spent the night with her. I used to leave her home and then go back to my place. Kate opened my eyes for me, and I would like to thank her personally for making me see that sharing my home with a woman is possible for me. A man can dream.

During her time with me, Kate did some research into stem cell treatment for spinal cord injuries. She suggested to me that I should look into it and she showed me the web sites that taught us about stem cell treatments. Stem cells have the ability to keep growing and dividing for long periods. The hope is that stem cells could repair or replace damaged cells by regenerating as specialised cells in a diseased or damaged area of the body. People with different types of cancer, Parkinson's disease and any number of other illnesses could, in theory, replace damaged cells with healthy stem cells and in that way combat some of the worst aspects of their sickness. New, healthy cells would replace the diseased cells and eventually outnumber them. That is the idea anyway. In my case, the research is still in the very early stages. But in the future, maybe a spinal cord injury could be repaired in some way with stem cells so that more movement and function are restored to the paralysed parts of the body. It is a long way off, but it is a ray of hope for people suffering from spinal cord injuries.

Kate had high hopes for me receiving the stem cell treatment. I must admit I was not so hopeful. Dr McCann had been very clear about my chances of ever walking again, even if there were great advances in spinal cord research. After Dr McCann told me that, just to be sure, I went back to the rehabilitation centre in Dun Laoghaire for a second opinion. The news was the same; I would never be able to walk again. The damage to my spinal cord is too severe and medical research is nowhere near finding any kind of a permanent treatment. But I was carried along by Kate's excitement. It was definitely worth a try and if she would be there with me, I was ready to give it a go.

We made contact with a clinic in Rotterdam in the Netherlands and planned to take a trip there to see the doctors for a consultation. I asked Rodney Stewart to organise the travel arrangements for me. He was able to do a lot of it on the Internet. Rodney got a very clear idea about how hard it is to arrange transport and accommodation for a disabled person. He found out the so-called disabled friendly hotels are anything but. You might be able to get a wheelchair in the door, but what happens after that? Most hotels don't have a flat level bathroom. They all have showers with trays that are raised a step off the floor. Mostly, hotel bathrooms are the size of a cupboard. Take it from me; it is impossible to get me and a shower chair into that kind of a shower. When he found the right hotel, Rodney then had to spend hours searching for a company that would hire out a hoist and a shower chair for the few days I was spending in Rotterdam. Plus there was the language barrier. Try explaining the word "hoist" to a non-English speaker. Rodney ended up getting pictures of hoists and emailing them to the people in Holland.

Rodney wrote me out a whole itinerary for the trip, with contact numbers for all the suppliers and companies he was using, as well as the flight and hotel details that most people would have on their itinerary. It was foolproof, or so he thought. I was in the middle of Rotterdam, sightseeing with Kate, when my wheelchair got a flat tyre. That is the same thing as a flat tyre on a car, except that wheelchairs don't carry a spare and you can't get a replacement down at Kwik Fit. I had to phone Rodney back in Cookstown and ask him to find the right kind of company to come and re-inflate the tyre for me, and then I had to wait in the middle of the street in the rain for the company to get to me. If Kate had not been there with me, I think I would have just taken the next flight home; I was that skundered with the whole business. But she was there and we made the best of it. The next day we went to the clinic for the consultation.

The doctors didn't give me any hope for a miracle cure, but they believed that stem cell treatment could help me. They arranged for me to come back to Rotterdam when I would receive the injection of stem cells into my neck at the site of my injury. After the consultation, I had to go on a strict diet. My weight was not a problem, but I had to cut out certain foods, such as dairy, to get into peak condition for the treatment to take place. It was hard to stick at first, but Kate was in charge of my meals, so I had no choice and I got used to it. I maintain that diet today and I am healthier for it. It would be very easy to take comfort in all the wrong types of food. But carrying extra weight increases my chances of other health complications, like ulcerated legs, pressure sores, and diabetes. All things I can do without. It was during this time after my consultation that Kate told me she was leaving. She had been called home to Poland by her family. I was heartbroken. There is no other word for it. If it had not been for Kate, I never would have gone for the stem cell treatment, and she would not be there when it happened. What if it was a great success? What if my chances of a normal life were 100% improved? But the treatment was the least of it really. If it had not been for Kate, life would have been boring. At the point of losing her, I realised how much Kate meant to me, and how much she had changed my life for the better. The trip to Rotterdam was like a holiday for me, and not just a trip to the doctors, and I know that Kate enjoyed herself too. But when she told me she was leaving, I buttoned up my feelings, like I always do. What could I say to Kate anyway? Could I really ask her not to go home to her family when they needed her? No, I couldn't.

I said my goodbyes to Kate and I asked my friends Maurice and Tom to come to Rotterdam with me to finish the stem cell treatment. Kate probably thought I didn't care a bit about her leaving. But if she did, she was dead wrong. By the time the date for the next trip to Rotterdam came around, Kate was gone. I felt as low as I have ever done since my accident. It was a kick in the teeth, another hard slap in my life. But when I thought about it, I said to myself, "*Philip, let it go. You can't keep that girl back. What have you got to offer her anyway? Her family needs her.*" I knew I was right, but it still felt like a hard slap.

Maurice and Tom had no idea how upset I was about Kate leaving. They thought I was low because I was nervous about the treatment. They did their best to keep my spirits up and they treated the trip to Rotterdam like a holiday. I went along with the lads as much as I could, but my heart wasn't in it. Maybe I wasn't in the right frame of mind for the treatment either. I felt very low in myself. I remembered my first trip to Rotterdam with Kate and how good I felt. Sitting in the plane with a glass of wine, we must have looked like any other happy couple, laughing and joking together. But when the plane landed, I had to wait until everyone got off and then I was carried off and strapped into my wheelchair. I was back to my normal life as a disabled person sitting on a wheelchair. The reality of my life hit me again and wiped out the brief fantasy I had lived on the plane with Kate sitting next to me.

On the flight to the Netherlands for the treatment, I was sitting between Maurice and Tom and they were winding me up about how bumpy it was. I was drinking a wee whiskey to steady my nerves. I still didn't like flying.

"Did you feel that? What's going on?" said Tom.

"I don't know, but it doesn't feel right, does it? Do you think this pilot knows what he's doing?" said Maurice.

"I doubt we won't get down in one piece, and look, they're taking Philly's wheelchair apart," said Tom.

This went on and on until I could take no more. Part of me knew they were winding me up, but part of me was genuinely terrified of crashing.

"Will you two shut the fuck up!" I told them. The whole trip was like that; the lads winding me up until I cracked, and then they would laugh and I would eventually join in. It was good for us to get away together. It was not exactly a holiday, but the lads did their best to keep it all going. Maurice and Tom say to this day that the trip to Rotterdam was like being away with the same old Philip, only in a wheelchair. I disagree with them in a way. It was the first time they saw the full extent of my disability and everything that had to be done for me. They were my carers for that trip. I was there telling them what had to be done and how to operate the equipment. I don't think they expected to have to do so much for me. I think their eyes were opened, maybe for the first time, to the reality of my life. They had to hoist me in and out of the wheelchair, shower me, get me dressed, get me in and out of taxis, get my food and drinks, all the things that my carers do for me at home. Of course, through it all I kept the banter going. I kept slagging them off every time they struggled to get something done for me, and they would give it right back to me with a mouthful of abuse. But most of the time, I used the oul' chat to turn attention away from my embarrassment about myself. I wanted to be the old Philip, but the reality is I will never be the old Philip again. But I would say, even though they have always stood by me, my friends proved themselves that time in Rotterdam. They did a brilliant job and I know they would do it again tomorrow if they had to.

I don't know what I expected from the stem cell treatment. Without Kate to keep me motivated, I kind of lost my enthusiasm for it. It was like I had forgotten what it was for. I went to the clinic and got the injection of stem cells into my neck. Then Maurice and Tom took me back to the hotel. I sat in my room and waited, but what for? I didn't expect to be able to walk again, nobody had given me that hope. But on the other hand, I had to see if there was anything different. What if the miracle happened and I missed it because I didn't bother trying? I sat there trying to feel if anything was different. I thought maybe I would feel tingling or something. Nothing happened. I was not really disappointed. It was about as much as I expected. I enjoyed a night out in Rotterdam with Maurice and Tom and then we came home. I sent Kate a text message to let her know I had the treatment but it had not made any difference.

In the year following the stem cell treatment, I would have to say it did make a difference. It was very gradual and probably nobody would notice it, except me. But I would say there is a small improvement in the mobility I have in my wrists and fingers. I have a bit more flexibility than I did before. There is no change at all in my upper body. It is still paralysed. A few months ago, I had a sensation of pressure in my feet and legs. It wasn't exactly pain, but it wasn't very pleasant either. Unfortunately, there was no sign of any movement, other than the spasms I still get since my accident. Stem cell treatment could be the way forward for people like me in the future, but it's not much help to me now.

Back home, I had to go about replacing Kate, except you can never replace a good worker who leaves. The trouble is, you get used to someone and used to their ways and habits. I was looking for Kate in other people and I was never going to find her. I said to myself, "*Looking for a new member of staff, it's like interviewing for a wife!*" I was looking for the same kind of qualities in a way; someone I could feel a connection with, someone with a certain kind of personality, and if she was good-looking as well, that would be a bonus! Living so close to someone under the same roof, it is like a marriage in a way. Whenever I find someone who seems just perfect, after a while, that person has to go home or go and do something else with her life. The marriage is over and it feels like a death. I get so used to having them around that there is a great big hole when they leave. I can't stop people from moving on, and I wouldn't do it even if I could, but I wonder if they realise the gap they leave in my life. They walk away to a new challenge somewhere else, and I am left behind. I can't walk away from my life or from my problems. I have no family to go home to; I have no new job to start. I am in the same position I have been in the last 10 years, in my wheelchair, going nowhere.

In the two years after Kate left, I lost count of the different members of staff who came and went: maybe 30, something like that. I made up my mind to keep a distance between me and the staff who work in my house. The trouble is, it is very hard to keep that distance. With all the intimate and personal things my workers have to do for me, I can't keep a very wide distance. Believe me, if I could manage without staff, I would. It is a pain hiring and rehiring staff. It is degrading having to rely on people, mostly strangers, to do everything for me. I need people to get me up in the morning, to take me to the shower, to clean me, to dress me, to get me into my wheelchair, to take me down the town, to make my tea and cook my meals, to clean my house and welcome my visitors. It is very personal and I think I have every right to be particular about it. I can't have people who are too nosy and looking into my business all the time. I can't have people who are cheeky to my friends. I can't have people who don't turn up. If a member of staff is in a bad mood and I am nearly afraid to ask them to do something for me, I say to myself, "*Is this my own house at the end of the day? What is the point of having this beautiful house when it doesn't feel like mine half the time? What is the point of having staff to do things if they are too grumpy to do their job right?*" The fact of the matter is that I pay strangers to work for me. I make all this effort and spend all this money to have as normal a life as I can. But at the end of it, I still feel like a dirty bastard at times. I still feel useless and dependent and as if I have very little control of my life.

But that's not to take away from the good people I have met in the last few years. Helen Dawson looked after me at weekends and is a really fantastic person. Helen is now at college training to be a speech therapist and she will be the best speech therapist of all time. Paula O'Neill is a good friend who comes and massages my shoulders the odd time, and she is another lovely person. I would often confide in Paula when I am feeling low and she always has good words of advice for me. The only trouble with Paula is she is going out with a Derry man, when she knows she would be better off with a Tyrone man! I would say Helen and Paula are two very good female friends I have at the minute. They just take me as I am, they let me be myself and I appreciate that in them. I also owe a big thank you to Bogdana, a housekeeper I had from Bulgaria. Bogdana, or Bogey as I called her, introduced me to a girl who has become very special in my life, and her name is Eva.

Eva is also from Bulgaria and she was living in England before I met her. When Bogey came to my house to work for me, I had my satellite dish tuned to pick up a Bulgarian TV channel and I got Skype so that Bogey could talk to her friends and family back home. I was trying to learn from the mistakes I made with Kate, and one of them was that she must have felt isolated so far away from Poland. Anyway, Bogey took a trip to London one weekend and when she came back, she told me she had made a new friend, Eva. They kept in touch through Skype and soon I was joining in their conversations. Eva was shy and not very confident about speaking English, but there was something about her. She was feeling a bit down in England and I invited her to come and see Bogey and stay with us for a few days.

I will never forget meeting Eva for the first time. The taxi dropped her off from the airport and she was standing there in the drive with her wee case looking that scared. She was probably wondering what she had got herself into. She hardly knew Bogey and she didn't know me at all, except from a bit of oul' chat on Skype. To me, Eva looked lovely, like an angel standing at my door. There was a feeling I can't describe that went through my whole body from head to toe when I met Eva, like someone switching on the power. I nearly felt like I could get up on my feet and open the door to her. Eva is one of the most beautiful looking girls I have ever known and I could hardly take my eyes off her, but it wasn't just her looks that impressed me for that week. The house was full of the sounds of women, with Bogey and Eva chatting away in Bulgarian. They had their own rooms in the house, and their own bathroom. They were getting ready to go out one night and doors were banging and heels were clicking on the floor. To be honest, I was a bit jealous I wasn't going out with them. There was a real buzz in the air as they got ready. I caught a quick look in the bathroom and it was full of bottles of make-up and perfume and hair gel and that. There was a box of tampax sitting on the top of the toilet, and it was the last thing I ever expected to see in my house.

"Jesus Eva," I said, "Will you take those buckin' things out of the bathroom." Eva looked at me, surprised and she said,

"Are you embarrassed Philip? In Bulgaria that is where we keep tampax, in the bathroom."

"There's a time and a place," I said, and I was laughing, "We're good Catholics over here. Get them out!"

And Eva said to me "You know Philip, you really haven't got a clue about women, have you?" It was not the only time Eva said that to me, and by God, she is right. It took Eva to put me straight about a few things that had been bothering me over the years. All the times a worker snapped my head off for no reason and the times I saw their grumpy faces and thought to myself, "*I better go easy today*," the word "hormones" never crossed my mind. My house must have been coming down with women's hormones all this time and I never even knew it. I only knew that I was afraid to open my mouth at times. I had a good laugh to myself. It was the first of many things Eva taught me.

When Eva went back to England, she left me her mobile phone number. Over the following months, I got to know her a lot better. She was friendly but also shy. I used to tease her, and send her silly text messages, but that's my way. It was only to let her know that I liked her. Bogey had planned to take a holiday back home in Bulgaria and we decided that if Eva was free and if she wanted to, she could do the holiday cover. I was taking a big chance on this girl, and I was nervous about it. It was one thing to have Eva in the house, helping Bogey out the odd time. But it was something else to have her in the house full-time, covering for Bogey while she was away. There was no need to worry. Eva just fitted into my life and my routine like a hand in a glove. I felt I already knew her well and it really wasn't that hard for her to pick up what she needed to do to help me in the house. By the time Bogey got back, me and Eva were the best of friends and that made it easier for Bogey to tell me that she had decided to go back to Bulgaria to finish her education. I was fairly sure that Eva would take Bogey's place. I wouldn't be left feeling like there was another death in the family. I was right.

Kate was the one who showed me that I could have a more normal life than I ever expected, but Eva was the one I wanted to have that life with. She gave me a reason to get up in the morning. I fell in love with Eva over the year she spent with me, and she fell in love with me. What happens next is up to Eva. She is back in Bulgaria now, and I miss her a lot, but we talk to each other and text each other every day. She has some decisions to make about her life and she has to make them by herself. I am here if she wants me and I will help her any way I can. But the final decision about what she wants to do and whether she wants a relationship with me is up to her. My ordeal in life is not hers. I wouldn't blame the girl if she decided she wanted a man with his independence. What I mean by that is a man who can do things for a woman, like go on holidays together and lie on the beach or swim in the sea, or go for a walk, or take her out for a dance. It would be a privilege for me to take Eva for a dance. I used to love dancing before my accident. I lived for my social life at the weekends. Not having that any more is one of the hardest things I have had to face. There is no social life for a young person in a wheelchair.

One of the reasons I wanted to live in my own home was so that I could have a social life. But it has been one of the hardest things for me to achieve. It's not just because of my disability. Life changes. I have great friends but they are all married now with beautiful young children. Even if I wasn't in the wheelchair, it would be hard for us lads to get together. We all have different things going on in our lives and taking up our time. Mostly when I see my friends, they come to visit me in my house, and that's great. But I like to get out too. It's not good for me to be at home all the time. To tell you the truth, I feel I have lost out on 10 years of a social life since my accident. Who knows how many women I might have met in those 10 years? That's a lot of time to do a bit of fishing, as we say in Co. Tyrone! The problem is, there are only a couple of pubs in Cookstown I can get into in the wheelchair. Not only that, the women I meet in these places haven't got a clue what to say to me. I might give a compliment to one of them and she just stares back at me and can't think of anything to say. How does that make me feel? Not good. I would like to say to all the women in Ireland, just talk to me normally when you see me out. Plenty of times, I have wanted to go and see Rodney's band, Juice, playing. But most of the time they play in an upstairs room in a pub with no disability access, or in some other place I can't get into. The message is clear enough: disabled people are not welcome; they are not entitled to a social life outside their own homes, and that is just not right.

When I do manage to get out with my friends, it is deadly. My uncle Joseph said to me one time, "I don't know what kind of friends you have, Philip, who would take you out in a wheelchair and get you flying drunk. What kind of friends are they?" All I can say is, "I wish it would happen more often". There are not too many people beating my door down to take me out. That's something else I would like to say to the women of Ireland, why don't you call up to see me and ask me out? I'm still free and single and I wouldn't turn you down! I would probably treat you better than some of these young lads I see around the place. I am the same old Philip. I still like to get out and act the goat. I still chat up the women and I still get wound up by my friends. That is the way I like it and it is a rare treat when it happens. My friends would never put me at risk, whatever family members might think. But they don't treat me like I was made of glass either. We muck about with the old wheelchair and yes, I do get flying drunk sometimes.

I was out with Rodney one night and we came to a pile of traffic cones in the street. I started weaving in and out of them in the chair, but I must have been a bit more far gone than I thought. I knocked the cones all over the place. Rodney was coming up behind me, laughing at me. He lifted his boot to one of the cones and sent it flying. The police were watching him, and as I sped off round the corner in my chair, Rodney got a bollocking for antisocial behaviour. Rodney, who never did a thing wrong in his life. It was priceless. For once, I didn't get the blame. If it had happened when I was walking, it would have been me who got caught. I am sure of that.

I drink wee whiskies now when I go out, rather than pints. I still love Budweiser, but it flies through the catheter. Before I know it, the bag is full and when that bag is full, it has to be emptied, no matter what. It is worse than a full bladder. Plenty of times I have had to get one of my friends to come into the street with me and open the catheter into the gutter. There isn't time to do it all properly in the bathroom with the surgical gloves. Whisky is easier to manage and it is in a better size of a glass than a pint. Although I drink water and cranberry juice from a pint glass at home, I feel a bit awkward with a pint when I am out. Somebody has to hand me the glass and I would be embarrassed if I dropped it. My hands are not always reliable and it feels safer and more natural to have a whisky glass in front of me. Sometimes I can just pretend that I am a normal man out in the pub having a drink with his friends.

The odd time I go out to a café or a restaurant for something to eat. Someone has to put the cup of coffee up to my lips because I can't manage the cup. At home I use a beaker with a lid, but I would be embarrassed to bring that out in public because it looks like something you would give to a very small child. I don't know which is worse, the beaker that I can hold myself, or having somebody lift the cup up for me. I use a feeding strap too to help me manage cutlery and I always feel people staring at me. Sometimes I wonder why I even want to have a social life because really it is an ordeal at times. I need to feel very comfortable with the people I go out with, otherwise it's not worth the embarrassment.

Most of my social life is at home. One of the things I was proud to be able to do when I had my own home was to invite my mother, Grace, to visit me. The thing about nursing homes and hospitals is that people can visit you without an invitation. That is good in a way, but you have no real control over who gets into the place. Also, you are expected to be on form for visitors all the time and that is not always the case. In my own home, as well as having my friends dropping by whenever they want, I can also invite people to stay, like Sr. Paula or Grace. Grace lives in a small apartment in a fold now. It is still connected to the Willow Hill hospital, and there are nurses on site all the time, but Grace has a bit more independence. It is strange that both of us are getting used to a new life in a new home at the same time. To be honest, I think

I am coping with it all better than Grace. I have more fight in me than she does, and I was desperate to achieve a home of my own. I have dreams and ambitions to aim for. Plus, I have the financial support. Grace didn't really want to move into her own apartment and she relies a lot on the nurses for little things like phoning a taxi or making an appointment with the hairdresser. These are all things she could do for herself, but I think she is lonely. Asking the nurses to do things for her gives her some social contact and company. Grace is used to living on a ward with patients around her. I am not sure it was such a good idea to put her out in the fold on her own after nearly 40 years in a hospital ward. She has friends in the next door apartments, but it is not the same as the ward. I know myself, when you close your front door, you are shutting the world out and yourself in. Grace would not be used to that and I think it is what she likes the least about living in the fold.

Grace has stayed with me a good few times now, but it is like having a nosy stranger in the house in a way. I need my privacy and I don't want Grace seeing what I have to go through just to get up and dressed in the mornings. It is degrading for me. If she had looked after me as a baby, maybe I would feel different about it. I feel like a baby now a lot of the time because I have to rely on people to do so many things for me. When Grace comes, I make sure she takes her tablets and goes to bed late in the evening so that she sleeps late in the morning and I can be up and dressed before she wakens. That way I feel more like the man of the house. With Sr. Paula, it is different. First, Sr. Paula cared for me as a baby, and also, I suppose you could say Sr. Paula knows her limits with me. She would know if I am feeling embarrassed about myself and she would know how to deal with it. Grace hasn't got a clue. It is hard to explain, but Sr. Paula would know to keep out of my way when I am with my carers in the morning. But Grace would want to come in for a chat with them, no matter what I think. Grace is used to everything being done in public on the wards. There is not much that would embarrass her.

On one of her visits, I gave Grace a necklace as a present. When she went back up to Omagh, I found out that she gave the necklace away. The next time she was up with me on a visit she told me she needed a new watch.

"Haven't I just given you a lovely necklace? What do you want a new watch for?" I asked her.

"I would just like to have a new watch, Philip. And I am not too keen on that necklace;" said Grace, "It doesn't suit me."

"I'll tell you what," I said, "Why don't you give me back the necklace and I'll exchange it for a new watch" Grace went very quiet and I never heard another word about the watch after that. It is sad, but that more or less sums up our relationship. Grace sees me as someone who can give her presents and take her on weekends away. I am happy to do it and to give Grace some pleasure in life. I would not deny her that after the life she has had. But I don't get anything in return, and I'm not talking about presents. What good are presents to me? Grace never telephones me out of the blue just to see how I am. She tells me how lucky I am to have a lovely house, but she doesn't seem to realise what all I had to give up to get my lovely house. When I told her I was writing a book about my life she thought it would be all about my disability and not my life before the accident or my dreams for the future. Grace sees everything in the present moment. The past means nothing to her and I don't know what she thinks about the future. We don't really relate to each other as mother and son yet. Grace is the demanding child and I am the parent, doing my best, but never really sure if I am doing the right thing. Grace will fight with me about what she wants to do on her visits. Sometimes I breathe a sigh of relief when the car comes to take her back to Omagh. Grace can be harder work than I am at times. But I still feel that I owe it to Grace to take her out for visits and weekends. It gives her a bit more variety in her life even if it does wear me out sometimes.

Life goes on. I do my work, I keep in contact with Grace, I watch my football, I see my friends, I manage my staff and I miss Eva. Would I say that I have achieved a normal life? I have come a long way from the days in the nursing homes. My health continues to be a worry, but my attitude is better. I take a better interest in life around me. I get down in the dumps sometimes. But yes, in some ways, I would say that I have achieved a normal life. I will never really get used to 24-hour care, but I have adapted to it the best I can. I hate my wheelchair, but I realise I need it the same way that other people need their cars.

I would say to any disabled person, don't let your disability hold you back and don't let it define who you are. There is more to you than your sickness, whatever it may be. There is more to me than being paralysed. There is still a lot of stuff you can do. You might surprise yourself with a talent you never knew you had. Nobody would have thought that I could be a good businessman, but I am and it is work I can do from home, sitting in my wheelchair, or sitting up in my bed, and I have made a good success of it so far. If I was walking, who knows what kind of business I would be in today. The thing is, although I was taken off my feet, I didn't sit back and do nothing. I still had the ambition and the fighting spirit to do some kind of work.

My biggest achievement so far is setting myself up in my own home. Would I recommend that to other disabled people? I would. It has been good for me. But what I would say is this. Make sure you have a good structure of support behind you, from your family and friends and the health service. You can't make it succeed on your own. I had no family to fall back on, but I have good friends and I have learned to harass the health service. It is a pity that you only get respect and a service from fighting with them, but that is the reality. Go against your nature if you have to and fight for what you are entitled to have. You also need to set yourself some goals and a way to achieve them. You can't just sit in your house doing nothing. I have had goals that keep me motivated and keep me busy. You don't need lots of money to achieve your goals. I never had any money when I got myself on TV or in the newspapers. I had nothing when I started my road safety work. But I had goals and the determination to achieve them.

A normal life is a lifelong project. I have ups and downs. I have had setbacks as well as successes. For me, the important thing is always to have things I want to achieve. I have done my main achievements and now I am putting my attention into my dreams. There are dreams that I have had for most of my life, from the time when I was walking, and I still have to achieve those.

Dreams

I dream about Eva. I dream about what might have been and I dream about what I hope might still happen for us in the future. I dream about the day when I look to the left side of the bed and see a wife there, sleeping. Maybe it will be Eva or maybe it will be somebody I haven't met yet. Eva wasn't the first person I shared my home with, but she was the first woman I shared my life with. Having Eva in my house was the best time I have spent since my accident. I had a real connection with her and I would have trusted her with my life. People ask me why that is important, and I say to them, "Put yourself in my position. I need help with everything. You try asking someone you don't trust to empty your catheter and then to sit down with you and watch TV." I feel exposed and vulnerable on the one hand. But on the other, I need the human contact and I need to trust a person to do things the right way. The people who care for me are brilliant, but they are doing a job. I want someone in my life who doesn't leave at the end of the day, someone who makes their home in my home.

Back in the time I was being fostered, my aunt Bernadette said to the social workers, "Philip is more fond of women. He seems to be afraid of men." That is true to this day. It is not so much fear as a lack of trust. The people I employ are mostly women. I feel more secure with them. I don't know if I could trust men to look after my personal needs, day in and day out. Danny Byrne said to me one time, "Philip, you are a good judge of character" and I respect the man for saying that to me. He is right. I can tell if I am going to get on with people nearly as soon as I meet them, and it is not just about getting on with people. I can tell if they are good, honest people. If they are going to work for me, I can tell if they will do a good job and be respectful. Having strangers around me 24 hours a day has made my judgment very sharp. I am always watching what is going on. The people who work for me have free access to my home and everything in it. Unless I am in my wheelchair, I am stuck in one place in the house. If I am in my bed, and someone decides to steal the money out of my wallet, they could do it right under my nose and I could do nothing about it. My live in worker could invite strangers into my house, and I would be lying there helpless and vulnerable. That is why I have to be able to trust people to do what I expect them to do, but also not to poke and pry into my private business. I am master of my own house at the end of the day, but I don't want to act like a boss all the time. It is a balancing act and the boundaries change all the time. If my housekeeper is pissing me off, then every little thing she does will annoy me and I will be looking to catch her out sticking her nose where it's not wanted. But then again I need to feel that I can relax in the company of my housekeeper. It is very hard to get the balance right, but when I do, it makes all the difference. It makes the ordeal of my life an easier burden to carry when I can share good times with another person.

When Kate left, it took me a long time to settle with a new housekeeper. Now that Eva has gone, I feel that I will never manage to do it. By God, sometimes I feel like I am a counsellor or a psychiatrist in my own house. I listen to that many problems and give out that much advice to these young women from all different countries who come here thinking they want to work for me, but who have too many other things on their minds. To tell you the truth, I think I should be getting paid for managing the workers in my home! It is a full time job at times, especially now when I am trying to replace everything that Eva meant to me, but I know that I can't. I can't have my bun and eat it, as they say.

It is all a matter of trust. I don't trust too many people. I never get close; I always hold something back. I hide behind the banter and the cheeky chat. But with Eva, it was different. In some ways, it was hard for me to give up control and trust her completely; I kept having to remind myself that Eva was just doing a job and I had to keep a bit of a distance between us. But it was more than a job to Eva and by the time she left, there was no distance between us. We were best friends and we were falling in love.

Eva stayed with me for over a year and I loved every minute of it. She used to fix my hair up with gel in the mornings and tell me I had beautiful eyes. It must be true; she is not the only woman to tell me that. I have my mother's eyes. We went out together for meals, or just down the town for a coffee and she would put her hand on my shoulder as we went down the street. I can't tell you how good that felt. I wanted to tell everyone we met that Eva wasn't my care assistant, but my friend and my girlfriend. But I was too embarrassed to say those things. Eva came with me to see my favourite band, Westlife, down in Croke Park. We went to see other bands together too in Belfast. I was still in the wheelchair but it felt a lot like a normal social life when I took Eva out. She took me clothes shopping with her and I had never been shopping with a woman before in my life. A lot of men don't like it when their wives or girlfriends ask for their opinion about clothes and stuff like that. To me it was a privilege to be asked for my opinion. It did no harm that Eva is the most beautiful woman I have ever known.

Eva said to me one time, "What do you think of this, Philip? Do you like it?" I was looking at Eva in a new dress and then she said,

"Stop looking at my ass, Philip."

"Looking at your ass?" I said, "I would look at your ass if I could find it, Eva, but I can't. It's not there. You're too skinny. You need to eat up a few Ulster fries, girl." That is a conversation I never expected to have with a woman since my accident.

The main thing about Eva is that we could talk to each other about anything. Eva has her problems, I have my problems, and the two of us would just talk things through. On my side, it felt good to be able to offer a young girl advice and it felt good to have her listening to some of my worries. I didn't tell Eva everything about my background, but she has met my mother and she knows how things are between us. Eva taught me a lot about Bulgaria and her family. Until she came to my home, Eva had never had her own bedroom in her life. In Bulgaria, she shared a room with her sister. The family lived in a small apartment and they didn't have central heating the way we do. It was freezing in the winter. Eva loved my house and the space she had there to do her own thing. Her sister Mimi came to stay with us for a holiday one time and they were great together, Eva and her sister. One night Eva was dancing in her room and I would have given anything to get up and dance with her. She asked me if I would visit her in Bulgaria and I said I would, but only in the summer. Eva says we have no summer in Ireland, and she hates the Irish weather.

During the time Eva was with me, she went home to Bulgaria several times for a break. Each time she left, I missed her, and each time she came back, I was the happiest man I have ever been. But finally the day came when Eva told me that she was going back home to make some decisions about her future. It was the day I dreaded, but I knew in my heart that it would come because you can never hold on to people no matter how much you want to. They have to make their own choices in life. I went with Eva to the airport and I could hardly talk to her on the journey I was that choked up. I wanted to tell Eva how I felt about her and how much I loved her, but I was afraid of putting pressure on her. In the end, I sent her a text message, even though she was sitting right next to me. The message said, "I love you." When Eva read it, she said, "I love you, Philip." Eva is the only woman who has ever said that to me. I believe she does love me and I am hoping she comes back to me, as my best friend and my girlfriend.

I am lost without Eva. I miss the feel of her hand on my shoulder when I go out. I had no heart in finding someone to live in after Eva left. Bernie Boyle, my home help, used to come in her own time at 11 o'clock at night to make me some tea and sit with me before I got settled for the night. She is solid gold, Bernie Boyle. Clare Monaghan also comes to see me at night after her shift as a student nurse in Belfast. But I still can't face finding a full-time housekeeper. Eva taught me how to empty my own catheter and how to put my toothpaste on my toothbrush. To a certain extent, I have gone back to thinking that I can manage on my own without a live in worker. But I am lonely as hell and I would say I have the pain of a broken heart. Even paralysed people feel that kind of pain.

I was sitting one day thinking about Eva and how much I missed her. I don't know how it happened, but one of my legs fell off the footplate of the wheelchair and I couldn't get it back up. It was hours before anyone was due to come. I could have phoned somebody, but I just left it. Nobody knew for weeks that the leg had broken, not even me. I was feeling that bad in myself and missing Eva so much that I paid no attention to the pain I was starting to feel in my leg. I couldn't understand it because I am not used to feeling much of anything in my legs. When I checked the leg, I could see that the flesh was red and inflamed. I could see where the broken bone was jutting up through the flesh. I was starting to get more spasms in the leg too, which were very uncomfortable. The bone wouldn't set even after months of treatment and I thought I would have to have an operation. The doctors were preparing me for the worst case. The problem was not so much the bone as the skin. If the surgeons had to cut me, it would be very difficult for my skin to close and heal normally. It was a huge risk and thankfully it was one decision I didn't have to make. Finally, the bone started to heal. But I wished I had somebody close to help me make difficult decisions.

The broken leg just proves one thing to me. I have good days and I have bad days, but one fact about my life stays the same: I need 24-hour care for the rest of my life. There is no point in thinking I can manage on my own. Time and again, circumstances have proved that I can't, no matter how much I want to. At Easter in 2009 I was hospitalised with an infection that became pneumonia. I received the last rites on Easter Monday. I needed to sign a consent form for the doctors to carry out a procedure to get rid of the fluid on my lungs. For the second time in my life, people thought I wouldn't make it. But the scariest part of that whole experience was that I felt so alone. Before the infection took hold, I couldn't seem to convince the doctors that I was really sick. I had no live in carer at the time. I could hardly breathe. The site of my catheter was becoming infected. My body was turning red all over. I was on the phone to the night service doctors, who didn't know me from Adam. I couldn't seem to get through to them that I needed a doctor to visit me at home and assess me. By the time a doctor finally came, it was nearly too late. In hospital, when the intensive care doctor was trying to get me to sign a consent form, I was nearly delirious. My friend, Maurice Byrne, was with me, telling me to sign. But I could hardly understand what was happening to me. I felt like I was signing my life away, not saving it. I was really scared. Thank God I came through, but it was touch and go for a few days. I don't want to be in that position again. I am breaking my heart over Eva, but I realise now that I have to replace her. I can't manage on my own. I have to have somebody with me all the time, somebody who can react quickly if I get sick, and who can help me to make life-saving decisions.

When Eva told me that she needed to go back to Bulgaria, I hid my feelings to a certain extent, but I let her know that if she needed my help in any way she had only to ask for it. I felt like the legs were kicked out from under me. What was I going to do without Eva? Inside my heart was breaking but the last thing I wanted to do was to put any pressure on her. At the end of the day, what have I got to offer Eva, or any woman: a man in a wheelchair, a man without a proper family, a man without his independence? That is a terrible ordeal to put on a woman. Who would blame Eva if she ran away from me? Eva told me that she loved me, but it didn't stop her from leaving. At least we are still in touch with each other. I haven't lost Eva. I just don't know yet if she is coming back to me. I want her to know that she will always have a home in Ireland, in my home. I have the most special memories of Eva, and if she ever does come back into my life, I will welcome her with open arms. I would be privileged to know her as my friend and my girlfriend. If she asked me to marry her, I would marry her tomorrow. Eva was there for me when I needed to feel like a normal man. She showed me that it was possible. I made some CDs for Eva of my favourite music. "Flying without wings" by Westlife is my song for Eva. It is a song that talks about holding on to your dreams because the one you let go of might be the one that makes you complete. I let Eva go. I couldn't and I wouldn't stop her. But I dream that when she decides what she wants to do, she will come back. Thank you Eva, so much, for giving me that buzz and making me feel like I had something to get up for in the morning.

When I first had to face the idea of having a live in housekeeper, I thought it would be a terrible and awkward experience for me and for the housekeeper. But I was wrong. It can be great. First Kate and then Eva taught me that it is possible for me to share my life with a woman. I am grateful to

Kate for opening my eyes and I am grateful to Eva for living the experience with me. I know now that with the right woman, I could have a proper relationship, the same as any other man. I have learned that the wheelchair, the hoist, and all the other stuff that makes me feel like a useless bastard, don't matter. They are there, and they are part of my life, but they are the least important part. They are just the tools. They are not the man. Kate and Eva have let me see that the dream I held on to all my life is possible. It was always my dream to have my own home, with a wife and two children. I have achieved the first part; I have a home that anybody would be proud of. I hope that I have the courage and the luck to achieve the second part, to meet a woman to share my home with. Whether it is Eva, or somebody else, it would be a privilege. But I'll say one thing, if Eva doesn't come back to me, I'm chasing no more women. They can come to me!

In my dream, I would not expect my wife to be my carer. It would be too much to ask. I will still have professional carers to support me. I want my wife to have her own work and her own interests. I want someone I can talk to and share my problems and my ideas with. I want to give a woman and a family as much love and support as I never had when I was growing up. I might have had a bad experience of family life myself, but I have seen how other families are, like the Byrnes. They stand out for me as a family who love and care for each other. That is the kind of family I dream about for myself.

The third part of my dream, having a couple of children in my life, would also be a privilege, and what I mean by that is, it is not something that I would take for granted. At the moment, I can't father my own children because of my injury, although fertility treatment might be an option in the future. I look at the people around me in Mid-Ulster. Some of them might be single mothers with children they are struggling to rear by themselves. Some of them are couples who have not been able to have a child and their hearts are broken over it.

The presence of children and the absence of children can cause a lot of grief in life. I think back to the childhood that I had, and of all the children in St Joseph's and the older children at Ballee. I know more than most people what it is like to be a child who is not loved. I was reared without the love of parents. My parents were not excited about my birth. They were not decorating a room and buying teddy bears and stuff like that. They were not making plans for me and telling each other that I was the most special baby in the world. I didn't have that kind of love ever in my life. I wouldn't want any child to go through what I went through in my childhood. To grow up believing that you are not loved and not wanted is a terrible experience and I carry it with me all my days. That is why I say I would be privileged to have children in my life, whether they were my own or adopted children, it wouldn't make any difference to me. I would show them that all they need for happiness is to be loved. Nothing else is as important as that: not money, not a nice house, not the best education or the best chances in life, just love that is never taken away.

Sometimes I go through my house in the wheelchair saying to myself, "*What is missing here? There is something missing.*" I go from room to room. Everything is neat and tidy and in its place. I go out into the garden and I look at the house, I look through the windows. Everything is beautiful and perfect and I realise that what is missing is the sights and sounds of family life. There are no toys lying about the place, there are no children playing together, there is no laughter from a wife and mother. I have this beautiful home and garden just for me and it feels wrong. This was a family home at one time and it should be a family home again. I can picture myself sitting on the wheelchair listening to children talking and laughing about their day at school. I love a bit of noise about the place. Some days all I hear is the hissing of the tyres on my wheelchair, as I move around an empty house. I can picture myself sitting with my wife in the evenings and talking about the events of the day and the plans for tomorrow. This is the life my friends have with their families, and I can't help but be jealous of them at times. When I go up to the Byrnes on Christmas day, and I see three generations of the family there, I say to myself, "*They are just the same as me. We are all good people doing the best we can. So why can't I have that kind of a family for myself?*" I think about all of my business ventures and the investments I have made and I think to myself, "*Who am I doing all this for?*" I would love to say I am building a future for my wife and a couple of children. It would give me real goals, making sure they are provided for when I drop off. But at the moment, I am building a future for nobody.

My friend Maurice Byrne brought his new baby son to see me. Eva was still with me at the time. Maurice put the baby on my knee and I held him there. It felt so special. Eva walked into the room and she went pure white in the face and stood there looking at me. She could see then what I wanted in life. She could see my dream lying on my knee, looking up at me and trusting me.

On the days when I am down in the dumps, I think it is an impossible dream to have a family of my own. But on my good days, I look at all the things I have achieved that everyone told me were impossible. I even believed it myself at times, but I have achieved them, like moving out of the nursing homes and having my own home, like getting on TV, like getting on a plane and going to Lourdes and the Netherlands, like meeting Eva and falling in love. I realise it is not impossible for me to have a family. Since the time of my accident, I have achieved everything I set my mind to do. What would stop me from achieving my ultimate dream of a family of my own?

I know one good reason. Just thinking about it brings me back to my old insecurity, the old problem of finding out who I am. I want to get my past sorted out and then I am going to put my full attention on building a relationship with a woman who will be my wife. My head is wrecked at the minute with trying to work out my past. It would not be fair on any woman to bring her into the middle of this. I want to get my past and my background all out in the open and then I want to move on with my life. When I know who I am and how I came to be in the world, I will feel secure enough in myself to settle down and be happy. I want to be able to say to a woman, "This is who I am. It is not a good story, but I am ready to move on from here." People say to me, "But Philip, there are no guarantees in this life. It might not make any difference to you to know who you are. It might even make things worse for you to know the truth." But what I say to that is, "Could I really be any worse off than I am today?" Not knowing the truth is wrecking my head and holding me back from achieving my full potential in life. I believe I will be better off when I know the truth, no matter what I find out about my father and my background. I will be better off because after more than 20 years, I can stop asking questions that nobody will answer. The truth can't be any worse than the thoughts I have had about my father over the years. Is he someone who doesn't give a damn about the children he leaves in the world? I have waited long enough for answers and for proof. I want to know who my father is, and then I will move on.

If Grace has told me the truth about my father, then that man is dead. I won't be able to get to know him, or even kick his ass for having a relationship with my mother and not supporting her after it. If he is my father, then that man's family is Protestant. Back when Grace got pregnant, that would have added to the scandal. I have been reared as a Catholic and when I was in hospitals and nursing homes, I met people from all kinds of background. We all had to cope with different types of sickness and disability. Religion didn't come into it. If my father was a nurse, the Willow Hill hospital has some explaining to do about their care of my mother. I have had a belly full of excuses from the hospital over the years. One minute my mother is a voluntary patient who makes her own decisions in life; the next she is incapable of managing her own affairs. One minute she is out in the community; the next she is back in the hospital in a locked up ward. Would the hospital say that it was alright for a woman like Grace to have a sexual relationship with one of its employees? I have been told there is no proof. Maybe it was a patient. I would still ask the same question about how the hospital cared for my mother. The hospital bosses are passing the buck and covering their own asses. I feel like I am spinning in circles for more than 20 years and I want it to stop.

I am now officially Grace's next of kin and the hospital is obliged to include me in decisions relating to my mother's care. Before me, my uncle Francis was my mother's next of kin, never her mother. He has been the gatekeeper all this time. The way I see it, uncle Francis has been involved in the cover up about my mother's pregnancy from the word go. I don't believe for one minute that he let the matter drop when Grace told the family she was pregnant. He might have told his brothers that nothing was to be done to find out who the father was, but I am certain that he made it his business to find out. He is not the kind of man to let it go. Maybe Grace has told me the truth, but until I have proof, there is always a shadow of a doubt. In that shadow is the thought that maybe my father is somebody much closer to home: a family friend, a neighbour, even, God forbid, a family member. Grace might have been told a story way back when she got pregnant and she has repeated it that often she might believe it herself. I just don't know for sure. If you want to know what it feels like when your head is wrecked thinking about your background, try imagining yourself as a child born out of incest. It kills me when people tell me that I look like the Donaghys. I know they mean I take after Grace, but I can't help wondering at times if I take after one of the brothers too. It is a thought that keeps me awake at night. How could I meet a woman and have a family with that hanging around in my head? I hope and pray it is not true. People say to me, "Forget about it, Philip, if it upsets you so much." Even Eva has said that to me. I put them straight. I tell them that I am not about to forget about my family background, not until I find out the truth. I tell them I will get it sorted out if it kills me and then I will let it go.

After all these years, I still don't understand why Grace and the Donaghy family haven't told me everything they know. What have they got to lose at this stage? What are they hiding? Back years ago was the time to do it. From the minute uncle Francis decided to foster me out of St Joseph's, he should have been thinking about how he was going to explain to me where I came from. Social services should have been part of it too. Just about every fostered or adopted child must face this at some time or another. There must be a way of handling it that doesn't wreck the child's head. When I was told at the age of 11 that it didn't matter who my father was, how could anyone think I would accept that? What was in their heads? Did they think I would be too retarded to worry about my background? Did they think I wouldn't care? Did they think I would forget? Maybe if they had left me in the children's home, I might have been happy enough to think of myself as an orphan. I didn't know any of my family back then. I might have traced them when I grew up and been proud to call myself a Donaghy. Instead, I am ashamed. As far as I am concerned, my family is made up of the people who care for me, and none of them is a Donaghy. Strangers who care for me in my own home are more of a family to me than the Donaghys.

My uncle Francis and aunt Bernadette chose to foster me out, but I knew from a very early age that I was a bastard. They didn't want me, or love me, and they made it clear they didn't consider me a part of their family. I knew I didn't belong there. My birth certificate proved that to me when I saw that my father's name was unknown.

There are people who say to me, "The problem isn't that you don't know who your father is, Philip. The problem is that you were abandoned as a baby by both sides of your family, your mother, your father and all of your relations. Finding out who your father is won't change that." That is true in a way, I was abandoned and I have to accept that. I can see that it affects my relationships with people to this day and it is why I never get too close. I always expect to be left behind. But I have not abandoned hope, and I hope when I prove who my father is, I will be able to lay my past to rest and move on with my life. Once I know the truth, I can try to have a better relationship with Grace. When I prove who my father is, whoever he is, I will say to my family, "You thought you could ignore me. You thought I would just go away and forget all about it. You thought when I had the accident I was brain damaged, and it wouldn't matter to me any more. But look at what I have achieved by myself without help from any of you. You knew all along and you refused to help me. You dumped your own sister in a mental hospital and you dumped her unwanted baby in a children's home until he was half reared. You thought he would come to nothing. But look what I have done without you. I am the can of worms you thought you had buried, but by God I have risen to the surface and it feels good." I dream about that moment. I dream about the past catching up with the Donaghys.

If I am really lucky, I will have the chance to get to know my father's side of the family. But that is down to them. I wouldn't blame them if they don't want anything to do with me when the truth comes out. They might just need time to get used to the idea of me. I remember what I felt like when I read the word "Unknown" in the space where my father's name should have been on my birth certificate. I imagine that my father's family who never knew, or never believed, I existed will feel something like the way I felt that day. It is like free falling and knowing your legs won't support you when you land. It is like being winded during a football game, when you don't know where your next breath is coming from. It is a terrible shock. It was for me, but at the same time, it explained some things for me too. At that moment, I realised why my uncle and aunt didn't love me. It was because I was a bastard and a reminder of my mother and the shame she brought on her family. Once my father's family get over the shock of knowing who I am and knowing that a scandal from years ago is out in the open, I hope they will see that the child of that scandal is innocent.

I believe I have the right to know who my father is. If he is alive, he has the right to acknowledge me or ignore me. If he is dead, then his family can choose. I hope some good can come out of this, I really do. I know it could hurt and shame a lot of people, but none more than me. When I think about finally knowing who my father is, I say to myself, "*Who is going to support me when I find out? If the news is good or bad, if the man is alive or dead, who am I going to turn to?*" I think about all the people who have been part of the cover up, and at the end of the day, they have their wives or husbands or their families to turn to, no matter what comes out. They will be comforted by another human being who is close to them and who loves them, in spite of everything. I have nobody. I just have myself. I am my own family. I hope I am strong enough to face the truth because, whatever happens, I will have to face it on my own, as usual.

A couple of years ago, I decided that when I sorted out my past, I would move house, make a fresh start. The way I was thinking, leaving my first home would be part of the process of moving on. I have proved that with the right support I can live independently of hospitals and nursing homes. I have installed the equipment and employed the staff to help me to live as normally as possible. I have entertained my friends in my home and welcomed my mother as my guest on weekend visits. I have promoted road safety here and shown young offenders what car crime can lead to. I have even had the house on television on the property show *Home Sweet Home*. I also fell in love here. The house holds a lot of memories, most of them good. It is a beautiful house and when I am ready to sell, it would be good if a disabled person bought it. But I am not sentimental about it. The house will be sold to the person who offers me the best price. I invested a lot of time and money in this house and, like anybody else, I want to see a return. The life I lead is not cheap and I don't have an endless supply of finance by any means. I need to keep filling the pot, and if the sale of my first home earns me a lock of pounds, that's good.

I had an idea to build my dream home. I found a bit of land with a house on it fronting the river outside Cookstown. It definitely had potential and I was excited about it. I made a few phone calls and very soon I had a plan. I decided I would redevelop the Cookstown house. While Feargal Logan was sorting out the legal work regarding my father, my plan was to project manage the building of my new home. I would be keeping myself busy, building a better home for me and the staff, while the most painful and personal aspects of my life and my mother's life were pulled through the legal system.

In the new house, I had planned to build a separate apartment for my housekeeper with an adjoining door to my living space that would be locked automatically at night. I would have a member of staff available, but not in my face, 24 hours a day. I would be able to play my music, sing my heart out, or cry my eyes out whenever I wanted. When I converted my first home, Collie McGurk, the architect, made most of the design decisions. Although Collie did a great job for me, no question about that, it was only by living in the house that I learned what I really needed. I never used some of the expensive customisations that seemed like a good idea at the time. I didn't need a sound system or an intercom system in every room. The only time I needed all the bells and whistles was when I was in bed. In the new house, I planned for my bedroom to be fully automated, right down to the blinds on the windows.

The more I thought about the house in Cookstown, the more ideas I had to make it perfect. I was working with an architect, but this time I was calling the shots and making the decisions. I was also working to a tighter budget than before. It really pisses me off the amount of money disabled people have to pay to customise their homes. I was not going to deny myself essential equipment for the sake of a few grand, but I was going to be a lot more shrewd with the suppliers. I had lined up my friend Rodney Stewart to handle the electronics for me again. I wanted voice-activated controls, as well as a PDA. Using my voice, I wanted to be able to open and close my windows and blinds; I wanted to control internal and external lighting; and I wanted to manage my CCTV and security.

Moving to Cookstown would bring me closer to my friends. Sometimes I worried that I would be too close for comfort. I always have that insecurity because I have always felt that I don't belong anywhere, not really. I am afraid of overstepping the mark with people. The Byrnes have built a ramp at their house for me to get in and out. You would think that would make me realise I am welcome there any time. But I still worry. Although the Byrnes are the type of parents I would have wanted in my life, we are not blood related at the end of the day. I would not want to cross that line and piss them off. The new place has a few acres of land around it. I have told Danny Byrne he can graze his sheep on the land if he wants. Mrs Byrne said she would cook me a dinner every day when I moved. The idea of living in Cookstown is like a dream for me. In a way, the thought of it is like reliving the time when I had the flat in Greenvale Drive and spent all my spare time at the Byrnes'.

I was waiting on news from the local planning office when I had a change of heart. Eva was still living with me at the time.

There was one day she was in bad form about something and I took myself off down the town and bought her a big bunch of flowers to cheer her up. She had hardly missed me from the house and there I was giving her the flowers and telling her that I hoped they would make her feel better. Eva smiled at me and said thank you, and I suddenly realised that in Cookstown I wouldn't have been able to do that. The land I had bought is out a country road without footpaths a few miles from the town. It would be dangerous for me to go on the roads out there in my wheelchair. I realised how much I enjoyed going down the town, especially when I went with Eva. It would be a lot harder in Cookstown. Then, when Eva went back to Bulgaria and I was sitting lonely in the house, I thought that it would even more lonely in Cookstown during the day when my friends were all at work. I realised that another nice house meant nothing to me. It was a project, a dream even, but it was mainly a distraction. I shelved the plans for Cookstown. I still have the land, but no plan to develop it yet. I thought of Eva and even if she came back to me, part of her heart would be in Bulgaria with her family and friends. If she wanted me to move to Bulgaria, if that would make her happy, I would do it. Maybe she could help me find a nice apartment there. We could spend our summers in Bulgaria and our winters in Ireland. I wonder would Eva like that?

Dreaming of a new home, dreaming of a life with Eva. If nothing else, they help me to pass the time. Even though I have come a very long way since the time of my accident, I still face the problem of how to pass the time. It is a lonely life on the wheelchair and you find out who your friends are when you are sick. Sometimes I think all my days are the same old routine and the routine brings me down. But then I might get a call to do some work with the Youth Justice Agency, or I might meet someone who has seen me on TV and needs to talk. I might get a call about a piece of property I have had my eye on, or there might be some progress on the case to find out who my father is. I am getting involved now in work with adult car criminals, and I still want to keep doing road safety work. I have to say to myself, "*Philip, you deserve a clap on the back and a gold star!*" There are not too many people walking who have achieved what I have achieved and whose lives are as full as mine is. I have campaigned for road safety, I have worked on my insurance settlement, I have spoken out on behalf of disabled people for better services, I have helped to design my own home and I have bought and sold property. That is not bad. That is more than a lot of people can say they have achieved. I have also written this book about my life. I am not able to write, but I have spoken my thoughts and ideas into a Dictaphone for hours. I remember when I decided to write a book. It was an idea I had when I was in rehabilitation and the title came to me first. I said to Feargal Logan, who was visiting me one day, "Feargal, I'm going to write a book about my life and I have the title of it. What do you think of "Life was just an accident"? Do you think that just about sums up my life so far?"

"Well, Philip, you are the man to do it," Feargal said, "If anyone can, you can."

"You're right there, boss," I said to him.

But I still have more work to do. I am a restless person. If I was walking, who knows what I would have achieved by now. I never really had the chance to find out. I was just starting to take my first steps into business when I was taken off my feet. Sitting on the wheelchair, I have plenty of time to think things over and to see them through to the end. I am good at telling people what to do. I am a natural boss in a way. I have noticed the best business people have good personalities and a lot of energy and I am like that in my own way. When I am up on the wheelchair, I can't stay still. I spin through the rooms of my house. When I have visitors, I change my position in the room constantly. Even though I have no feeling, it is hard to sit in the chair for hours at a time. I feel the strain of it in my shoulders, my neck and my backside. It wears me out and I have to keep on the move. My mind is restless too. I am always turning over my thoughts and ideas. I need to keep my mind occupied, I need to have lots of different ideas on the go. If I get an idea, I am on the phone straight away asking my friends and contacts what they think of it, and what they can do to help me get it going. I like to be able to see what I have achieved at the end of every month. It is not about money in the bank, but it is about making progress and getting things done. I like to be able to see it happening. When things stand still, my mind goes into dark places

When Eva left towards the end of 2008, and just past my 10-year anniversary of my accident, I must admit I went into a bit of a slump. I stopped looking after myself. I lost my appetite; I broke my leg. I got a new housekeeper, a nice, hardworking girl, but I could hardly look at her. She didn't last a week. The next girl didn't work out either. I just couldn't replace Eva. I was behaving like I did when I went "on strike" at the Musgrave Park Hospital, before Dr McCann kicked my ass and told me that I had choices in life. After Eva left, I didn't want to play the game any more. I was fed up being paralysed. I thought to myself, "*If I was walking, I would get on a plane and go to Bulgaria and bring Eva back.*" But I knew deep down that wasn't it. The problem was that I couldn't face being rejected. What if Eva decided she wanted a man from her own culture? I could understand that, but it would break my heart. Although Eva explained to me that she needed to go home and make some decisions about her life, it felt as though she was leaving me. I felt abandoned by her in a way. I had opened up to Eva and shared my life with her. I had gone against my instincts of a lifetime and got close to her. Then she left me. She probably didn't realise how close I felt to her. But when she left, it made me feel the same way I felt when I was a child and a teenager, like an unwanted bastard.

I say to myself, "*I have been 10 years sitting on this wheelchair, is this how I am going to spend the next 10 years of my life?*" It is one hell of a thought. I worked out that I have been lifted in a hoist about 30,000 times in the last 10 years. Is that what I have to look forward to in the next 10 years, another 30,000 lifts in a hoist? Some days, I just can't face that. I feel I am getting older too and I wonder who will be looking after me when I am 45 or 55. I have had housekeepers from all different countries in the world, Ireland, China, Poland, Bulgaria, the Philippines. Is that my future? I never got to travel outside Ireland when I was walking. Now all the different cultures are coming to me. Will there even be foreign workers coming into this country in 10 years' time or 20 years' time? I don't know. Sometimes I think that I can't face my future sitting in this chair. I don't really feel pain, but I feel boredom and it goes right through me. People say, "Take yourself down the town Philip and buy yourself something. Treat yourself." But that's no good to me. I go into the shops and there's very little there I can use. I can't use computer games, fancy clothes are no use to me, even a pint of beer has to be handed down to me. People say, "Go on a holiday, Philip." If I could leave my disability behind and get away for two weeks in the sun I would. But going on a holiday means I have to take a care assistant with me and I have to hire out all the equipment. I can't even sit in the sun because my skin would break out if it got sun burned. A holiday is okay but it isn't a break from my life or from my routine. I read in the papers about the young rugby lad who went to Switzerland to die and I don't blame that man or his family one bit. He couldn't face the ordeal of his life and sometimes I feel the same about mine. It is always there in the back of my mind that when I can't stand it any more I will take the decision to end it. I put this in to show the people reading this book that not all dreams are good. Some of them are nightmares.

But that's life. I am lucky in a way. My days being down in the dumps pass. That is why it is important for all disabled people to set themselves goals to achieve in life, no matter how small they might be. Every achievement is a celebration. Every goal gives you a reason to get up in the morning.

I have one dream that will be harder to achieve than the others. It might even be harder than finding a wife! One day, I hope to open a unit for young disabled people to meet and relax with their friends and families. I am the ideal man for that job, because I have lived in all different kinds of institutions throughout my life. I know what works and what doesn't work. The health service says they can't justify a unit aimed at the young disabled, but I see it differently. I lived in nursing homes for the elderly and it was not the right environment for a young man. There weren't enough activities and stimulation. I know first hand what it is like to live without the necessary facilities and equipment. It got me down; it added to my embarrassment about myself and it took away my confidence. I felt degraded when I had to watch my carers struggling to lift me using a manual hoist instead of an electric one. I lost some self-respect because the simple things were not there to help me. But simple things, like electric hoists, electric wheelchairs, shower chairs and exercise bikes are also expensive. They might add to the quality of my life, but they aren't available to everybody who needs them. That is why I want to open the unit, so that for a few hours a few times a week, young disabled people get the benefit of the right kind of equipment in an atmosphere created just for them.

I want a place where disabled people can go and socialise with their friends without feeling embarrassed or feeling like a bloody nuisance. I have been out in places where I couldn't get into the building without someone putting out a ramp and then someone had to hold open the door for me. When I finally got inside, they had to move the tables and chairs for me, and then I was sticking out like a sore thumb and the other customers had to squeeze past me. How can a disabled person even try to lead a normal life when just getting into a place is so awkward? My idea is to have a unit where the needs of the disabled come first. It should be easy to get into and get around with wide open spaces for wheelchairs.

I have the first hand experience and I have the dream to open the unit. But, I need more than that. There is a lot of red tape involved with it and it will be impossible for me to achieve on my own. I hate red tape. It slows me down. Building a place for members of the public to use is very different from building my own home. The planning laws are different, the liability and insurance are different and the health and safety issues are different. Plus, I need qualified staff to run the unit. I might be able to run the business end of things, but I would need a team of physical instructors, therapists, nurses, cooks, carers and administrators too. I have had enough trouble employing the people I need just for myself. This would be on a completely different scale. But there is a need for the unit I dream of. There are enough young victims of accidents, and young people disabled from birth, and young people with degenerative diseases to justify it, in my opinion. It will take time and I will need to go into different partnerships to get the project going. That will be a new experience for me because up to now I am used to being the boss and calling the shots. I have already had one planning application turned down, but I will keep trying.

That is what I say to myself, to other disabled people, and to all the bastards in children's homes, keep trying. You only have one life. If you want something, get out there and grab hold of it. If you have the imagination to dream about it, then you will find a way to achieve it. That has been my experience since my accident and it is a lesson I wish I had learned when I was walking. There are a lot of people out there who can bring you down. Look at me. I was told from a very early age that I was a bastard born on the dung heap. I was told I was retarded.

I was told I was mad, like my poor mother. I was told I would come to nothing in life. Sometimes I feel so down that I think maybe I am brain damaged. But what kind of a life would I have if I believed those things? A miserable one. I might even have committed suicide by now. But deep down I don't believe them. I believe I am here for a reason and I do what I have to do to make my life the best it can be and to prove my family wrong who put me down for years when I was a child. When I had my accident, they probably thought I would be better off living in a nursing home and wasting away. They thought I had a brain injury and they probably hoped I would be so far gone that I would stop asking questions about my father and my background. It would have been easier for my family if I had just shut up and kept out of the limelight. But it is not my job to make life easier for my family. It is my job to make life easier for myself, for other disabled people, for young drivers and car criminals and for all the children who were reared in children's homes. I will share my experience with anybody if it will help them to achieve their best potential in life. If my family doesn't like it, tough luck on them.

And just in case anyone out there is thinking, "*This Philip Donaghy sounds too good to be true,*" I have other dreams too, just like everybody else's. I suppose they are fantasies. When I was a child, my foster family and social services thought I lived in a fantasy. In some ways I still do. I would love to meet my favourite footballers, Steven Gerrard and Bruce Grobbelaar from Liverpool FC, present and past. The greatest football team in the world and I have supported them since I was no age. I loved playing my football when I was on my feet, and now I am the greatest fan of Liverpool. I watch all the matches on TV. My friends support different clubs, and we sometimes watch matches together, slagging each other's team off all through the match. If we are not together, we are on the phone or sending texts, passing abuse on the performance of one team or the other. A football night is always a good night.

I would like to meet the model Danielle Lloyd. I have a few posters of her on the walls of my bedroom and she is beautiful. Bernie Boyle says to me, "Philip, will you get those dirty pictures off the walls" and I make sure there are a few more there the next time Bernie comes round. She always looks away, pretending to be disgusted. But Danielle Lloyd is only doing what anybody with a beautiful face and body should do, show it off. There is no point in hiding it away, that is what I say.

My favourite band is Westlife. My friends don't like them, but I go to nearly all their concerts in Ireland. Some people say I look a bit like Shane Filan. I would love to meet the boys in Westlife, then Shane Filan could see for himself that I have far better looks than he does. When I was walking, I used to love going out dancing and I used to listen to dance music. I don't listen to it any more because it reminds me of the good times I have lost out on. I listen to Westlife songs and I listen to the words.

Maybe when my book gets published, I will go on *The Late Late Show* again and Westlife will be there too. By then, I might be married and my wife will be with me. Maybe she will be Eva, looking beautiful and with her hand on my shoulder, or maybe she will be somebody else. I will tell Ryan Tubridy that I listen to the Westlife version of a Frank Sinatra song when I need to give myself a boost. It is called "My Way". Westlife will perform that song for me, and I will say to people watching, "That is how I do things now, my way, and let me tell you something, it feels good."

Epilogue – Who am I?

Long before I started writing this book, I was working with my legal team to find out for once and for all who my father was and how I came to be in the world. Feargal Logan scribbled on my file "On hold due to serious RTA" back in October 1998. He probably thought that was the end of it. I was expected to die because of the accident. Case closed. When I didn't die, maybe he thought that I would be too taken up with living as a paralysed man to bother any more with looking into my background. Well, the file was reopened. I needed the truth to come out. I know it will hurt a lot of people, not least myself.

I have invested time, money and personal stress in this journey. I have nearly wrecked my life over it. I got myself a criminal conviction at the age of 17 because social services told me they weren't going to help me any further to find out about my background. I have come very close to falling out with my mother for good over the head of it. I have listened to people all my life telling me to forget about it and move on. Some of them had bad intentions and wanted to cover up the truth. Others, I know, had my best interests at heart. But to all of them I would like to say, "The time to move on and leave the past to itself is when I know who I am." I am nearly there, but not yet. I was nearly there at the age of 17 when social services dropped me like a hot brick. That's not going to happen again.

When I moved to Omagh, shortly after I left care, I took matters into my own hands. I couldn't afford to employ a solicitor. I made a mess of things and I upset a lot of people. I was threatened and warned off. When I was in Sligo and earning a wage, I asked Feargal Logan to look into the matter of my paternity. After my accident, when I was finally settled in my new home, I asked Feargal Logan to start again. People probably hoped that my search for my identity was over. They hoped that the accident would take my mind off my other problems. That is not how it works. I can't do too much about my paralysis, but, by God, I can hunt down my father and I can do it all legal and above board.

I have the finances now. I nearly had to die to get them. But what use is money to me once the wages are paid and the bills are settled? It doesn't buy my happiness, but it might just buy peace of mind for what I have been through and what my mother has suffered all her adult life.

I have been asking questions about my father since I was 11 years old. For more than 20 years, I have been drip-fed bits and pieces of answers. I have had enough of it. My head is wrecked with wondering who he was, what happened to him, how my mother was treated, and why so little thought was given to me. I am the innocent victim in all of this, in the same way that I was the innocent victim of a car accident. I don't want to cause any trouble, but too much has been hidden for too long. I have the right to know the truth, and if the truth hurts, it will hurt nobody as much as it hurts me. I am prepared to take that risk. I have an open mind about my father. I have listened to what the Willow Hill Hospital told me when I was a teenager and the different account my mother gave me at the same time. I accuse nobody. I just want to know the truth. I have said all along that everyone involved in my mother's life at the time I was born will have someone to turn to when the truth comes out. They all have families who will support them, no matter what. The only ones who have nobody to turn to are Grace, my mother, and me. Whatever happens, we have to deal with it on our own. We are not even close enough to rely on each other for support.

In 2008, I asked my mother, Grace Donaghy, for a sworn affidavit confirming the name of the man she says is my father and describing the circumstances of my conception and birth. Let me tell you, there are not too many people who would want to know that much detail about how they came to be in the world. Most people would see it as a private matter between their parents. But I never had parents to rear me the normal way. The details are important to me even though the health service, social services and my own blood relations all told me to forget about it.

It took a long time to persuade Grace to do it and towards the end of 2008, my uncle Joseph brought Grace to a solicitor's office to sign her affidavit. I have to thank both of them for that. It was not easy for Grace. It was a very big thing for her to do. I know that it vexes her to talk about it, but in the end she did it, of her own free will. She swore on the bible and she signed the affidavit. Grace is a good Catholic woman and she would never swear lies on the bible, I know that. Joseph was a good support to me and to his sister over this and he deserves credit for it. Grace probably wonders if she did the right thing. She probably wonders what her brother Francis will make of it.

It was a very hard thing for Grace to do, signing that affidavit, and I thank her for it. Reading it nearly tore my heart out of me, with pity for Grace and for myself. It was like reading my children's home and social work files for the first time. When I got those files, I kept expecting to read something good about myself, something personal that would make me smile or trigger a happy memory. But there was nothing like that. The files were very good, very correct. My name was at the top of every report and the facts of my life in care were there to be read in every detail. But they could be about anybody. There was nothing that made them "Philip".

The files might say that I was struggling to learn my words, but they didn't go on to describe the funny things I said. They said I was lively, but they didn't say how I showed my lively personality. They said I was chastised, but they didn't say how or why. Grace's affidavit was a bit like that too. It described the very beginning of my existence, but there was no "Philip" in it. How could there be when Grace never knew me and never got the chance?

"Well?" people said, when they heard Grace was going to sign the affidavit, "How did it go? Did your mother sign? What did she say?" I didn't tell too many people about the affidavit, but the people who know me the best wanted to know all about it. I never had nothing in writing before. Grace told me bits and pieces; the social workers back when I was in Ballee wrote some information in their reports. I never saw those reports until I requested them under the Freedom of Information Act. I never got the full story; I still don't have it because I only got Grace's version, and that is the only version I am ever likely to have. When my friends asked me what the affidavit said, I thought to myself, "*I have waited more than 20 years for this information.*" I wasn't too sure how to handle it. It was painful so I did what I always do when I am under stress. I started to joke about, and I kept everyone going. I turned myself into the butt of the joke.

"Do you know what?" I said to my friends, "I was conceived in a laundry bag." I was hiding behind the banter and the jokes, as usual. "I should be sponsored by Daz Ultra", I said, "I am the best advertisement for dirty laundry," I told them, and I kept the whole thing going.

We all had a good laugh about the beginnings of Philip Donaghy. But at the end of the day, it was not one bit funny.

The story Grace has sworn her oath on was that she was in a relationship with a nurse at the Willow Hill Psychiatric Hospital, a married man, a Protestant. To this day, as my book goes to press, I can't bring myself to name the man. I won't name him until the law tells me I can. I still have a small seed of doubt; what if it isn't him? Grace used to meet him for coffee in the hospital canteen. He took her to the laundry room and I was conceived among the industrial sized bags of dirty linen from all the hundreds of hospital beds they had there at that time. When it was discovered that Grace was pregnant, she was sent away to the nuns in Newry. The man, my alleged father, was moved to a different part of the hospital and worked different shifts so that he wouldn't have the opportunity to meet my mother again. When I was born, I was sent to the Nazareth nuns in Belfast to be reared. After a while, Grace went back to the hospital. She never saw the man again. He died of cancer when I was around three years old. Grace said he knew about me. I don't know if he knew where I was at, because Grace herself hardly knew that the whole time I was growing up. I don't know if he ever tried to contact me. If he did, he never succeeded. I'm told he asked about me when he was dying. I don't know if that is true.

That's it. That's the story. I am a laundry room accident. I am the dirty linen that gets washed in public. Neither my mother nor my father got the chance to know me or rear me as a baby. I may as well have been bundled out the door with the dirty sheets. I understand now why Grace doesn't really see me as her son, her own flesh and blood. We are no more than strangers to each other at the end of the day. I will look after Grace through the rest of her life as best as I can. I will support her in ways that her brothers and sister, and her own mother didn't, back when she was a young woman with problems. I feel sorry for Grace and a great pity for what she has been through. I think my life has been hard, I think I have lost out on a lot of things. But Grace has lost out too. On the days when I think I have a shit life, I remind myself that the person in this story who has really had a shit life is Grace, my mother.

I looked elsewhere for mothers in my life and I was lucky enough to find two brilliant ones. Sr. Paula was my mother in my early years. Mrs Byrne is like a mother to me since I was dumped out on the streets at the age of 18. Grace Donaghy is my mother's name on my birth certificate and I owe her respect for that. But she never knew me as a baby; she wasn't there when I cut my first tooth, or took my first step, or went to school for the first time, or made my first holy communion. She wasn't there when her brother fostered me out. She wasn't there for my unhappiness in her home place. She wasn't there when I first learned that I was a bastard. She wasn't there at Ballee children's home. She was never there for Christmas, and it was the Byrne family who took me in for Christmas dinner when I turned 18 and was left to fend for myself. She wasn't there even when I moved to Omagh to be closer to her. She didn't defend me when I was run out of that town. She wasn't there when I had my accident. But the bonds of a natural mother are strong. I will respect and support Grace, but I can't say that I really owe her much.

Grace's sworn affidavit is not the end of the story. I know that she believes what she said because she would never have sworn it on the bible if she knew it to be a pack of lies. But for all I know, Grace is repeating the story she was told to tell all those years ago. There could be another truth that she has forgotten. The affidavit is due to be presented to the High Court in Belfast. If it is accepted by the judge, then my birth certificate can be altered to include for the first time my father's name. But an affidavit is not proof and I believe a judge will want proof. DNA holds the truth. If I have a living relative on my father's side who would give a sample to be DNA tested, the truth will come out. Just as I have always said, blood is thicker than water. The true DNA proof is lying 30 years in a graveyard in Co. Tyrone.

If the man Grace has named is proved as my father, then that man was a nurse at the Willow Hill Psychiatric Hospital. If he was in a sexual relationship with a patient, what does that say about the standards of care in the hospital at the time? Was it the done thing for employees to have sex with the patients? Are there any other hidden pregnancies that were covered up? Was he the only nurse who was in a relationship with a patient in his care? Is there anyone reading this book who has had a similar cover up in their background? The way I see it, even though I am exposing my mother, my alleged late father, their families and the hospital to the public eye, the person who is most exposed is me, the wee bastard. At the end of the day, I might be the only one. But there might be other people out there whose backgrounds will be blown open by what I have discovered about myself. I make no apology for it.

Part of me wants to hide myself away with my mother's statement. It is not easy to sit here and know that I came out of an unplanned and unwanted pregnancy in a hospital laundry. But part of me wants to let the world know the circumstances and the consequences of that pregnancy. What happened to my mother was wrong. What happened to me was wrong. If I can help other people to face the truth in their backgrounds, then it will be worth the effort of exposing my private tragedy in public.

If, after all the legal proceedings, I still don't know who my father is, I don't know what I will do. I will be back at square one, looking up the road to Mullabeg for answers. But I know this much, I will find out. But then what? When I finally prove who my father is, what will I do then? I have spent more than 20 years looking for him. What will take the place of that search and that effort in my life? There are some days I honestly don't know. I say to myself, "*Maybe the time will come to take the final decision in life,*" and what I mean by that is suicide. I have faced that thought plenty of times in the last 10 years sitting on the wheelchair. I face it again every time I look into the future and I say to myself "*Do I want this life? Do I want another 10 years or 20 years of this?*" But those are dark days when I have those thoughts. There are still things for me to do. I will be looking to see what investigation the

Willow Hill did into my mother's pregnancy. I will speak out on behalf of the bastards in children's homes who have the right to know who they are. I will speak out on behalf of the disturbed women, like my mother, who were taken advantage of in psychiatric hospitals and whose stories were covered up. I will speak out on behalf of the children who were hidden away because their families and the authorities were embarrassed of them. I will speak out on behalf of the living victims of road carnage. I will speak out for all disabled people who can't even get into a café for a cup of coffee when they go out. I will speak out for the elderly people in nursing homes who paid taxes all their lives to end their days sitting in their own waste, staring at the four walls. I will get justice for all the forgotten people. That's a lot of work for any man. I have achieved everything I set out to achieve since the time of my accident, so I have no doubt that I will do it.

The readers of this book know as much about me as I know myself. My whole life feels like the story of a dream at the minute. My life before my accident is like somebody else's dream and not mine. But there are two things that I want to see to the finish. I want to prove who my father is; that has been my dream since the age of 11. I want to meet and marry the woman of my dreams and raise a family of two children. I will stick around until those dreams come true.

Printed in the United States
by Baker & Taylor Publisher Services